DOORWAY
to
DILEMMA

DOORWAY
to
DILEMMA

Bewildering Tales
of Dark Fantasy

Edited by
MIKE ASHLEY

This collection first published in 2019 by
The British Library
96 Euston Road
London NWI 2DB

Dates attributed to each story relate to first publication.

Cataloguing in Publication Data
A catalogue record for this publication is available from the British Library

ISBN 978 0 7123 5263 5
e-ISBN 978 0 7123 6494 2

Frontispiece illustration by Enrique Bernardou, 2019

Cover design by Mauricio Villamayor with illustration by Enrique Bernardou

Text design and typesetting by Tetragon, London
Printed in England by CPI Group (UK) Ltd, Croydon, CRO 4YY

Contents

INTRODUCTION

What Is Dark Fantasy?

Fantasy, in its broadest sense, covers the entire field of weird and supernatural fiction. Fantasy is about the impossible, at least in our understanding of the natural world. It includes magic, monsters, ghosts, anything and everything that seems to defy the laws of science.

In the last fifty years or so, especially since the phenomenal success of J.R.R. Tolkien's *Lord of the Rings* and Robert E. Howard's stories featuring Conan the Barbarian, and all their off-shoots, fantasy has tended to be marketed as either stories set entirely in a secondary world, or where some secondary or hidden world impinges upon our own. As a consequence, this became dubbed heroic fantasy or sword-and-sorcery which distinguishes it from other stories of the supernatural. When we think of the supernatural, our immediate thoughts go to ghost stories, or vampires, werewolves, zombies or the occult. So, although these are as much fantasy as stories of swordsmen and sorcerers, they tend to be grouped separately as supernatural fiction.

There is another genre of fiction labelled "horror". It's not a very helpful label, because it describes a mood of fiction, not its content. Any fiction can contain scenes of horror, especially crime fiction, and does not need to be related to supernatural fiction or fantasy, but horror has tended to become attached to stories of zombies, vampires and the like, with the catch-all term of supernatural horror.

You'd think that covered all forms of fantasy, but it doesn't. There are those stories which deal with the inexplicable, the strange, the unsettling, and the just plain bizarre. They don't include ghosts or vampires or sorcerers or dragons. They tend to be set in our world, often the here-and-now, but where the characters experience things they cannot explain and which become unnerving and frightening. In the past these have been classified as horror or strange tales or weird fiction, but they now revel in the term "dark fantasy".

The coinage of the term is usually attributed to the author Charles L. Grant where he regarded it as referring to events affecting individuals which are beyond their understanding. But the term itself had been around for decades. It was used by the *Illustrated London News* to describe a picture by Sidney H. Sime, "The Floating Island", in its special Christmas issue in 1931. Sime is a good example of an artist whose images were often dark reflections of the fantastic, particularly when he illustrated the work of Lord Dunsany.

Dunsany, one of whose stories is included in this book, had specifically requested that Sime illustrate the stories in his first collection, *The Gods of Pegana* in 1905, resulting in a partnership that lasted over twenty years and saw some of the most remarkable if grotesque black-and-white illustrations of the fantastic ever printed. Sime had already established a reputation for his artwork in the pages of such magazines as *Pick-Me-Up* and *Pall Mall* during the 1890s, the decade of decadence which saw the real emergence of dark fantasy as a distinct if, at that stage, unnamed genre. This was the decade that saw such supreme dark fantasies as *The Picture of Dorian Gray* (1891) by Oscar Wilde, "The Great God Pan" (1894) and *The Three Impostors* (1895) by Arthur Machen, *The King in Yellow* (1895) by Robert W. Chambers and *Shapes in the Fire* (1896) by M. P. Shiel to name but a few.

But the roots of dark fantasy go back much further. As far back as the stories of our childhood.

What have long been mistitled as "fairy tales", a mistranslation from the French *conte des fées*, are the many oral folk tales passed down the generations from long before anyone can remember. It's not until someone wrote them down that we have a permanent record, but there's no doubt many of the popular stories go back to the early Middle Ages or before, and they show many of the features of dark fantasy.

Take the story "Sleeping Beauty", best known from versions by Charles Perrault in 1697 and the Brothers Grimm in 1812. It is in the Grimms' version that the princess is awoken from her enchanted sleep by a kiss. But there are earlier versions dating back as far as the fourteenth century under the title "Troylus and Zellandine", where the prince does not simply kiss the sleeping princess, he assaults her, and she does not wake until she gives birth.

Then there is "Little Red Riding Hood", again collected by Perrault, but already long known as a folk tale. In the early version the wolf kills and devours the young girl's grandmother, keeping some of the flesh and blood in bowls to offer to the girl when she arrives. The wolf then seduces the girl in bed and is about to eat her but she escapes.

These are bleak and dark tales. Throughout folk tales we find child abuse, mutilation, rape and murder. In the first edition of their *Kinder und Hausmärchen* in 1812 the Grimm Brothers included a tale "How Some Children Played at Slaughtering" in which a young boy kills another but, after a simple test where the boy must choose between money or an apple, the judge sets him free. That story was dropped from later editions because it was too violent!

There are plenty of similar stories but these are sufficient to show that many folk tales were, in themselves, dark fantasies. They were created as warning stories to educate children about life and its dangers and how to deal with the strange and inexplicable. They also dealt with how children cope with the loss of innocence, which is reflected in the stories by Mary Wilkins and Lucy Clifford reprinted here.

As the roots of dark fantasy took hold and sprouted so other features emerged, most notably the element of fear and confusion arising from bewilderment with the bizarre circumstances in the story. In these stories the main protagonist struggles to cope with the unknown and their fear and horror propels the story along. Writers like Edgar Allan Poe and Nathaniel Hawthorne had explored this territory but the author who really took hold of it and, to all intents, brought the dark fantasy into the open, was Fitz-James O'Brien with his classic story "What Was It?". Although this story has been reprinted many times I make no apologies for including it here because it sets the benchmark for the dark fantasy. That feeling of helplessness against the unknown was further explored in the stories included here by Morley Roberts, Catherine Wells, Thomas Burke and David H. Keller.

The sister to the story of fear was the puzzle or dilemma story. Frank R. Stockton, who created many of his own fairy tales, established this form with his classic "The Lady, or the Tiger?", which drew upon the fairy/folktale background and raised a classic dilemma which has intrigued readers ever since. The popularity of this form led to other puzzle stories and I have included here a few of the best, "The Little Room", "The Mysterious Card" and "The Woman in Red" along with their sequels.

The heuristic nature of the folktale—or more significantly the tragedy of *not* learning from your experiences—also fed into the dark fantasy and amongst those books which saw a transition from traditional fairy tale to modern weird tale, one of the most remarkable is *Anyhow Stories* by Lucy Clifford, which included "The New Mother", a children's fantasy unlike any other of its period. What begins as a story about naughty children reaches a climax with anything but a happy ending.

By the 1880s the dark fantasy had firmly established itself by the fusion of the folk-tale and supernatural horror. Perhaps the most striking story to mutate the fairy realm into dark fantasy is Arthur Machen's "The White People" which has a story within a story which is unsettling from start to finish.

This anthology includes a representation of the range of dark fantasy from the 1880s to the 1930s showing how this sub-genre of dark fantasy took shape and form and delivered some of the most unsettling and unnerving fiction of its day.

MIKE ASHLEY, 2019

WHAT WAS IT?

Fitz-James O'Brien (1826–1862)

The life of Fitz-James O'Brien is every bit as exciting and almost as
fanciful as his fiction. A bohemian and dandy and almost certainly
homosexual, he lived way beyond his means, despite (or more likely
because of) a significant inheritance that allowed him to leave his
native Ireland and venture to the temptations of London and Paris.
He apparently sold some stories and poems while in England but as
these appeared anonymously few have been identified. It was not
until he went to New York in 1852 and captured the literary scene
with his flamboyance and gaiety that he established himself as a writer
to watch. It has been argued that it was thanks to O'Brien that the
American short story became established as a literary form when the
first issue of *The Atlantic Monthly* published "The Diamond Lens" in
1858. O'Brien fits solidly in the evolution of the macabre and supernatural tale in the United States between his forebears Edgar Allan
Poe and Nathaniel Hawthorne and his successor Ambrose Bierce.
O'Brien died as he lived. Despite his excessive and exuberant life
style he was athletic and fit and had long been known as an excellent horseman, swordsman and pistol-shot. So, when the American
Civil War began he signed up. Alas he was shot in an exchange of
fire and whilst he had the strength to fire back and kill his opponent,
one arm was shattered from shoulder to elbow. O'Brien still had the
strength to ride twenty miles to find a doctor, who unfortunately
seemed less than competent, and it was two weeks before he died of

complications from the wound. His work remained popular for the rest of the nineteenth century but his reputation has steadily faded. Yet, as the story reprinted here demonstrates, his work is as vivid and exciting today as it was a hundred and fifty years ago.

It is, I confess, with considerable diffidence that I approach the strange narrative which I am about to relate. The events which I purpose detailing are of so extraordinary a character that I am quite prepared to meet with an unusual amount of incredulity and scorn. I accept all such beforehand. I have, I trust, the literary courage to face unbelief. I have, after mature consideration, resolved to narrate, in as simple and straightforward a manner as I can compass, some facts that passed under my observation, in the month of July last, and which, in the annals of the mysteries of physical science, are wholly unparalleled.

I live at No.—— Twenty-sixth Street, in New York. The house is in some respects a curious one. It has enjoyed for the last two years the reputation of being haunted. It is a large and stately residence, surrounded by what was once a garden, but which is now only a green enclosure used for bleaching clothes. The dry basin of what has been a fountain, and a few fruit-trees ragged and unpruned, indicate that this spot in past days was a pleasant, shady retreat, filled with fruit and flowers and the sweet murmur of waters.

The house is very spacious. A hall of noble size leads to a large spiral staircase winding through its centre, while the various apartments are of imposing dimensions. It was built some fifteen or twenty years since by Mr. A——, the well-known New York merchant, who five years ago threw the commercial world into convulsions by a stupendous bank fraud. Mr. A——, as every one knows, escaped to Europe, and died not long after, of a broken heart. Almost immediately after the news of his decease reached this country and was verified, the report spread in Twenty-sixth Street that No.—— was haunted. Legal measures had dispossessed the widow of its former owner, and it was inhabited merely by a caretaker and his wife, placed there by the house-agent into whose hands it had passed for the purposes of renting or sale. These people declared that they were troubled with unnatural noises. Doors were opened without any visible agency. The remnants of furniture scattered through the various rooms were, during the night, piled one upon the other by unknown hands. Invisible feet passed up and down the stairs in broad daylight, accompanied by the rustle of unseen silk dresses, and the gliding of viewless hands along the massive balusters. The caretaker and his wife declared they would live there no longer. The house-agent laughed, dismissed them, and put others in their place. The noises and supernatural manifestations continued. The neighbourhood caught up the story, and the house remained untenanted for three years. Several persons negotiated for it; but, somehow, always before the bargain was closed they heard the unpleasant rumours and declined to treat any further.

It was in this state of things that my landlady, who at that time kept a boarding-house in Bleecker Street, and who wished to move further up town, conceived the bold idea of renting No.——, Twenty-sixth Street. Happening to have in her house rather a plucky and philosophical set of boarders, she laid her scheme before us, stating candidly everything she had heard respecting the ghostly qualities of the establishment to which she wished to remove us. With the exception of two timid persons—a sea captain and a returned Californian, who immediately gave notice that they would leave—all of Mrs. Moffat's guests declared that they would accompany her in her chivalric incursion into the abode of spirits.

Our removal was effected in the month of May, and we were charmed with our new residence. The portion of Twenty-sixth Street where our house is situated, between Seventh and Eighth Avenues, is one of the pleasantest localities in New York. The gardens back of the houses, running down nearly to the Hudson, form, in the summer time, a perfect avenue of verdure. The air is pure and invigorating, sweeping, as it does, straight across the river from the Weehawken heights, and even the ragged garden which surrounded the house, although displaying on washing days rather too much clothes-line, still gave us a piece of greensward to look at, and a cool retreat in the summer evenings, where we smoked our cigars in the dusk, and watched the fireflies flashing their dark-lanterns in the long grass.

Of course we had no sooner established ourselves at No.—— than we began to expect ghosts. We absolutely awaited their advent with eagerness. Our dinner conversation was supernatural. One of the boarders who had purchased Mrs. Crowe's "Night Side of Nature" for his own private delectation, was regarded as a public enemy by the entire household for not having bought twenty copies. The man led a life of supreme wretchedness while he was reading this volume. A system of espionage was established, of which he was the victim. If he incautiously laid the book down for an instant and left the room, it was immediately seized and read aloud in secret places to a select few. I found myself a person of immense importance, it having leaked out that I was tolerably well versed in the history of supernaturalism, and had once written a story the foundation of which was a ghost. If a table or a wainscot panel happened to warp when we were assembled in the large drawing room, there was an instant silence, and every one was prepared for an immediate clanking of chains and a spectral form.

After a month of psychological excitement, it was with the utmost dissatisfaction that we were forced to acknowledge that nothing in the remotest degree approaching the supernatural had manifested itself. Once the black butler asseverated that his candle had been blown out by some invisible agency while he was undressing himself for the night; but as I had more than once discovered this coloured gentleman in a condition when one candle must have appeared to him like two, I thought it possible that, by going a step further in his potations, he might have reversed this phenomenon, and seen no candle at all where he ought to have beheld one.

Things were in this state when an incident took place so awful and inexplicable that my reason fairly reels at the bare memory of the occurrence. It was the tenth of July. After dinner was over I repaired, with my friend Dr. Hammond, to the garden to smoke my evening pipe. Independent of certain mental sympathies which existed between the Doctor and myself, we were linked together by a vice. We both smoked opium. We knew each other's secret, and respected it. We enjoyed together that wonderful expansion of thought, that marvellous intensifying of the perceptive faculties, that boundless feeling of existence when we seem to have points of contact with the whole universe,—in short, unimaginable spiritual bliss, which I would not surrender for a throne, and which I hope you, reader, will never—never taste.

Those hours of opium happiness which the Doctor and I spent together in secret were regulated with a scientific accuracy. We did not blindly smoke the drug of paradise, and leave our dreams to chance. While smoking, we carefully steered our conversation through the brightest and calmest channels of thought. We talked of the East, and endeavoured to recall the magical panorama of its glowing scenery. We criticized the most sensuous poets—those who painted life ruddy with health, brimming with passion, happy in the possession of youth and strength and beauty. If we talked of Shakespeare's "Tempest", we lingered over Ariel, and avoided Caliban. Like the Guebers, we turned our faces to the East, and saw only the sunny side of the world.

This skilful colouring of our train of thought produced in our subsequent visions a corresponding tone. The splendours of Arabian fairyland dyed our dreams. We paced that narrow strip of grass with the tread and port of kings. The song of the *rana arborea*, while he clung to the bark of the ragged plum-tree, sounded like the strains of divine musicians. Houses, walls, and streets melted like rain clouds, and vistas of unimaginable glory stretched away before us. It was a rapturous companionship. We enjoyed the vast delight more perfectly because, even in our most ecstatic moments, we were conscious of each other's presence. Our pleasures, while individual, were still twin, vibrating and moving in musical accord.

On the evening in question, the tenth of July, the Doctor and myself drifted into an unusually metaphysical mood. We lit our large meerschaums, filled with fine Turkish tobacco, in the core of which burned a little black nut of opium, that, like the nut in the fairy tale, held within its narrow limits wonders beyond the reach of kings; we paced to and fro, conversing. A strange perversity dominated the currents of our thoughts. They would *not* flow through the sunlit channels into which we strove to divert them. For some unaccountable reason, they constantly diverged into dark and lonesome beds, where a continual gloom brooded. It was in vain that, after our old fashion, we flung ourselves on the shores of the East, and talked of its gay bazaars, of the splendours of the time of Haroun, of harems and golden palaces. Black afreets continually arose from the depths of our talk, and expanded, like the one the fisherman released from the copper vessel, until they blotted everything bright from our vision. Insensibly, we yielded to the occult force that swayed us, and indulged in gloomy speculation. We had talked some time upon the proneness of the human mind to mysticism, and the almost universal love of the terrible, when Hammond suddenly said to me, "What do you consider to be the greatest element of terror?"

The question puzzled me. That many things were terrible, I knew. Stumbling over a corpse in the dark; beholding, as I once did, a woman floating down a steep and rapid river, with wildly lifted arms, and awful, upturned face, uttering, as she drifted, shrieks that rent one's heart while we, the spectators, stood frozen at a window which overhung the river at a height of sixty feet, unable to make the slightest effort to save her, but dumbly watching her last supreme agony and her disappearance. A shattered wreck, with no life visible, encountered floating listlessly on the ocean, is a terrible object, for it suggests a huge terror, the proportions of which are veiled. But it now struck me, for the first time, that there must be one great and ruling embodiment of fear,—a King of Terrors, to which all others must succumb. What might it be? To what train of circumstances would it owe its existence?

"I confess, Hammond," I replied to my friend, "I never considered the subject before. That there must be one Something more terrible than any other thing, I feel. I cannot attempt, however, even the most vague definition."

"I am somewhat like you, Harry," he answered. "I feel my capacity to experience a terror greater than anything yet conceived by the human mind;—something combining in fearful and unnatural amalgamation hitherto supposed in-compatable elements. The calling of the voices in Brockden Brown's novel of 'Wieland' is awful; so is the picture of the Dweller of the Threshold, in Bulwer's 'Zanoni'; but," he added, shaking his head gloomily, "there is something more horrible still than these."

"Look here, Hammond," I rejoined, "let us drop this kind of talk, for heaven's sake! We shall suffer for it, depend on it."

"I don't know what's the matter with me tonight,' he replied, "but my brain is running upon all sorts of weird and awful thoughts. I feel as if I could write a story like Hoffmann, tonight, if I were only master of a literary style."

"Well, if we are going to be Hoffmannesque in our talk, I'm off to bed. Opium and nightmares should never be brought together. How sultry it is! Goodnight, Hammond."

"Goodnight, Harry. Pleasant dreams to you."

"To you, gloomy wretch, afreets, ghouls, and enchanters."

We parted, and each sought his respective chamber. I undressed quickly and got into bed, taking with me, according to my usual custom, a book, over which I generally read myself to sleep. I opened the volume as soon as I had laid my head upon the pillow, and instantly flung it to the other side of the room. It was Goudon's "History of Monsters",—a curious French work, which I had lately imported from Paris, but which, in the state of mind I had then reached, was anything but an agreeable companion. I resolved to go to sleep at once; so, turning down my gas until nothing but a little blue point of light glimmered on the top of the tube, I composed myself to rest.

The room was in total darkness. The atom of gas that still remained alight did not illuminate a distance of three inches round the burner. I desperately drew my arm across my eyes, as if to shut out even the darkness, and tried to think of nothing. It was in vain. The confounded themes touched on by Hammond in the garden kept obtruding themselves on my brain. I battled against them. I erected ramparts of would-be blankness of intellect to keep them out. They still crowded upon me. While I was lying still as a corpse, hoping that by a perfect physical inaction I should hasten mental repose, an awful incident occurred. A Something dropped, as it seemed, from the ceiling, plumb upon my chest, and the next instant I felt two bony hands encircling my throat, endeavouring to choke me.

I am no coward, and am possessed of considerable physical strength. The suddenness of the attack, instead of stunning me, strung every nerve to its highest tension. My body acted from instinct, before my brain had time to realize the terrors of my position. In an instant I wound two muscular arms around the creature, and squeezed it, with all the strength of despair, against my chest. In a few seconds the bony hands that had fastened on my throat loosened their hold, and I was free to breathe once more. Then commenced a struggle of awful intensity. Immersed in the most profound darkness, totally ignorant of the nature of the Thing by which I was so suddenly attacked, finding my grasp slipping every moment, by reason, it seemed to me, of the entire nakedness, neck, and chest, having every moment to protect my throat against a pair of sinewy, agile hands, which my utmost efforts could not confine,—these were a combination of circumstances to combat which required all the strength, skill, and courage that I possessed.

At last, after a silent, deadly, exhausting struggle, I got my assailant under by a series of incredible efforts of strength. Once pinned, with my knee on what I made out to be its chest, I knew that I was victor. I rested for a moment to breathe. I heard the creature beneath me panting in the darkness, and felt the violent throbbing of a heart. It was apparently as exhausted as I was; that was one comfort. At this moment I remembered that I usually placed under my pillow, before going to bed, a large yellow silk pocket-handkerchief. I felt for it instantly; it was there. In a few seconds more I had, after a fashion, pinioned the creature's arms.

I now felt tolerably secure. There was nothing more to be done but to turn on the gas, and, having first seen what my midnight assailant was like, arouse the household. I will confess to being actuated by a certain pride in not giving the alarm before; I wished to make the capture alone and unaided.

Never losing my hold for an instant, I slipped from the bed to the floor, dragging my captive with me. I had but a few steps to make to reach the gas burner; these I made with the greatest caution, holding the creature in a grip like a vice. At last I got within arm's length of the tiny speck of blue light which told me where the gas burner lay. Quick as lightning I released my grasp with one hand and let on the full flood of light. Then I turned to look at my captive.

I cannot even attempt to give any definition of my sensations the instant after I turned on the gas. I suppose I must have shrieked with terror, for in less than a minute afterwards my room was crowded with the inmates of the house. I shudder now as I think of that awful moment. *I saw nothing!* Yes; I had one arm firmly clasped round a breathing, panting, corporeal shape, my other hand gripped with all its strength a throat as warm, and apparently fleshly, as my own; and yet with living substance in my grasp, with its body pressed against my own, and all in the bright glare of a large jet of gas, I absolutely beheld nothing! Not even an outline—a vapour!

I do not, even at this hour, realize the situation in which I found myself. I cannot recall the astounding incident thoroughly. Imagination in vain tries to compass the awful paradox.

It breathed. I felt its warm breath upon my cheek. It struggled fiercely. It had hands. They clutched me. Its skin was smooth, like my own. There it lay, pressed close up against me, solid as stone—and yet utterly invisible!

I wonder that I did not faint or go mad on the instant. Some wonderful instinct must have sustained me; for, absolutely, in place of loosening my hold on the terrible Enigma, I seemed to gain an additional strength in my moment of horror, and tightened my grasp with such wonderful force that I felt the creature shivering with agony.

Just then Hammond entered my room at the head of the household. As soon as he beheld my face—which, I suppose, must have been an awful sight to look at—he hastened forward, crying, "Great heaven, Harry! what has happened?"

"Hammond! Hammond!" I cried, "come here. O, this is awful! I have been attacked in bed by something or other, which I have hold of; but I can't see it,—I can't see it!"

Hammond, doubtless struck by the unfeigned horror expressed in my countenance, made one or two steps forward with an anxious yet puzzled expression. A very audible titter burst from the remainder of my visitors. This suppressed laughter made me furious. To laugh at a human being in my position! It was the worst species of cruelty. *Now*, I can understand why the appearance of a man struggling violently, as it would seem, with an airy nothing, and calling for assistance against a vision, should have appeared ludicrous. *Then*, so great was my rage against the mocking crowd that had I the power I would have stricken them dead where they stood.

"Hammond! Hammond!" I cried again, despairingly, "for God's sake come to me. I can hold the—the thing but a short while longer. It is overpowering me. Help me! Help me!"

"Harry," whispered Hammond, approaching me, "you have been smoking too much opium."

"I swear to you, Hammond, that this is no vision," I answered, in the same low tone. "Don't you see how it shakes my whole frame with its struggles? If you don't believe me, convince yourself. Feel it,—touch it."

Hammond advanced and laid his hand in the spot I indicated. A wild cry of horror burst from him. He had felt it!

In a moment he had discovered somewhere in my room a long piece of cord, and was the next instant winding it and knotting it about the body of the unseen being that I clasped in my arms.

"Harry," he said, in a hoarse, agitated voice, for, though he preserved his presence of mind, he was deeply moved. "Harry, it's all safe now. You may let go, old fellow, if you're tired. The Thing can't move."

I was utterly exhausted, and I gladly loosed my hold.

Hammond stood holding the ends of the cord that bound the Invisible, twisted round his hand, while before him, self-supporting as it were, he held a rope laced and interlaced, and stretching tightly around a vacant space. I never saw a man so thoroughly stricken with awe. Nevertheless his face expressed all the courage and determination which I knew him to possess. His lips, although white, were set firmly, and one could perceive at a glance that, although stricken with fear, he was not daunted.

The confusion that ensued among the guests of the house who were witnesses of this extraordinary scene between Hammond and myself,—who beheld the pantomime of binding this struggling Something,—who beheld me almost sinking from physical exhaustion when my task of jailer was over,—the confusion and terror that took possession of the bystanders, when they saw all this, was beyond description. The weaker ones fled from the apartment. The few who remained clustered near the door and could not be induced to approach Hammond and his Charge. Still incredulity broke out through their terror. They had not the courage to satisfy themselves and yet they doubted. It was in vain that I begged of some of the men to come near and convince themselves by touch of the existence in that room of a living being which was invisible. They were incredulous, but did not dare to undeceive themselves. How could a solid, living, breathing body be invisible, they asked. My reply was this. I gave a sign to Hammond, and both of us—conquering our fearful repugnance to touch the invisible creature—lifted it from the ground, manacled as it was, and took it to my bed. Its weight was about that of a boy of fourteen.

"Now, my friends," I said, as Hammond and myself held the creature suspended over the bed, "I can give you self-evident proof that here is a solid, ponderable body which, nevertheless, you cannot see. Be good enough to watch the surface of the bed attentively."

I was astonished at my own courage in treating this strange event so calmly; but I had recovered from my first terror, and felt a sort of scientific pride in the affair, which dominated every other feeling.

The eyes of the bystanders were immediately fixed on my bed. At a given signal Hammond and I let the creature fall. There was the dull sound of a heavy body alighting on a soft mass. The timbers of the bed creaked. A deep impression marked itself distinctly on the pillow, and on the bed itself. The crowd who witnessed this gave a low cry, and rushed from the room. Hammond and I were left alone with our Mystery.

We remained silent for some time, listening to the low, irregular breathing of the creature on the bed, and watching the rustle of the bed clothes as it impotently struggled to free itself from confinement. Then Hammond spoke.

"Harry, this is awful."

"Ay, awful."

"But not unaccountable."

"Not unaccountable! What do you mean? Such a thing has never occurred since the birth of the world. I know not what to think, Hammond. God grant that I am not mad, and that this is not an insane fantasy!"

"Let us reason a little, Harry. Here is a solid body which we touch, but which we cannot see. The fact is so unusual that it strikes us with terror. Is there no parallel, though, for such a phenomenon? Take a piece of pure glass. It is tangible and transparent. A certain chemical coarseness is all that prevents its being entirely transparent as to be totally invisible. It is not *theoretically impossible*, mind you, to make a glass which shall not reflect a single ray of light,—a glass so pure and homogeneous in its atoms that the rays from the sun will pass through it as they do through the air, refracting but not reflecting. We do not see the air, and yet we feel it."

"That's all very well, Hammond, but these are inanimate substances. Glass does not breathe, air does not breathe. *This* thing has a heart that palpitates—a will that moves it—lungs that play, and inspire and respire."

"You forget the phenomena of which we have so often heard of late," answered the Doctor gravely. "At the meetings called 'spirit circles', invisible hands have been thrust into the hands of those persons round the table—warm, fleshly hands that seemed to pulsate with mortal life."

"What? Do you think, then, that this thing is—"

"I don't know what it is," was the solemn reply; "but please the gods I will, with your assistance, thoroughly investigate it."

We watched together, smoking many pipes, all night long, by the bedside of the unearthly being that tossed and panted until it was apparently wearied out. Then we learned by the low, regular breathing that it slept.

The next morning the house was all astir. The boarders congregated on the landing outside my room, and Hammond and myself were lions. We had to answer a thousand questions as to the state of our extraordinary prisoner, for as yet not one person in the house except ourselves could be induced to set foot in the apartment.

The creature was awake. This was evidenced by the convulsive manner in which the bed clothes were moved in its efforts to escape. There was something truly terrible in beholding, as it were, those secondhand indications of the terrible writhings and agonized struggles for liberty which themselves were invisible.

Hammond and myself had racked our brains during the long night to discover some means by which we might realize the shape and general appearance of the Enigma. As well as we could make out by passing our hands over the creature's form, its outlines and lineaments were human. There was a mouth; a round, smooth head without hair; a nose, which, however, was little elevated above the cheeks; and its hands and feet felt like those of a boy. At first we thought of placing the being on a smooth surface and tracing its outline with chalk, as shoemakers trace the outline of a foot. This plan was given up as being of no value. Such an outline would give not the slightest idea of its conformation.

A happy thought struck me. We would make a cast of it in plaster of Paris. This would give us the solid figure, and satisfy all our wishes. But how to do it? The movements of the creature would disturb the setting of the plastic covering, and distort the mould. Another thought. Why not give it chloroform? It has respiratory organs—that was evident by its breathing. Once reduced to a state of insensibility, we could do with it what we would. Doctor X—— was sent for;

and after the worthy physician had recovered from the first shock of amazement, he proceeded to administer the chloroform. In three minutes afterward we were enabled to remove the fetters from the creature's body, and a modeller was busily engaged in covering the invisible form with the moist clay. In five minutes more we had a mould, and before evening a rough facsimile of the Mystery. It was shaped like a man,—distorted, uncouth, and horrible, but still like a man. It was small, not over four feet and some inches in height, and its limbs revealed a muscular development that was unparalleled. Its face surpassed in hideousness anything I have ever seen. Gustave Doré, or Callot, or Tony Johannot, never conceived anything so horrible. There is a face in one of the latter's illustrations to *Un Voyage où il vous plaira*, which somewhat approaches the countenance of this creature, but does not equal it. It was the physiognomy of what I should fancy a ghoul might be. It looked as if it was capable of feeding on human flesh.

Having satisfied our curiosity, and bound every one in the house to secrecy, it became a question what was to be done with our Enigma? It was impossible that we should keep such a horror in our house; it was equally impossible that such an awful being should be let loose upon the world. I confess that I would have gladly voted for the creature's destruction. But who would shoulder the responsibility? Who would undertake the execution of this horrible semblance of a human being? Day after day this question was deliberated gravely. The boarders all left the house. Mrs. Moffat was in despair, and threatened Hammond and myself with all sorts of legal penalties if we did not remove the Horror. Our answer was, "We will go if you like, but we decline taking this creature with us. Remove it yourself if you please. It appeared in your house. On you the responsibility rests." To this there was, of course, no answer. Mrs. Moffat could not obtain for love or money a person who would even approach the Mystery.

The most singular part of the affair was that we were entirely ignorant of what the creature habitually fed on. Everything in the way of nutriment that we could think of was placed before it, but was never touched. It was awful to stand by, day after day, and see the clothes toss, and hear the hard breathing, and know that it was starving.

Ten, twelve days, a fortnight passed, and it still lived. The pulsations of the heart, however, were daily growing fainter, and had now nearly ceased. It was evident that the creature was dying for want of sustenance. While this terrible life-struggle was going on, I felt miserable. I could not sleep. Horrible as the creature was, it was pitiful to think of the pangs it was suffering.

At last it died. Hammond and I found it cold and stiff one morning in the bed. The heart had ceased to beat, the lungs to inspire. We hastened to bury it in the garden. It was a strange funeral, the dropping of that viewless corpse into the damp hole. The cast of its form I gave to Doctor X——, who keeps it in his museum in Tenth Street.

As I am on the eve of a long journey from which I may not return, I have drawn up this narrative of an event the most singular that has ever come to my knowledge.

THE ANTICIPATOR

Morley Roberts (1857–1942)

In his youth Morley Roberts did not seem he would make much of his life. A failed academic, having argued with his father he left England at the age of twenty-one and headed for Australia where he became a sheep farmer for three years. Upon his return he tried to work as a civil servant which was not to his liking and he set off again on his travels, this time to the United States and Canada: he fell in love with British Columbia which he felt was about as remote as he could be. That was until he travelled around the Pacific and South Africa. When he returned again to England his friend George Gissing advised that he ought to write about his experiences and from then on Roberts never stopped, producing over three hundred short stories, more than thirty novels, and much else besides. Amongst his many collections, most of which feature sea stories or episodes in far-flung corners of the world, are a few with a number of strange tales, including *The Keeper of the Waters* (1898) and *Midsummer Madness* (1909). The first of those includes the story reprinted here, "The Anticipator", which has one of the most original ideas of any story.

"Of course, I admit it isn't plagiarism," said Carter Esplan, savagely; "it's fate, it's the devil, but is it the less irritating on that account? No, no!" And he ran his hand through his hair till it stood on end. He shook with febrile excitement, a red spot burned on either cheek, and his bitten lip quivered.

"Confound Burford and his parents and his ancestors! The tools to him that can handle them," he added, after a pause, during which his friend Vincent curiously considered him.

"It's your own fault, my dear wild man," said he; "you are too lazy. Besides, remember these things—these notions, motives—are in the air. Originality is only the art of catching early worms. Why don't you do the things as soon as you invent them?"

"Now you talk like a bourgeois, like a commercial traveller," returned Esplan, angrily. "Why doesn't an apple-tree yield apples when the blossoms are fertilized? Why wait for summer, and the influences of wind and sky? Why don't live chickens burst new-laid eggs? Shall parturition tread sudden on conception? Didn't the mountain labour to bring forth a mouse? And shall—"

"Your works of genius do not require a portion of the eternity to which they are destined?"

"Stuff!" snarled Esplan; "but you know my method. I catch the suggestion, the floating thistledown of thought, the title, maybe; and then I leave it, perhaps without a note, to the brain, to the subliminal

33

consciousness, the subconscious self. The story grows in the dark of the inner, perpetual, sleepless soul. It may be rejected by the artistic tribunal sitting there; it may be bidden to stand aside. I, the outer I, the husk-case of heredities, know nothing of it, but one day I take the pen and the hand writes it. This is the automatism of art, and I—I am nothing, the last only of the concealed individualities within me. Perhaps a dumb ancestor attains speech, and yet the Complex Ego Esplan must be anticipated in this way."

He rose and paced the lonely club smoking-room with irregular steps. His nerves were evidently quivering, his brain was wild. But Vincent, who was a physician, saw deeper. For Esplan's speech was jerky, at times he missed the right word; the locomotor centres were not under control.

"What of morphine?" he thought. "I wonder if he's at it again, and is today without his quantum." But Esplan burst out once more.

"I should not care so much if Burford did them well, but he doesn't know how to write a story. Look at this last thing of mine—of his. I saw it leaping and alive; it ran and sang, a very Maenad; it had red blood. With him it wasn't even born dead; it squeaks puppetry, and leaks sawdust, and moves like a lay figure, and smells of most manifest manufacture. But I can't do it now. He has spoilt it for ever. It's the third time. Curse him, and my luck! I work when I must."

"Your calling is very serious to you," said Vincent, lazily. "After all, what does it matter? What are stories? Are they not opiates for cowards' lives? I would rather invent some little instrument, or build a plank bridge across a muddy stream, than write the best of them."

Esplan turned on him.

"Well, well," he almost shouted; "the man who invented chloroform was great, and the makers of it are useful. Call stories chloral, morphia, bromides, if you will, but we give ease."

"When it might be better to use blisters."

"Rot!" answered Esplan, rudely. "In any case, your talk is idle. I am I, and writers are writers—small, if you will, but a result and a force, Give me a rest. Don't talk ideal poppycock!"

He ordered liqueur brandy. After drinking it his aspect changed a little, and he smiled.

"Perhaps it won't occur again. If it does, I shall feel that Burford is very much in my way, I shall have to—"

"Remove him?" asked Vincent.

"No, but work quicker. I have something to write soon. It would just suit him to spoil."

The talk changed, and soon afterwards the friends parted. Esplan went to his chambers in Bloomsbury. He paced his sitting-room idly for a few minutes, but after a while he began to feel the impulse in his brain; his fingers itched, the semi-automatic mood came on. He sat down and wrote, at first slowly, then quicker, and at last furiously.

It was three in the afternoon when he commenced work. At ten o'clock he was still at his desk, and the big table on which it stood was strewn with tobacco-ashes and many pipes. His hair again stood on end, for at intervals he ran his damp hands through it. His eyes altered like opals; at times they sparkled and almost blazed, and then grew dim. He changed at each sentence; he mouthed his written talk audibly; each thought was reflected in his pale, mobile face. He laughed and then groaned; at the crisis, tears ran down and blurred the already undecipherable script. But at eleven he rose, stiff in every limb, and staggering. With difficulty he picked the unpaged leaves from the floor, and sorted them in due order. He fell into his chair.

"It's good, it's good!" he said, chuckling; "what a queer devil I am! My dumb ancestors pipe oddly in me. It's strange, devilish strange; man's but a mouthpiece, and crazy at that. How long has this last thing been hatching? The story is old, yet new. Gibbon shall have it. It will just suit him. Little beast, little horror, little hog, with a divine gold ring of appreciation in his grubbing snout."

He drank half a tumbler of whisky, and tumbled into bed. His mind ran riot.

"My ego's a bit fissured," he said. "I ought to be careful."

And ere he fell asleep he talked conscious nonsense. Incongruous ideas linked themselves together, he sneered at his brain's folly, and yet he was afraid. He used morphine at last in such a big dose that it touched the optic centre and subjective lightnings flashed in his dark room. He dreamed of an "At Home," where he met big, brutal Burford wearing a great diamond in his shirt-front.

"Bought by my conveyed thoughts," he said. But looking down he perceived that he had yet a greater jewel of his own, and soon his soul melted in the contemplation of its rays, till his consciousness was dissipated by a divine absorption into the very Nirvana of Light.

When he woke the next day, it was already late in the afternoon. He was overcome by yesterday's labour, and, though much less irritable, he walked feebly. The trouble of posting his story to Gibbon seemed almost too much for him, but he sent it, and took a cab to his club, where he sat almost comatose for many hours.

Two days afterwards he received a note from the editor, returning his story. It was good, but—

"Burford sent me a tale with the same motive weeks ago, and I accepted it."

Esplan smashed his thin white hand on his mantelpiece, and made it bleed. That night he got drunk on champagne, and the brilliant wine seemed to nip and bite and twist every nerve and brain-cell. His irritability grew so extreme that he lay in wait for subtle, unconceived insults, and meditated morbidly on the aspect of innocent strangers.

He gave the waiter double what was necessary, not because it was particularly deserved, but because he felt that the slightest sign of discontent on the man's part might lead to an uncontrollable outburst of anger on his own.

Next day, he met Burford in Piccadilly, and cut him dead with a bitter sneer.

"I daren't speak to him—I daren't!" he muttered.

And Burford, who could not quite understand, felt outraged. He himself hated Esplan with the hatred of an outpaced, outsailed rival. He knew his own work lacked the diabolical certainty of Esplan's—it wanted the fine phrase, the right red word of colour, the rush and onward march to due finality, the bitter, exact conviction, the knowledge of humanity that lies in inheritance, the exalted experience that proves received intuitions. He was, he knew, a successful failure, and his ambition was greater even than Esplan's. For he was greedy, grasping, esurient, and his hollowness was obvious even before Esplan proved it with his ringing touch.

"He takes what I have done, and does it better. It's malice, malice," he urged to himself.

And when Esplan placed his last story, and the world remembered, only to forget in its white-hot brilliance, the cold paste of Burford's Paris jewel, he felt hell surge within him. But he beat his thoughts down for a while, and went on his little, laboured way.

The success of this story and Burford's bitter eclipse helped Esplan greatly, and he might have got saner if other influences working for misery in his life had not hurt him. For a certain woman died, one whom none knew to be his friend, and he clung to morphine, which, in its increase, helped to throw him later.

And at last the crash did come, for Burford had two stories, better far than his usual work, in a magazine that Esplan looked on as his own, They were on Esplan's very motives; he had them almost ready to write. The sting of this last bitter blow drove him off his tottering balance; he conceived murder, and plotted it brutally, and then subtly, and became dominated by it, till his life was the flower of the insane motive. It altered nothing that a reviewer pointed out the close resemblance between the two men's work, and, exalting Esplan's genius, placed one writer beyond all cavil, the other below all place.

But that drove Burford crazy. It was so bitterly true. He ground his teeth, and hating his own work, hated worse the man who destroyed his own conceit. He wanted to do harm. How should he do it?

Esplan had long since gone under. He was a homicidal maniac, with one man before him. He conceived and wrote schemes. His stories ran to murder. He read and imagined means. At times he was in danger of believing he had already done the deed. One wild day he almost gave himself up for this proleptic death. Thus his imagination burnt and flamed before his conceived path.

"I'll do it, I'll do it," he muttered; and at the club the men talked about him.

"Tomorrow," he said, and then he put it off. He must consider the art of it. He left it to bourgeon in his fertile brain. And at last, just as he wrote, action, lighted up by strange circumstance, began to loom big before him. Such a murder would wake a vivid world, and be an epoch in crime. If the red earth were convulsed in war, even then would it stay to hear that incredible, true story, and, soliciting deeper knowledge, seek out the method and growth of means and motive. He chuckled audibly in the street, and laughed thin laughter in his room of fleeting visions. At night he walked the lonely streets near at hand, considering eagerly the rush of his own divided thoughts, and, leaning against the railings of the leafy gardens, he saw ghosts in the moon shadows and beckoned them to converse, He became a nightbird and was rarely seen.

"Tomorrow," he said at last. Tomorrow he would really take the first step. He rubbed his hands and laughed as he pondered near home, in his own lonely square, the finer last details which his imagination multiplied.

"Stay, enough, enough!" he cried to his separate mad mind; "it is already done."

And the shadows were very dark about him. He turned to go home.

Then came immortality to him in strange shape. For it seemed as though his ardent and confined soul burst out of his narrow brain and sparkled marvellously. Lights showered about him, and from a rose sky lightnings flashed, and he heard awful thunder. The heavens opened in a white blaze, and he saw unimaginable things. He reeled, put his hand to his stricken head, and fell heavily in a pool of his own blood.

And the Anticipator, horribly afraid, ran down a by-street.

THE LADY, OR THE TIGER?

and

THE DISCOURAGER OF HESITANCY

Frank R. Stockton (1834–1902)

In his day Stockton was one of America's most popular humorists. He carved for himself a special niche using fairy tales and fables as a way of satirizing society and pricking the bubble of pomposity. These began with "Ting-a-Ling" in 1867 and continued right through to his death in 1902 and even beyond. *The Return of Frank R. Stockton* (1913) were stories purportedly narrated by Stockton through the medium Etta de Camp. His collected works, *The Novels and Stories of Frank R. Stockton* (1899–1904) runs to twenty-three volumes. Of all his stories, though, the one for which he is best remembered is "The Lady, or the Tiger?" which effectively launched the fascination for puzzle stories. Far less known is its sequel, and both are reprinted here.

I n the very olden time there lived a semi-barbaric king, whose ideas, though somewhat polished and sharpened by the progressiveness of distant Latin neighbours, were still large, florid, and untrammelled, as became the half of him which was barbaric. He was a man of exuberant fancy, and, withal, of an authority so irresistible that, at his will, he turned his varied fancies into facts. He was greatly given to self-communing, and, when he and himself agreed upon anything, the thing was done. When every member of his domestic and political systems moved smoothly in its appointed course, his nature was bland and genial; but, whenever there was a little hitch, and some of his orbs got out of their orbits, he was blander and more genial still, for nothing pleased him so much as to make the crooked straight and crush down uneven places.

Among the borrowed notions by which his barbarism had become semified was that of the public arena, in which, by exhibitions of manly and beastly valour, the minds of his subjects were refined and cultured.

But even here the exuberant and barbaric fancy asserted itself. The arena of the king was built, not to give the people an opportunity of hearing the rhapsodies of dying gladiators, nor to enable them to view the inevitable conclusion of a conflict between religious opinions and hungry jaws, but for purposes far better adapted to widen and develop the mental energies of the people. This vast amphitheatre, with its encircling galleries, its mysterious vaults, and its unseen passages, was an agent of poetic justice, in which crime was punished, or virtue rewarded, by the decrees of an impartial and incorruptible chance.

When a subject was accused of a crime of sufficient importance to interest the king, public notice was given that on an appointed day the fate of the accused person would be decided in the king's arena, a structure which well deserved its name, for, although its form and plan were borrowed from afar, its purpose emanated solely from the brain of this man, who, every barleycorn a king, knew no tradition to which he owed more allegiance than pleased his fancy, and who ingrafted on every adopted form of human thought and action the rich growth of his barbaric idealism.

When all the people had assembled in the galleries, and the king, surrounded by his court, sat high up on his throne of royal state on one side of the arena, he gave a signal, a door beneath him opened, and the accused subject stepped out into the amphitheatre. Directly opposite him, on the other side of the inclosed space, were two doors, exactly alike and side by side. It was the duty and the privilege of the person on trial to walk directly to these doors and open one of them. He could open either door he pleased; he was subject to no guidance or influence but that of the aforementioned impartial and incorruptible chance. If he opened the one, there came out of it a hungry tiger, the fiercest and most cruel that could be procured, which immediately sprang upon him and tore him to pieces as a punishment for his guilt. The moment that the case of the criminal was thus decided, doleful iron bells were clanged, great wails went up from the hired mourners posted on the outer rim of the arena, and the vast audience, with bowed heads and downcast hearts, wended slowly their homeward way, mourning greatly that one so young and fair, or so old and respected, should have merited so dire a fate.

But, if the accused person opened the other door, there came forth from it a lady, the most suitable to his years and station that his majesty could select among his fair subjects, and to this lady he was immediately married, as a reward of his innocence. It mattered not that he might already possess a wife and family, or that his affections might be engaged upon an object of his own selection; the king allowed no such subordinate arrangements to interfere with his great scheme of retribution and reward. The exercises, as in the other instance, took place immediately, and in the arena. Another door opened beneath the king, and a priest, followed by a band of choristers, and dancing maidens blowing joyous airs on golden horns and treading an epithalamic measure, advanced to where the pair stood, side by side, and the wedding was promptly and cheerily solemnized. Then the gay brass bells rang forth their merry peals, the people shouted glad hurrahs, and the innocent man, preceded by children strewing flowers on his path, led his bride to his home.

This was the king's semi-barbaric method of administering justice. Its perfect fairness is obvious. The criminal could not know out of which door would come the lady; he opened either he pleased, without having the slightest idea whether, in the next instant, he was to be devoured or married. On some occasions the tiger came out of one door, and on some out of the other. The decisions of this tribunal were not only fair, they were positively determinate: the accused person was instantly punished if he found himself guilty, and, if innocent, he was rewarded on the spot, whether he liked it or not. There was no escape from the judgments of the king's arena.

The institution was a very popular one. When the people gathered together on one of the great trial days, they never knew whether they were to witness a bloody slaughter or a hilarious wedding. This element of uncertainty lent an interest to the occasion which it could not otherwise have attained. Thus, the masses were entertained and pleased, and the thinking part of the community could bring no charge of unfairness against this plan, for did not the accused person have the whole matter in his own hands?

This semi-barbaric king had a daughter as blooming as his most florid fancies, and with a soul as fervent and imperious as his own. As is usual in such cases, she was the apple of his eye, and was loved by him above all humanity. Among his courtiers was a young man of that fineness of blood and lowness of station common to the conventional heroes of romance who love royal maidens. This royal maiden was well satisfied with her lover, for he was handsome and brave to a degree unsurpassed in all this kingdom, and she loved him with an ardour that had enough of barbarism in it to make it exceedingly warm and strong. This love affair moved on happily for many months, until one day the king happened to discover its existence. He did not hesitate nor waver in regard to his duty in the premises. The youth was immediately cast into prison, and a day was appointed for his trial in the king's arena. This, of course, was an especially important occasion, and his majesty, as well as all the people, was greatly interested in the workings and development of this trial. Never before had such a case occurred; never before had a subject dared to love the daughter of the king. In after years such things became commonplace enough, but then they were in no slight degree novel and startling.

The tiger-cages of the kingdom were searched for the most savage and relentless beasts, from which the fiercest monster might be selected for the arena; and the ranks of maiden youth and beauty throughout the land were carefully surveyed by competent judges in order that the young man might have a fitting bride in case fate did not determine for him a different destiny. Of course, everybody knew that the deed with which the accused was charged had been done.

He had loved the princess, and neither he, she, nor any one else, thought of denying the fact; but the king would not think of allowing any fact of this kind to interfere with the workings of the tribunal, in which he took such great delight and satisfaction. No matter how the affair turned out, the youth would be disposed of, and the king would take an aesthetic pleasure in watching the course of events, which would determine whether or not the young man had done wrong in allowing himself to love the princess.

The appointed day arrived. From far and near the people gathered, and thronged the great galleries of the arena, and crowds, unable to gain admittance, massed themselves against its outside walls. The king and his court were in their places, opposite the twin doors, those fateful portals, so terrible in their similarity.

All was ready. The signal was given. A door beneath the royal party opened, and the lover of the princess walked into the arena. Tall, beautiful, fair, his appearance was greeted with a low hum of admiration and anxiety. Half the audience had not known so grand a youth had lived among them. No wonder the princess loved him! What a terrible thing for him to be there!

As the youth advanced into the arena he turned, as the custom was, to bow to the king, but he did not think at all of that royal personage. His eyes were fixed upon the princess, who sat to the right of her father. Had it not been for the moiety of barbarism in her nature it is probable that lady would not have been there, but her intense and fervid soul would not allow her to be absent on an occasion in which she was so terribly interested. From the moment that the decree had gone forth that her lover should decide his fate in the king's arena, she had thought of nothing, night or day, but this great event and the various subjects connected with it. Possessed of more power, influence, and force of character than any one who had ever before been interested in such a case, she had done what no other person had done,—she had possessed herself of the secret of the doors. She knew in which of the two rooms, that lay behind those doors, stood the cage of the tiger, with its open front, and in which waited the lady. Through these thick doors, heavily curtained with skins on the inside, it was impossible that any noise or suggestion should come from within to the person who should approach to raise the latch of one of them. But gold, and the power of a woman's will, had brought the secret to the princess.

And not only did she know in which room stood the lady ready to emerge, all blushing and radiant, should her door be opened, but she knew who the lady was. It was one of the fairest and loveliest of the damsels of the court who had been selected as the reward of the accused youth, should he be proved innocent of the crime of aspiring to one so far above him; and the princess hated her. Often had she seen, or imagined that she had seen, this fair creature throwing glances of admiration upon the person of her lover, and sometimes she thought these glances were perceived, and even returned. Now and then she had seen them talking together; it was but for a moment or two, but much can be said in a brief space; it may have been on most unimportant topics, but how could she know that? The girl was lovely, but she had dared to raise her eyes to the loved one of the princess; and, with all the intensity of the savage blood transmitted to her through long lines of wholly barbaric ancestors, she hated the woman who blushed and trembled behind that silent door.

When her lover turned and looked at her, and his eye met hers as she sat there, paler and whiter than any one in the vast ocean of anxious faces about her, he saw, by that power of quick perception which is given to those whose souls are one, that she knew behind which door crouched the tiger, and behind which stood the lady.

He had expected her to know it. He understood her nature, and his soul was assured that she would never rest until she had made plain to herself this thing, hidden to all other lookers-on, even to the king. The only hope for the youth in which there was any element of certainty was based upon the success of the princess in discovering this mystery; and the moment he looked upon her, he saw she had succeeded, as in his soul he knew she would succeed.

Then it was that his quick and anxious glance asked the question: "Which?" It was as plain to her as if he shouted it from where he stood. There was not an instant to be lost. The question was asked in a flash; it must be answered in another.

Her right arm lay on the cushioned parapet before her. She raised her hand, and made a slight, quick movement toward the right. No one but her lover saw her. Every eye but his was fixed on the man in the arena.

He turned, and with a firm and rapid step he walked across the empty space. Every heart stopped beating, every breath was held, every eye was fixed immovably upon that man. Without the slightest hesitation, he went to the door on the right, and opened it.

Now, the point of the story is this: Did the tiger come out of that door, or did the lady?

The more we reflect upon this question, the harder it is to answer. It involves a study of the human heart which leads us through devious mazes of passion, out of which it is difficult to find our way. Think of it, fair reader, not as if the decision of the question depended upon yourself, but upon that hot-blooded, semi-barbaric princess, her soul at a white heat beneath the combined fires of despair and jealousy. She had lost him, but who should have him?

How often, in her waking hours and in her dreams, had she started in wild horror, and covered her face with her hands as she thought of her lover opening the door on the other side of which waited the cruel fangs of the tiger!

But how much oftener had she seen him at the other door! How in her grievous reveries had she gnashed her teeth, and torn her hair, when she saw his start of rapturous delight as he opened the door of the lady! How her soul had burned in agony when she had seen him rush to meet that woman, with her flushing cheek and sparkling eye of triumph; when she had seen him lead her forth, his whole frame kindled with the joy of recovered life; when she had heard the glad shouts from the multitude, and the wild ringing of the happy bells; when she had seen the priest, with his joyous followers, advance to the couple, and make them man and wife before her very eyes; and when she had seen them walk away together upon their path of flowers, followed by the tremendous shouts of the hilarious multitude, in which her one despairing shriek was lost and drowned!

Would it not be better for him to die at once, and go to wait for her in the blessed regions of semi-barbaric futurity?

And yet, that awful tiger, those shrieks, that blood!

Her decision had been indicated in an instant, but it had been made after days and nights of anguished deliberation. She had known she would be asked, she had decided what she would answer, and, without the slightest hesitation, she had moved her hand to the right.

The question of her decision is one not to be lightly considered, and it is not for me to presume to set myself up as the one person able to answer it. And so I leave it with all of you: Which came out of the opened door—the lady, or the tiger?

I t was nearly a year after the occurrence of that event in the arena
of the semi-barbaric king known as the incident of the lady or the
tiger, that there came to the palace of this monarch a deputation
of five strangers from a far country. These men, of venerable and
dignified aspect and demeanour, were received by a high officer of
the court, and to him they made known their errand.

"Most noble officer," said the speaker of the deputation, "it so
happened that one of our countrymen was present here, in your
capital city, on that momentous occasion when a young man who had
dared to aspire to the hand of your king's daughter had been placed
in the arena, in the midst of the assembled multitude, and ordered to
open one of two doors, not knowing whether a ferocious tiger would
spring out upon him, or a beauteous lady would advance, ready to
become his bride. Our fellow citizen who was then present was a
man of supersensitive feelings, and at the moment when the youth
was about to open the door he was so fearful lest he should behold a
horrible spectacle that his nerves failed him, and he fled precipitately
from the arena, and, mounting his camel, rode homeward as fast as
he could go."

"We were all very much interested in the story which our countryman told us, and we were extremely sorry that he did not wait to see
the end of the affair. We hoped, however, that in a few weeks some
traveller from your city would come among us and bring us further

news, but up to that day when we left our country no such traveller had arrived. At last it was determined that the only thing to be done was to send a deputation to this country, and to ask the question: 'Which came out of the open door, the lady or the tiger?'"

When the high officer had heard the mission of this most respectable deputation, he led the five strangers into an inner room, where they were seated upon soft cushions, and where he ordered coffee, pipes, sherbet, and other semi-barbaric refreshments to be served to them. Then, taking his seat before them, he thus addressed the visitors.

"Most noble strangers, before answering the question you have come so far to ask, I will relate to you an incident which occurred not very long after that to which you have referred. It is well known in all regions hereabout that our great king is very fond of the presence of beautiful women about his court. All the ladies in waiting upon the queen and royal family are most lovely maidens, brought here from every part of the kingdom. The fame of this concourse of beauty, unequalled in any other royal court, has spread far and wide, and had it not been for the equally wide-spread fame of the systems of impetuous justice adopted by our king, many foreigners would doubtless have visited our court."

"But not very long ago there arrived here from a distant land a prince of distinguished appearance and undoubted rank. To such a one, of course, a royal audience was granted, and our king met him very graciously, and begged him to make known the object of his visit. Thereupon the prince informed his Royal Highness that, having heard of the superior beauty of the ladies of his court, he had come to ask permission to make one of them his wife."

"When our king heard this bold announcement, his face reddened, he turned uneasily on his throne, and we were all in dread lest some quick words of furious condemnation should leap from out his quivering lips. But by a mighty effort he controlled himself, and after a moment's silence he turned to the prince and said: 'Your request is granted. Tomorrow at noon you shall wed one of the fairest damsels of our court.' Then turning to his officers he said: 'Give orders that everything be prepared for a wedding in the palace at high noon tomorrow. Convey this royal prince to suitable apartments. Send to him tailors, bootmakers, hatters, jewellers, armourers, men of every craft whose services he may need. Whatever he asks, provide. And let all be ready for the ceremony tomorrow.'"

"'But, your Majesty,' exclaimed the prince, 'before we make these preparations, I would like—'

"'Say no more!' roared the king. 'My royal orders have been given, and nothing more is needed to be said. You asked a boon. I granted it, and I will hear no more on the subject. Farewell, my prince, until tomorrow noon.'"

"At this the king arose and left the audience chamber, while the prince was hurried away to the apartments selected for him. Here came to him tailors, hatters, jewellers, and every one who was needed to fit him out in grand attire for the wedding. But the mind of the prince was much troubled and perplexed."

"'I do not understand,' he said to his attendants, 'this precipitancy of action. When am I to see the ladies, that I may choose among them? I wish opportunity, not only to gaze upon their forms and faces, but to become acquainted with their relative intellectual development.'"

"'We can tell you nothing,' was the answer. 'What our king thinks right, that will he do. More than this we know not.'"

"'His Majesty's notions seem to be very peculiar,' said the prince, 'and, so far as I can see, they do not at all agree with mine.'"

"At that moment an attendant whom the prince had not noticed came and stood beside him. This was a broad-shouldered man of cheery aspect, who carried, its hilt in his right hand, and its broad back resting on his broad arm, an enormous scimitar, the upturned edge of which was keen and bright as any razor. Holding this formidable weapon as tenderly as though it had been a sleeping infant, this man drew closer to the prince and bowed."

"'Who are you?' exclaimed his Highness, starting back at the sight of the frightful weapon.'"

"'I,' said the other, with a courteous smile, 'am the Discourager of Hesitancy. When the king makes known his wishes to any one, a subject or visitor, whose disposition in some little points may be supposed not wholly to coincide with that of his Majesty, I am appointed to attend him closely, that, should he think of pausing in the path of obedience to the royal will, he may look at me, and proceed.'"

"The prince looked at him, and proceeded to be measured for a coat."

"The tailors and shoemakers and hatters worked all night, and the next morning, when everything was ready, and the hour of noon was drawing nigh, the prince again anxiously inquired of his attendants when he might expect to be introduced to the ladies."

"'The king will attend to that,' they said. 'We know nothing of the matter.'"

"'Your Highness,' said the Discourager of Hesitancy, approaching with a courtly bow, 'will observe the excellent quality of this edge.' And drawing a hair from his head, he dropped it upon the upturned edge of his scimitar, upon which it was cut in two at the moment of touching."

"The prince glanced, and turned upon his heel."

"Now came officers to conduct him to the grand hall of the palace, in which the ceremony was to be performed. Here the prince found the king seated upon his throne, with his nobles, his courtiers, and his officers standing about him in magnificent array. The prince was led to a position in front of the king, to whom he made obeisance, and then said:

"'Your majesty, before I proceed further—'

"At this moment an attendant, who had approached with a long scarf of delicate silk, wound it about the lower part of the prince's face so quickly and adroitly that he was obliged to cease speaking. Then, with wonderful dexterity, the rest of the scarf was wound around the prince's head, so that he was completely blindfolded. Thereupon the attendant quickly made openings in the scarf over the mouth and ears, so that the prince might breathe and hear, and fastening the ends of the scarf securely, he retired."

"The first impulse of the prince was to snatch the silken folds from his head and face, but, as he raised his hands to do so, he heard beside him the voice of the Discourager of Hesitancy, who gently whispered: 'I am here, your Highness.' And, with a shudder, the arms of the prince fell down by his side."

"Now before him he heard the voice of a priest, who had begun the marriage service in use in that semi-barbaric country. At his side he could hear a delicate rustle, which seemed to proceed from fabrics of soft silk. Gently putting forth his hand, he felt folds of such silk close behind him. Then came the voice of the priest requesting him to take the hand of the lady by his side; and reaching forth his right hand, the prince received within it another hand, so small, so soft, so delicately fashioned, and so delightful to the touch, that a thrill went through his being. Then, as was the custom of the country, the priest first asked the lady would she have this man to be her husband;

to which the answer gently came, in the sweetest voice he had ever heard: 'I will.'"

"Then ran raptures rampant through the prince's blood. The touch, the tone, enchanted him. All the ladies of that court were beautiful, the Discourager was behind him, and through his parted scarf he boldly answered: 'Yes, I will.'"

"Whereupon the priest pronounced them man and wife."

"Now the prince heard a little bustle about him, the long scarf was rapidly unrolled from his head, and he turned, with a start, to gaze upon his bride. To his utter amazement, there was no one there. He stood alone. Unable on the instant to ask a question or say a word, he gazed blankly about him."

"Then the king arose from his throne, and came down, and took him by the hand."

"'Where is my wife?' gasped the prince."

"'She is here,' said the king, leading him to a curtained doorway at the side of the hall."

"'The curtains were drawn aside, and the prince, entering, found himself in a long apartment, near the opposite wall of which stood a line of forty ladies, all dressed in rich attire, and each one apparently more beautiful than the rest.'"

"Waving his hand toward the line, the king said to the prince: "There is your bride! Approach, and lead her forth! But, remember this: that if you attempt to take away one of the unmarried damsels of our court, your execution will be instantaneous. Now, delay no longer. Step up and take your bride.'"

"The prince, as in a dream, walked slowly along the line of ladies, and then walked slowly back again. Nothing could he see about any one of them to indicate that she was more of a bride than the others. Their dresses were all similar, they all blushed, they all looked up and then looked down. They all had charming little hands. Not one spoke a word. Not one lifted a finger to make a sign. It was evident that the orders given them had been very strict."

"'Why this delay?' roared the king. 'If I had been married this day to one so fair as the lady who wedded you, I should not wait one second to claim her.'"

"The bewildered prince walked again up and down the line. And this time there was a slight change in the countenances of two of the ladies. One of the fairest gently smiled as he passed her. Another, just as beautiful, slightly frowned."

"'Now,' said the prince to himself, 'I am sure that it is one of those two ladies whom I have married. But which? One smiled. And would not any woman smile when she saw in such a case, her husband coming toward her? Then again, on the other hand, would not any woman frown when she saw her husband come toward her and fail to claim her? Would she not knit her lovely brows? Would she not inwardly say 'It is I! Don't you know it? Don't you feel it? Come!' But if this woman had not been married, would she not frown when she saw the man looking at her? Would she not say inwardly, "Don't stop at me! It is the next but one. It is two ladies above. Go on!" Then again, the one who married me did not see my face. Would she not now smile if she thought me comely? But if I wedded the one who frowned, could she restrain her disapprobation if she did not like me? Smiles invite the approach of true love. A frown is a reproach to a tardy advance. A smile—"

"'Now, hear me!' loudly cried the king. 'In ten seconds, if you do not take the lady we have given you, she who has just been made your bride shall be made your widow.'"

"And, as the last word was uttered, the Discourager of Hesitancy stepped close behind the prince and whispered: 'I am here!'"

"Now the prince could not hesitate an instant; he stepped forward and took one of the two ladies by the hand."

"Loud rang the bells, loud cheered the people, and the king came forward to congratulate the prince. He had taken his lawful bride."

"'Now, then,' said the officer to the deputation of five strangers from a far country, "when you can decide among yourselves which lady the prince chose, the one who smiled or the one who frowned, then I will tell you which came out of the open door, the lady or the tiger!"

At the latest accounts the five strangers had not yet decided.

THE WHITE PEOPLE

Arthur Machen (1863–1947)

Along with Bram Stoker, M. R. James and Algernon Blackwood, Arthur Machen was one of the major writers of supernatural fiction at the end of the nineteenth century. He developed an interest in mysticism and local folklore as a child and, when he travelled to London from his native Wales in 1880 with the intention of undertaking medical studies, Machen started to read as much esoterica as he could find as became evident from his 1881 poem "Eleusinia". Rather than complete his medical studies he became a journalist and also worked as a publisher's clerk and a translator. He fell under the influence of Robert Louis Stevenson and turned to writing fiction much of which included an underlying theme that the "little people" we think of as fairies or elves really exist but in a very different and more dangerous form than we understand. These beliefs emerge as background in *The Great God Pan*, "The Inmost Light", "The Shining Pyramid", *The Three Impostors* and, most vividly, in the story presented here, "The White People".

"Sorcery and sanctity," said Ambrose, "these are the only realities. Each is an ecstasy, a withdrawal from the common life."

Cotgrave listened, interested. He had been brought by a friend to this mouldering house in a northern suburb, through an old garden to the room where Ambrose the recluse dozed and dreamed over his books.

"Yes," he went on, "magic is justified of her children. There are many, I think, who eat dry crusts and drink water, with a joy infinitely sharper than anything within the experience of the 'practical' epicure."

"You are speaking of the saints?"

"Yes, and of the sinners, too. I think you are falling into the very general error of confining the spiritual world to the supremely good; but the supremely wicked, necessarily, have their portion in it. The merely carnal, sensual man can no more be a great sinner than he can be a great saint. Most of us are just indifferent, mixed-up creatures; we muddle through the world without realizing the meaning and the inner sense of things, and, consequently, our wickedness and our goodness are alike second-rate, unimportant."

"And you think the great sinner, then, will be an ascetic, as well as the great saint?"

"Great people of all kinds forsake the imperfect copies and go to the perfect originals. I have no doubt but that many of the very highest among the saints have never done a 'good action' (using the words in their ordinary sense). And, on the other hand, there have been those who have sounded the very depths of sin, who all their lives have never done an 'ill deed.'"

He went out of the room for a moment, and Cotgrave, in high delight, turned to his friend and thanked him for the introduction.

"He's grand," he said. "I never saw that kind of lunatic before."

Ambrose returned with more whisky and helped the two men in a liberal manner. He abused the teetotal sect with ferocity, as he handed the seltzer, and pouring out a glass of water for himself, was about to resume his monologue, when Cotgrave broke in—

"I can't stand it, you know," he said, "your paradoxes are too monstrous. A man may be a great sinner and yet never do anything sinful! Come!"

"You're quite wrong," said Ambrose. "I never make paradoxes; I wish I could. I merely said that a man may have an exquisite taste in Romanée Conti, and yet never have even smelt four ale. That's all, and it's more like a truism than a paradox, isn't it? Your surprise at my remark is due to the fact that you haven't realized what sin is. Oh, yes, there is a sort of connexion between Sin with the capital letter, and actions which are commonly called sinful: with murder, theft, adultery, and so forth. Much the same connexion that there is between the A, B, C and fine literature. But I believe that the misconception—it is all but universal—arises in great measure from our looking at the matter through social spectacles. We think that a man who does evil to *us* and to his neighbours must be very evil. So he is, from a social standpoint; but can't you realize that Evil in its essence is a lonely thing, a passion of the solitary, individual soul? Really, the average murderer, *quâ* murderer, is not by any means a sinner in the true sense of the word. He is simply a wild beast that we have to get rid of to save our own necks from his knife. I should class him rather with tigers than with sinners."

"It seems a little strange."

"I think not. The murderer murders not from positive qualities, but from negative ones; he lacks something which non-murderers possess. Evil, of course, is wholly positive—only it is on the wrong side. You may believe me that sin in its proper sense is very rare; it is probable that there have been far fewer sinners than saints. Yes, your standpoint is all very well for practical, social purposes; we are naturally inclined to think that a person who is very disagreeable to us must be a very great sinner! It is very disagreeable to have one's pocket picked, and we pronounce the thief to be a very great sinner. In truth, he is merely an undeveloped man. He cannot be a saint, of course; but he may be, and often is, an infinitely better creature than thousands who have never broken a single commandment. He is a great nuisance to *us*, I admit, and we very properly lock him up if we catch him; but between his troublesome and unsocial action and evil—Oh, the connexion is of the weakest."

It was getting very late. The man who had brought Cotgrave had probably heard all this before, since he assisted with a bland and judicious smile, but Cotgrave began to think that his "lunatic" was turning into a sage.

"Do you know," he said, "you interest me immensely? You think, then, that we do not understand the real nature of evil?"

"No, I don't think we do. We over-estimate it and we under-estimate it. We take the very numerous infractions of our social 'bye-laws'—the very necessary and very proper regulations which keep the human company together—and we get frightened at the prevalence of 'sin' and 'evil.' But this is really nonsense. Take theft, for example. Have you any *horror* at the thought of Robin Hood, of the

Highland caterans of the seventeenth century, of the moss-troopers, of the company promoters of our day?

"Then, on the other hand, we underrate evil. We attach such an enormous importance to the 'sin' of meddling with our pockets (and our wives) that we have quite forgotten the awfulness of real sin."

"And what is sin?" said Cotgrave.

"I think I must reply to your question by another. What would your feelings be, seriously, if your cat or your dog began to talk to you, and to dispute with you in human accents? You would be over-whelmed with horror. I am sure of it. And if the roses in your garden sang a weird song, you would go mad. And suppose the stones in the road began to swell and grow before your eyes, and if the pebble that you noticed at night had shot out stony blossoms in the morning?

"Well, these examples may give you some notion of what sin really is."

"Look here," said the third man, hitherto placid, "you two seem pretty well wound up. But I'm going home. I've missed my tram, and I shall have to walk."

Ambrose and Cotgrave seemed to settle down more profoundly when the other had gone out into the early misty morning and the pale light of the lamps.

"You astonish me," said Cotgrave. "I had never thought of that. If that is really so, one must turn everything upside down. Then the essence of sin really is—"

"In the taking of heaven by storm, it seems to me," said Ambrose. "It appears to me that it is simply an attempt to penetrate into another and a higher sphere in a forbidden manner. You can understand why it is so rare. They are few, indeed, who wish to penetrate into other spheres, higher or lower, in ways allowed or forbidden. Men, in the mass, are amply content with life as they find it. Therefore there are few saints, and sinners (in the proper sense) are fewer still, and men of genius, who partake sometimes of each character, are rare also. Yes; on the whole, it is, perhaps, harder to be a great sinner than a great saint."

"There is something profoundly unnatural about sin? Is that what you mean?"

"Exactly. Holiness requires as great, or almost as great, an effort; but holiness works on lines that *were* natural once; it is an effort to recover the ecstasy that was before the Fall. But sin is an effort to gain the ecstasy and the knowledge that pertain alone to angels, and in making this effort man becomes a demon. I told you that the mere murderer is not *therefore* a sinner; that is true, but the sinner is sometimes a murderer. Gilles de Raiz is an instance. So you see that while the good and the evil are unnatural to man as he now is—to man the social, civilized being—evil is unnatural in a much deeper sense than good. The saint endeavours to recover a gift which he has lost; the sinner tries to obtain something which was never his. In brief, he repeats the Fall."

"But are you a Catholic?" said Cotgrave.

"Yes; I am a member of the persecuted Anglican Church."

"Then, how about those texts which seem to reckon as sin that which you would set down as a mere trivial dereliction?"

"Yes; but in one place the word 'sorcerers' comes in the same sentence, doesn't it? That seems to me to give the key-note. Consider: can you imagine for a moment that a false statement which saves an innocent man's life is a sin? No; very good, then, it is not the mere liar who is excluded by those words; it is, above all, the "sorcerers" who use the material life, who use the failings incidental to material life as instruments to obtain their infinitely wicked ends. And let me tell you this: our higher senses are so blunted, we are so drenched

65

with materialism, that we should probably fail to recognize real wickedness if we encountered it."

"But shouldn't we experience a certain horror—a terror such as you hinted we would experience if a rose tree sang—in the mere presence of an evil man?"

"We should if we were natural: children and women feel this horror you speak of, even animals experience it. But with most of us convention and civilization and education have blinded and deafened and obscured the natural reason. No, sometimes we may recognize evil by its hatred of the good—one doesn't need much penetration to guess at the influence which dictated, quite unconsciously, the "Blackwood" review of Keats—but this is purely incidental; and, as a rule, I suspect that the Hierarchs of Tophet pass quite unnoticed, or, perhaps, in certain cases, as good but mistaken men."

"But you used the word 'unconscious' just now, of Keats' reviewers. Is wickedness ever unconscious?"

"Always. It must be so. It is like holiness and genius in this as in other points; it is a certain rapture or ecstasy of the soul; a transcendent effort to surpass the ordinary bounds. So, surpassing these, it surpasses also the understanding, the faculty that takes note of that which comes before it. No, a man may be infinitely and horribly wicked and never suspect it. But I tell you, evil in this, its certain and true sense, is rare, and I think it is growing rarer."

"I am trying to get hold of it all," said Cotgrave. "From what you say, I gather that the true evil differs generically from that which we call evil?"

"Quite so. There is, no doubt, an analogy between the two; a resemblance such as enables us to use, quite legitimately, such terms as the 'foot of the mountain' and the 'leg of the table.' And, sometimes, of course, the two speak, as it were, in the same language. The rough miner, or 'puddler,' the untrained, undeveloped 'tiger-man,' heated by a quart or two above his usual measure, comes home and kicks his irritating and injudicious wife to death. He is a murderer. And Gilles de Raiz was a murderer. But you see the gulf that separates the two? The 'word,' if I may so speak, is accidentally the same in each case, but the 'meaning' is utterly different. It is flagrant 'Hobson Jobson' to confuse the two, or rather, it is as if one supposed that Juggernaut and the Argonauts had something to do etymologically with one another. And no doubt the same weak likeness, or analogy, runs between all the 'social' sins and the real spiritual sins, and in some cases, perhaps, the lesser may be 'schoolmasters' to lead one on to the greater—from the shadow to the reality. If you are anything of a Theologian, you will see the importance of all this."

"I am sorry to say," remarked Cotgrave, "that I have devoted very little of my time to theology. Indeed, I have often wondered on what grounds theologians have claimed the title of Science of Sciences for their favourite study; since the "theological" books I have looked into have always seemed to me to be concerned with feeble and obvious pieties, or with the kings of Israel and Judah. I do not care to hear about those kings."

Ambrose grinned.

"We must try to avoid theological discussion," he said.

"I perceive that you would be a bitter disputant. But perhaps the 'dates of the kings' have as much to do with theology as the hobnails of the murderous puddler with evil."

"Then, to return to our main subject, you think that sin is an esoteric, occult thing?"

"Yes. It is the infernal miracle as holiness is the supernal. Now and then it is raised to such a pitch that we entirely fail to suspect its exist-ence; it is like the note of the great pedal pipes of the organ, which is so deep that we cannot hear it. In other cases it may lead to the lunatic asylum, or to still stranger issues. But you must never confuse it with mere social misdoing. Remember how the Apostle, speaking of the 'other side,' distinguishes between 'charitable' actions and charity. And as one may give all one's goods to the poor, and yet lack charity; so, remember, one may avoid every crime and yet be a sinner."

"Your psychology is very strange to me," said Cotgrave, "but I confess I like it, and I suppose that one might fairly deduce from your premises the conclusion that the real sinner might very possibly strike the observer as a harmless personage enough?"

"Certainly; because the true evil has nothing to do with social life or social laws, or if it has, only incidentally and accidentally. It is a lonely passion of the soul—or a passion of the lonely soul—whichever you like. If, by chance, we understand it, and grasp its full significance, then, indeed, it will fill us with horror and with awe. But this emotion is widely distinguished from the fear and the disgust with which we regard the ordinary criminal, since this latter is largely or entirely founded on the regard which we have for our own skins or purses. We hate a murderer, because we know that we should hate to be murdered, or to have any one that we like murdered. So, on the 'other side,' we venerate the saints, but we don't 'like' them as we like our friends. Can you persuade yourself that you would have 'enjoyed' St. Paul's company? Do you think that you and I would have 'got on' with Sir Galahad?

"So with the sinners, as with the saints. If you met a very evil man, and recognized his evil; he would, no doubt, fill you with horror and awe; but there is no reason why you should 'dislike' him. On the contrary, it is quite possible that if you could succeed in putting the sin out of your mind you might find the sinner capital company, and in a little while you might have to reason yourself back into horror.

Still, how awful it is. If the roses and the lilies suddenly sang on this coming morning; if the furniture began to move in procession, as in De Maupassant's tale!"

"I am glad you have come back to that comparison," said Cotgrave, "because I wanted to ask you what it is that corresponds in humanity to these imaginary feats of inanimate things. In a word—what is sin? You have given me, I know, an abstract definition, but I should like a concrete example."

"I told you it was very rare," said Ambrose, who appeared willing to avoid the giving of a direct answer. "The materialism of the age, which has done a good deal to suppress sanctity, has done perhaps more to suppress evil. We find the earth so very comfortable that we have no inclination either for ascents or descents. It would seem as if the scholar who decided to 'specialize' in Tophet, would be reduced to purely antiquarian researches. No palæontologist could show you a *live* pterodactyl."

"And yet you, I think, have 'specialized,' and I believe that your researches have descended to our modern times."

"You are really interested, I see. Well, I confess, that I have dabbled a little, and if you like I can show you something that bears on the very curious subject we have been discussing."

Ambrose took a candle and went away to a far, dim corner of the room. Cotgrave saw him open a venerable bureau that stood there, and from some secret recess he drew out a parcel, and came back to the window where they had been sitting.

Ambrose undid a wrapping of paper, and produced a green pocket-book.

"You will take care of it?" he said. "Don't leave it lying about. It is one of the choicer pieces in my collection, and I should be very sorry if it were lost."

He fondled the faded binding.

"I knew the girl who wrote this," he said. "When you read it, you will see how it illustrates the talk we have had tonight. There is a sequel, too, but I won't talk of that."

"There was an odd article in one of the reviews some months ago," he began again, with the air of a man who changes the subject. "It was written by a doctor—Dr. Coryn, I think, was the name. He says that a lady, watching her little girl playing at the drawing-room window, suddenly saw the heavy sash give way and fall on the child's fingers. The lady fainted, I think, but at any rate the doctor was summoned, and when he had dressed the child's wounded and maimed fingers he was summoned to the mother. She was groaning with pain, and it was found that three fingers of her hand, corresponding with those that had been injured on the child's hand, were swollen and inflamed, and later, in the doctor's language, purulent sloughing set in."

Ambrose still handled delicately the green volume.

"Well, here it is," he said at last, parting with difficulty, it seemed, from his treasure.

"You will bring it back as soon as you have read it," he said, as they went out into the hall, into the old garden, faint with the odour of white lilies.

There was a broad red band in the east as Cotgrave turned to go, and from the high ground where he stood he saw that awful spectacle of London in a dream.

THE GREEN BOOK

The morocco binding of the book was faded, and the colour had grown faint, but there were no stains nor bruises nor marks of usage. The book looked as if it had been bought "on a visit to London" some seventy or eighty years ago, and had somehow been forgotten and suffered to lie away out of sight. There was an old, delicate, lingering odour about it, such an odour as sometimes haunts an ancient piece of furniture for a century or more. The end-papers, inside the binding, were oddly decorated with coloured patterns and faded gold. It looked small, but the paper was fine, and there were many leaves, closely covered with minute, painfully formed characters.

I found this book (the manuscript began) in a drawer in the old bureau that stands on the landing. It was a very rainy day and I could not go out, so in the afternoon I got a candle and rummaged in the bureau. Nearly all the drawers were full of old dresses, but one of the small ones looked empty, and I found this book hidden right at the back. I wanted a book like this, so I took it to write in. It is full of secrets. I have a great many other books of secrets I have written, hidden in a safe place, and I am going to write here many of the old secrets and some new ones; but there are some I shall not put down at all. I must not write down the real names of the days and months which I found out a year ago, nor the way to make the Aklo letters, or the Chian language, or the great beautiful Circles, nor the Mao Games, nor the chief songs. I may write something about all these things but not the way to do them, for peculiar reasons. And I must not say who the Nymphs are, or the Dôls, or Jeelo, or what voolas mean. All these are most secret secrets, and I am glad when I remember what they are, and how many wonderful languages I know, but there are some things that I call the secrets of the secrets of the secrets that I dare not think of unless I am quite alone, and then I shut my eyes, and put my hands over them and whisper the word, and the Alala comes. I only do this at night in my room or in certain woods that I know, but I must not describe them, as they are secret woods. Then there are the Ceremonies, which are all of them important, but some are more delightful than others—there are the White Ceremonies, and the Green Ceremonies, and the Scarlet Ceremonies. The Scarlet Ceremonies are the best, but there is only one place where they can be performed properly, though there is a very nice imitation which I have done in other places. Besides these, I have the dances, and the Comedy, and I have done the Comedy sometimes when the others were looking, and they didn't understand anything about it. I was very little when I first knew about these things.

When I was very small, and mother was alive, I can remember remembering things before that, only it has all got confused. But I remember when I was five or six I heard them talking about me when they thought I was not noticing. They were saying how queer I was a year or two before, and how nurse had called my mother to come and listen to me talking all to myself, and I was saying words that nobody could understand. I was speaking the Xu language, but I only remember a very few of the words, as it was about the little white faces that used to look at me when I was lying in my cradle. They used to talk to me, and I learnt their language and talked to them in it about some great white place where they lived, where the trees and the grass were all white, and there were white hills as high up as the moon, and a cold wind. I have often dreamed of it afterwards, but the faces went away when I was very little. But a wonderful thing happened when I was about five. My nurse was carrying me on her shoulder; there was a field of yellow corn, and we went through it, it was very hot. Then we came to a path through a wood, and a tall man came after us, and went with us till we came to a place where there was a deep pool, and it was very dark and shady. Nurse put me down on the soft moss under a tree, and she said: "She can't get to the pond now." So they left me there, and I sat quite still and watched, and out of the water and out of the wood came two wonderful white people, and they began to play and dance and sing. They were a kind of creamy white like the old ivory figure in the drawing-room; one was a beautiful lady with kind dark eyes, and a grave face, and long black hair, and she smiled such a strange sad smile at the other, who laughed and came to her. They played together, and danced round and round the pool, and they sang a song till I fell asleep. Nurse woke me up when she came back, and she was looking something like the lady had looked, so I told her all about it, and asked her why she looked like that. At first she cried, and then she looked very frightened, and turned quite pale. She put me down on the grass and stared at me, and I could see she was shaking all over. Then she said I had been dreaming, but I knew I hadn't. Then she made me promise not to say a word about it to anybody, and if I did I should be thrown into the black pit. I was not frightened at all, though nurse was, and I never forgot about it, because when I shut my eyes and it was quite quiet, and I was all alone, I could see them again, very faint and far away, but very splendid; and little bits of the song they sang came into my head, but I couldn't sing it.

I was thirteen, nearly fourteen, when I had a very singular adventure, so strange that the day on which it happened is always called the White Day. My mother had been dead for more than a year, and in the morning I had lessons, but they let me go out for walks in the afternoon. And this afternoon I walked a new way, and a little brook led me into a new country, but I tore my frock getting through some of the difficult places, as the way was through many bushes, and beneath the low branches of trees, and up thorny thickets on the hills, and by dark woods full of creeping thorns. And it was a long, long way. It seemed as if I was going on for ever and ever, and I had to creep by a place like a tunnel where a brook must have been, but all the water had dried up, and the floor was rocky, and the bushes had grown overhead till they met, so that it was quite dark. And I went on and on through that dark place; it was a long, long way. And I came to a hill that I never saw before. I was in a dismal thicket full of black twisted boughs that tore me as I went through them, and I cried out because I was smarting all over, and then I found that I was climbing, and I went up and up a long way, till at last the thicket stopped and I came out crying just under the top of a big bare place, where there were ugly grey stones lying all about on the grass, and here and there a little twisted, stunted tree came out from under a stone, like a snake. And I went up, right to the top, a long way. I never saw such big ugly stones before; they came out of the earth some of them, and some looked as if they had been rolled to where they were, and they went on and on as far as I could see, a long, long way. I looked out from them and saw the country, but it was strange. It was winter time, and there were black terrible woods hanging from the hills all round; it was like seeing a large room hung with black curtains, and the shape of the trees seemed quite different from any I had ever seen before. I was afraid. Then beyond the woods there were other hills round in a great ring, but I had never seen any of them; it all looked black, and everything had a voor over it. It was all so still and silent, and the sky was heavy and grey and sad, like a wicked voorish dome in Deep Dendo. I went on into the dreadful rocks. There were hundreds and hundreds of them. Some were like horrid-grinning men; I could see their faces as if they would jump at me out of the stone, and catch hold of me, and drag me with them back into the rock, so that I should always be there. And there were other rocks that were like animals, creeping, horrible animals, putting out their tongues, and others were like words that I could not say, and others like dead people lying on the grass. I went on among them, though they frightened me, and my heart was full of wicked songs that they put into it; and I wanted to make faces and twist myself about in the way they did, and I went on and on a long way till at last I liked the rocks, and they didn't frighten me any more. I sang the songs I thought of; songs full of words that must not be spoken or written down. Then I made faces like the faces on the rocks, and I twisted myself about like the twisted ones, and I lay down flat on the ground like the dead ones, and I went up to one that was grinning, and put my arms round him and hugged him. And so I went on and on through the rocks till I came to a round mound in the middle of them. It was higher than a mound, it was nearly as high as our house, and it was like a great basin turned upside down, all smooth and round and green, with one stone, like a post, sticking up at the top. I climbed up the sides, but they were so steep I had to stop or I should have rolled all the way down again, and I should have knocked against the stones at the bottom, and perhaps been killed. But I wanted to get up to the very top of the big round mound, so I lay down flat on my face, and took hold of the grass with my hands and drew myself up, bit by bit, till I was at the top. Then I sat down on the stone in the middle, and looked all round about. I felt I had come such a long, long way, just as if I were a hundred miles from home, or in some other country, or in one of the strange places I had read about in the "Tales of the Genie" and the "Arabian Nights," or as if I had gone across the sea, far away, for years and I had found another world that nobody had ever seen or heard of before, or as if I had somehow flown through the sky and fallen on one of the stars I had read about where everything is dead and cold and grey, and there is no air, and the wind doesn't blow. I sat on the stone and looked all round and down and round about me. It was just as if I was sitting on a tower in the middle of a great empty town, because I could see nothing all around but the grey rocks on the ground. I couldn't make out their shapes any more, but I could see them on and on for a long way, and I looked at them, and they seemed as if they had been arranged into patterns, and shapes, and figures. I knew they couldn't be, because I had seen a lot of them coming right out of the earth, joined to the deep rocks below, so I looked again, but still I saw nothing but circles, and small circles inside big ones, and pyramids, and domes, and spires, and they seemed all to go round and round the place where I was sitting, and the more I looked, the more I saw great big rings of rocks, getting bigger and bigger, and I stared so long that it felt as if they were all moving and turning, like a great wheel, and I was turning, too, in the middle. I got quite dizzy and queer in the head, and everything began to be hazy and not clear, and I saw little sparks of blue light, and the stones looked as if they were springing and dancing and twisting as they went round and round and round. I was frightened again, and I cried out loud, and jumped up from the stone I was sitting on, and fell down. When I got up I was so glad they all looked still, and I sat down on the top and slid down the mound, and went on again. I danced as I went in the peculiar way the rocks had danced when I got giddy, and I was so glad I could do it quite well, and I danced and danced along, and sang extraordinary songs that came into my head. At last I came to the edge of that great flat hill, and there were no more rocks, and the way went again through a dark thicket in a hollow. It was just as bad as the other one I went through climbing up, but I didn't mind this one, because I was so glad I had seen those singular dances and could imitate them. I went down, creeping through the bushes, and a tall nettle stung me on my leg, and made me burn, but I didn't mind it, and I tingled with the boughs and the thorns, but I only laughed and sang. Then I got out of the thicket into a close valley, a little secret place like a dark passage that nobody ever knows of, because it was so narrow and deep and the woods were so thick round it. There is a steep bank with trees hanging over it, and there the ferns keep green all through the winter, when they are dead and brown upon the hill, and the ferns there have a sweet, rich smell like what oozes out of fir trees. There was a little stream of water running down this valley, so small that I could easily step across it. I drank the water with my hand, and it tasted like bright, yellow wine, and it sparkled and bubbled as it ran down over beautiful red and yellow and green stones, so that it seemed alive and all colours at once. I drank it, and I drank more with my hand, but I couldn't drink enough, so I lay down and bent my head and sucked the water up with my lips. It tasted much better, drinking it that way, and a ripple would come up to my mouth and give me a kiss, and I laughed, and drank again, and pretended there was a nymph, like the one in the old picture at home, who lived in the water and was kissing me. So I bent low down to the water, and put my lips softly to it, and whispered to the nymph that I would come again. I felt sure it could not be common water, I was so glad when I got up and went on; and I danced again and went up and up the valley, under hanging hills. And when I came to the top, the ground rose up in front of me, tall and steep as a wall, and there was nothing but the green wall and the sky. I thought of "for ever and for ever, world without end, Amen"; and I thought I must have really found the end of the world, because it was like the end of everything, as if there could be nothing at all beyond, except the kingdom of Voor, where the light goes when it is put out, and the water goes when the sun takes it away. I began to think of all the long, long way I had journeyed, how I had found a brook and followed it, and followed it on, and gone through bushes and thorny thickets, and dark woods full of creeping thorns. Then I had crept up a tunnel under trees, and climbed a thicket, and seen all the grey rocks, and sat in the middle of them when they turned round, and then I had gone on through the grey rocks and come down the hill through the stinging thicket and up the dark valley, all a long, long way. I wondered how I should get home again, if I could ever find the way, and if my home was there any more, or if it were turned and everybody in it into grey rocks, as in the "Arabian Nights." So I sat down on the grass and thought what I should do next. I was tired, and my feet were hot with walking, and as I looked about I saw there was a wonderful well just under the high, steep wall of grass. All the ground round it was covered with bright, green, dripping moss; there was every kind of moss there, moss like beautiful little ferns, and like palms and fir trees, and it was all green as jewellery, and drops of water hung on it like diamonds. And in the middle was the great well, deep and shining and beautiful, so clear that it looked as if I could touch the red sand at the bottom, but it was far below. I stood by it and looked in, as if I were looking in a glass. At the bottom of the well, in the middle of it, the red grains of sand were moving and stirring all the time, and I saw how the water bubbled up, but at the top it was quite smooth, and full and brimming. It was a great well, large like a bath, and with the shining, glittering green moss about it, it looked like a great white jewel, with green jewels all round. My feet were so hot and tired that I took off my boots and stockings, and let my feet down into the water, and the water was soft and cold, and when I got up I wasn't tired any more, and I felt I must go on, farther and farther, and see what was on the other side of the wall. I climbed up it very slowly, going sideways all the time, and when I got to the top and looked over, I was in the queerest country I had seen, stranger even than the hill of the grey rocks. It looked as if earth-children had been playing there with their spades, as it was all hills and hollows, and castles and walls made of earth and covered with grass. There were two mounds like big beehives, round and great and solemn, and then hollow basins, and then a steep mounting wall like the ones I saw once by the seaside where the big guns and the soldiers were. I nearly fell into one of the round hollows, it went away from under my feet so suddenly, and I ran fast down the side and stood at the bottom and looked up. It was strange and solemn to look up. There was nothing but the grey, heavy sky and the sides of the hollow; everything else had gone away, and the hollow was the whole world, and I thought that at night it must be full of ghosts and moving shadows and pale things when the moon shone down to the bottom at the dead of the night, and the wind wailed up above. It was so strange and solemn and lonely, like a hollow temple of dead heathen gods. It reminded me of a tale my nurse had told me when I was quite little; it was the same nurse that took me into the wood where I saw the beautiful white people. And I remembered how nurse had told me the story one winter night, when the wind was beating the trees against the wall, and crying and moaning in the nursery chimney. She said there was, somewhere or other, a hollow pit, just like the one I was standing in, everybody was afraid to go into it or near it, it was such a bad place. But once upon a time there was a poor girl who said she would go into the hollow pit, and everybody tried to stop her, but she would go. And she went down into the pit and came back laughing, and said there was nothing there at all, except green grass and red stones, and white stones and yellow flowers. And soon after people saw she had most beautiful emerald earrings, and they asked how she got them, as she and her mother were quite poor. But she laughed, and said her earrings were not made of emeralds at all, but only of green grass. Then, one day, she wore on her breast the reddest ruby that any one had ever seen, and it was as big as a hen's egg, and glowed and sparkled like a hot burning coal of fire. And they asked her how she got it, as she and her mother were quite poor. But she laughed, and said it was not a ruby at all, but only a red stone. Then one day she wore round her neck the loveliest necklace that any one had ever seen, much finer than the queen's finest, and it was made of great bright diamonds, hundreds of them, and they shone like all the stars on a night in June. So they asked her how she got it, as she and her mother were quite poor. But she laughed, and said they were not diamonds at all, but only white stones. And one day she went to the Court, and she wore on her head a crown of pure angel-gold, so nurse said, and it shone like the sun, and it was much more splendid than the crown the king was wearing himself, and in her ears she wore the emeralds, and the big ruby was the brooch on her breast, and the great diamond necklace was sparkling on her neck. And the king and queen thought she was some great princess from a long way off, and got down from their thrones and went to meet her, but somebody told the king and queen who she was, and that she was quite poor. So the king asked why she wore a gold crown, and how she got it, as she and her mother were so poor. And she laughed, and said it wasn't a gold crown at all, but only some yellow flowers she had put in her hair. And the king thought it was very strange, and said she should stay at the Court, and they would see what would happen next. And she was so lovely that everybody said that her eyes were greener than the emeralds, that her lips were redder than the ruby, that her skin was whiter than the diamonds, and that her hair was brighter than the golden crown. So the king's son said he would marry her, and the king said he might. And the bishop married them, and there was a great supper, and afterwards the king's son went to his wife's room. But just when he had his hand on the door, he saw a tall, black man, with a dreadful face, standing in front of the door, and a voice said—

Venture not upon your life,
This is mine own wedded wife.

Then the king's son fell down on the ground in a fit. And they came
and tried to get into the room, but they couldn't, and they hacked at
the door with hatchets, but the wood had turned hard as iron, and
at last everybody ran away, they were so frightened at the screaming
and laughing and shrieking and crying that came out of the room.
But next day they went in, and found there was nothing in the room
but thick black smoke, because the black man had come and taken
her away. And on the bed there were two knots of faded grass and a
red stone, and some white stones, and some faded yellow flowers. I
remembered this tale of nurse's while I was standing at the bottom
of the deep hollow; it was so strange and solitary there, and I felt
afraid. I could not see any stones or flowers, but I was afraid of bringing them away without knowing, and I thought I would do a charm
that came into my head to keep the black man away. So I stood right
in the very middle of the hollow, and I made sure that I had none of
those things on me, and then I walked round the place, and touched
my eyes, and my lips, and my hair in a peculiar manner, and whispered
some queer words that nurse taught me to keep bad things away.
Then I felt safe and climbed up out of the hollow, and went on
through all those mounds and hollows and walls, till I came to the
end, which was high above all the rest, and I could see that all the
different shapes of the earth were arranged in patterns, something
like the grey rocks, only the pattern was different. It was getting late,
and the air was indistinct, but it looked from where I was standing
something like two great figures of people lying on the grass. And I
went on, and at last I found a certain wood, which is too secret to be
described, and nobody knows of the passage into it, which I found

out in a very curious manner, by seeing some little animal run into the wood through it. So I went after the animal by a very narrow dark way, under thorns and bushes, and it was almost dark when I came to a kind of open place in the middle. And there I saw the most wonderful sight I have ever seen, but it was only for a minute, as I ran away directly, and crept out of the wood by the passage I had come by, and ran and ran as fast as ever I could, because I was afraid, what I had seen was so wonderful and so strange and beautiful. But I wanted to get home and think of it, and I did not know what might not happen if I stayed by the wood. I was hot all over and trembling, and my heart was beating, and strange cries that I could not help came from me as I ran from the wood. I was glad that a great white moon came up from over a round hill and showed me the way, so I went back through the mounds and hollows and down the close valley, and up through the thicket over the place of the grey rocks, and so at last I got home again. My father was busy in his study, and the servants had not told about my not coming home, though they were frightened, and wondered what they ought to do, so I told them I had lost my way, but I did not let them find out the real way I had been. I went to bed and lay awake all through the night, thinking of what I had seen. When I came out of the narrow way, and it looked all shining, though the air was dark, it seemed so certain, and all the way home I was quite sure that I had seen it, and I wanted to be alone in my room, and be glad over it all to myself, and shut my eyes and pretend it was there, and do all the things I would have done if I had not been so afraid. But when I shut my eyes the sight would not come, and I began to think about my adventures all over again, and I remembered how dusky and queer it was at the end, and I was afraid it must be all a mistake, because it seemed impossible it could happen. It seemed like one of nurse's tales, which I didn't really believe in, though I was frightened at the bottom of the hollow; and the stories she told me when I was little came back into my head, and I wondered whether it was really there what I thought I had seen, or whether any of her tales could have happened a long time ago. It was so queer; I lay awake there in my room at the back of the house, and the moon was shining on the other side towards the river, so the bright light did not fall upon the wall. And the house was quite still. I had heard my father come upstairs, and just after the clock struck twelve, and after the house was still and empty, as if there was nobody alive in it. And though it was all dark and indistinct in my room, a pale glimmering kind of light shone in through the white blind, and once I got up and looked out, and there was a great black shadow of the house covering the garden, looking like a prison where men are hanged; and then beyond it was all white; and the wood shone white with black gulfs between the trees. It was still and clear, and there were no clouds on the sky. I wanted to think of what I had seen but I couldn't, and I began to think of all the tales that nurse had told me so long ago that I thought I had forgotten, but they all came back, and mixed up with the thickets and the grey rocks and the hollows in the earth and the secret wood, till I hardly knew what was new and what was old, or whether it was not all dreaming. And then I remembered that hot summer afternoon, so long ago, when nurse left me by myself in the shade, and the white people came out of the water and out of the wood, and played, and danced, and sang, and I began to fancy that nurse told me about something like it before I saw them, only I couldn't recollect exactly what she told me. Then I wondered whether she had been the white lady, as I remembered she was just as white and beautiful, and had the same dark eyes and black hair; and sometimes she smiled and looked like the lady had looked, when she was telling me some of her stories, beginning with "Once on a time," or "In the time of the fairies." But I thought she couldn't be the lady, as she seemed to have gone a different way into the wood, and I didn't think the man who came after us could be the other, or I couldn't have seen that wonderful secret in the secret wood. I thought of the moon: but it was afterwards when I was in the middle of the wild land, where the earth was made into the shape of great figures, and it was all walls, and mysterious hollows, and smooth round mounds, that I saw the great white moon come up over a round hill. I was wondering about all these things, till at last I got quite frightened, because I was afraid something had happened to me, and I remembered nurse's tale of the poor girl who went into the hollow pit, and was carried away at last by the black man. I knew I had gone into a hollow pit too, and perhaps it was the same, and I had done something dreadful. So I did the charm over again, and touched my eyes and my lips and my hair in a peculiar manner, and said the old words from the fairy language, so that I might be sure I had not been carried away. I tried again to see the secret wood, and to creep up the passage and see what I had seen there, but somehow I couldn't, and I kept on thinking of nurse's stories. There was one I remembered about a young man who once upon a time went hunting, and all the day he and his hounds hunted everywhere, and they crossed the rivers and went into all the woods, and went round the marshes, but they couldn't find anything at all, and they hunted all day till the sun sank down and began to set behind the mountain. And the young man was angry because he couldn't find anything, and he was going to turn back, when just as the sun touched the mountain, he saw come out of a brake in front of him a beautiful white stag. And he cheered to his hounds, but they whined and would not follow, and he cheered to his horse, but it shivered and stood stock still, and the young man jumped off the horse and left the hounds and began to follow the white stag all alone. And soon it was quite dark, and the sky was black, without a single star shining in it, and the stag went away into the darkness. And though the man had brought his gun with him he never shot at the stag, because he wanted to catch it, and he was afraid he would lose it in the night. But he never lost it once, though the sky was so black and the air was so dark, and the stag went on and on till the young man didn't know a bit where he was. And they went through enormous woods where the air was full of whispers and a pale, dead light came out from the rotten trunks that were lying on the ground, and just as the man thought he had lost the stag, he would see it all white and shining in front of him, and he would run fast to catch it, but the stag always ran faster, so he did not catch it. And they went through the enormous woods, and they swam across rivers, and they waded through black marshes where the ground bubbled, and the air was full of will-o'-the-wisps, and the stag fled away down into rocky narrow valleys, where the air was like the smell of a vault, and the man went after it. And they went over the great mountains and the man heard the wind come down from the sky, and the stag went on and the man went after. At last the sun rose and the young man found he was in a country that he had never seen before; it was a beautiful valley with a bright stream running through it, and a great, big round hill in the middle. And the stag went down the valley, towards the hill, and it seemed to be getting tired and went slower and slower, and though the man was tired, too, he began to run faster, and he was sure he would catch the stag at last. But just as they got to the bottom of the hill, and the man stretched out his hand to catch the stag, it vanished into the earth, and the man began to cry; he was so sorry that he had lost it after all his long hunting. But as he was crying he saw there was a door in the hill, just in front of him, and he went in, and it was quite dark, but he went on, as he thought he would find the white stag. And all of a sudden it got light, and there was the sky, and the sun shining, and birds singing in the trees, and there was a beautiful fountain. And by the fountain a lovely lady was sitting, who was the queen of the fairies, and she told the man that she had changed herself into a stag to bring him there because she loved him so much. Then she brought out a great gold cup, covered with jewels, from her fairy palace, and she offered him wine in the cup to drink. And he drank, and the more he drank the more he longed to drink, because the wine was enchanted. So he kissed the lovely lady, and she became his wife, and he stayed all that day and all that night in the hill where she lived, and when he woke he found he was lying on the ground, close to where he had seen the stag first, and his horse was there and his hounds were there waiting, and he looked up, and the sun sank behind the mountain. And he went home and lived a long time, but he would never kiss any other lady because he had kissed the queen of the fairies, and he would never drink common wine any more, because he had drunk enchanted wine. And sometimes nurse told me tales that she had heard from her great-grandmother, who was very old, and lived in a cottage on the mountain all alone, and most of these tales were about a hill where people used to meet at night long ago, and they used to play all sorts of strange games and do queer things that nurse told me of, but I couldn't understand, and now, she said, everybody but her great-grandmother had forgotten all about it, and nobody knew where the hill was, not even her great-grandmother. But she told me one very strange story about the hill, and I trembled when I remembered it. She said that people always went there in summer, when it was very hot, and they had to dance a good deal. It would be all dark at first, and there were trees there, which made it much darker, and people would come, one by one, from all directions, by a secret path which nobody else knew, and two persons would keep the gate, and every one as they came up had to give a very curious sign, which nurse showed me as well as she could, but she said she couldn't show me properly. And all kinds of people would come; there would be gentle folks and village folks, and some old people and boys and girls, and quite small children, who sat and watched. And it would all be dark as they came in, except in one corner where some one was burning something that smelt strong and sweet, and made them laugh, and there one would see a glaring of coals, and the smoke mounting up red. So they would all come in, and when the last had come there was no door any more, so that no one else could get in, even if they knew there was anything beyond. And once a gentleman who was a stranger and had ridden a long way, lost his path at night, and his horse took him into the very middle of the wild country, where everything was upside down, and there were dreadful marshes and great stones everywhere, and holes underfoot, and the trees looked like gibbet-posts, because they had great black arms that stretched out across the way. And this strange gentleman was very frightened, and his horse began to shiver all over, and at last it stopped and wouldn't go any farther, and the gentleman got down and tried to lead the horse, but it wouldn't move, and it was all covered with a sweat, like death. So the gentleman went on all alone, going farther and farther into the wild country, till at last he came to a dark place, where he heard shouting and singing and crying, like nothing he had ever heard before. It all sounded quite close to him, but he couldn't get in, and so he began to call, and while he was calling, something came behind him, and in a minute his mouth and arms and legs were all bound up, and he fell into a swoon. And when he came to himself, he was lying by the roadside, just where he had first lost his way, under a blasted oak with a black trunk, and his horse was tied beside him. So he rode on to the town and told the people there what had happened, and some of them were amazed; but others knew. So when once everybody had come, there was no door at all for anybody else to pass in by. And when they were all inside, round in a ring, touching each other, some one began to sing in the darkness, and some one else would make a noise like thunder with a thing they had on purpose, and on still nights people would hear the thundering noise far, far away beyond the wild land, and some of them, who thought they knew what it was, used to make a sign on their breasts when they woke up in their beds at dead of night and heard that terrible deep noise, like thunder on the mountains. And the noise and the singing would go on and on for a long time, and the people who were in a ring swayed a little to and fro; and the song was in an old, old language that nobody knows now, and the tune was queer. Nurse said her great-grandmother had known some one who remembered a little of it, when she was quite a little girl, and nurse tried to sing some of it to me, and it was so strange a tune that I turned all cold and my flesh crept as if I had put my hand on something dead. Sometimes it was a man that sang and sometimes it was a woman, and sometimes the one who sang it did it so well that two or three of the people who were there fell to the ground shrieking and tearing with their hands. The singing went on, and the people in the ring kept swaying to and fro for a long time, and at last the moon would rise over a place they called the Tole Deol, and came up and showed them swinging and swaying from side to side, with the sweet thick smoke curling up from the burning coals, and floating in circles all around them. Then they had their supper. A boy and a girl brought it to them; the boy carried a great cup of wine, and the girl carried a cake of bread, and they passed the bread and the wine round and round, but they tasted quite different from common bread and common wine, and changed everybody that tasted them. Then they all rose up and danced, and secret things were brought out of some hiding place, and they played extraordinary games, and danced round and round and round in the moonlight, and sometimes people would suddenly disappear and never be heard of afterwards, and nobody knew what had happened to them. And they drank more of that curious wine, and they made images and worshipped them, and nurse showed me how the images were made one day when we were out for a walk, and we passed by a place where there was a lot of wet clay. So nurse asked me if I would like to know what those things were like that they made on the hill, and I said yes. Then she asked me if I would promise never to tell a living soul a word about it, and if I did I was to be thrown into the black pit with the dead people, and I said I wouldn't tell anybody, and she said the same thing again and again, and I promised. So she took my wooden spade and dug a big lump of clay and put it in my tin bucket, and told me to say if any one met us that I was going to make pies when I went home. Then we went on a little way till we came to a little brake growing right down into the road, and nurse stopped, and looked up the road and down it, and then peeped through the hedge into the field on the other side, and then she said, "Quick!" and we ran into the brake, and crept in and out among the bushes till we had gone a good way from the road. Then we sat down under a bush, and I wanted so much to know what nurse was going to make with the clay, but before she would begin she made me promise again not to say a word about it, and she went again and peeped through the bushes on every side, though the lane was so small and deep that hardly anybody ever went there. So we sat down, and nurse took the clay out of the bucket, and began to knead it with her hands, and do queer things with it, and turn it about. And she hid it under a big dock-leaf for a minute or two and then she brought it out again, and then she stood up and sat down, and walked round the clay in a peculiar manner, and all the time she was softly singing a sort of rhyme, and her face got very red. Then she sat down again, and took the clay in her hands and began to shape it into a doll, but not like the dolls I have at home, and she made the queerest doll I had ever seen, all out of the wet clay, and hid it under a bush to get dry and hard, and all the time she was making it she was singing these rhymes to herself, and her face got redder and redder. So we left the doll there, hidden away in the bushes where nobody would ever find it. And a few days later we went the same walk, and when we came to that narrow, dark part of the lane where the brake runs down to the bank, nurse made me promise all over again, and she looked about, just as she had done before, and we crept into the bushes till we got to the green place where the little clay man was hidden. I remember it all so well, though I was only eight, and it is eight years ago now as I am writing it down, but the sky was a deep violet blue, and in the middle of the brake where we were sitting there was a great elder tree covered with blossoms, and on the other side there was a clump of meadowsweet, and when I think of that day the smell of the meadowsweet and elder blossom seems to fill the room, and if I shut my eyes I can see the glaring blue sky, with little clouds very white floating across it, and nurse who went away long ago sitting opposite me and looking like the beautiful white lady in the wood. So we sat down and nurse took out the clay doll from the secret place where she had hidden it, and she said we must "pay our respects," and she would show me what to do, and I must watch her all the time. So she did all sorts of queer things with the little clay man, and I noticed she was all streaming with perspiration, though we had walked so slowly, and then she told me to "pay my respects," and I did everything she did because I liked her, and it was such an odd game. And she said that

if one loved very much, the clay man was very good, if one did certain
things with it, and if one hated very much, it was just as good, only
one had to do different things, and we played with it a long time, and
pretended all sorts of things. Nurse said her great-grandmother had
told her all about these images, but what we did was no harm at all,
only a game. But she told me a story about these images that frightened
me very much, and that was what I remembered that night when I
was lying awake in my room in the pale, empty darkness, thinking of
what I had seen and the secret wood. Nurse said there was once a
young lady of the high gentry, who lived in a great castle. And she
was so beautiful that all the gentlemen wanted to marry her, because
she was the loveliest lady that anybody had ever seen, and she was
kind to everybody, and everybody thought she was very good. But
though she was polite to all the gentlemen who wished to marry her,
she put them off, and said she couldn't make up her mind, and she
wasn't sure she wanted to marry anybody at all. And her father, who
was a very great lord, was angry, though he was so fond of her, and
he asked her why she wouldn't choose a bachelor out of all the handsome young men who came to the castle. But she only said she didn't
love any of them very much, and she must wait, and if they pestered
her, she said she would go and be a nun in a nunnery. So all the
gentlemen said they would go away and wait for a year and a day, and
when a year and a day were gone, they would come back again and
ask her to say which one she would marry. So the day was appointed
and they all went away; and the lady had promised that in a year and
a day it would be her wedding day with one of them. But the truth
was, that she was the queen of the people who danced on the hill on
summer nights, and on the proper nights she would lock the door of
her room, and she and her maid would steal out of the castle by a
secret passage that only they knew of, and go away up to the hill in

the wild land. And she knew more of the secret things than any one else, and more than any one knew before or after, because she would not tell anybody the most secret secrets. She knew how to do all the awful things, how to destroy young men, and how to put a curse on people, and other things that I could not understand. And her real name was the Lady Avelin, but the dancing people called her Cassap, which meant somebody very wise, in the old language. And she was whiter than any of them and taller, and her eyes shone in the dark like burning rubies; and she could sing songs that none of the others could sing, and when she sang they all fell down on their faces and worshipped her. And she could do what they called shib-show, which was a very wonderful enchantment. She would tell the great lord, her father, that she wanted to go into the woods to gather flowers, so he let her go, and she and her maid went into the woods where nobody came, and the maid would keep watch. Then the lady would lie down under the trees and begin to sing a particular song, and she stretched out her arms, and from every part of the wood great serpents would come, hissing and gliding in and out among the trees, and shooting out their forked tongues as they crawled up to the lady. And they all came to her, and twisted round her, round her body, and her arms, and her neck, till she was covered with writhing serpents, and there was only her head to be seen. And she whispered to them, and she sang to them, and they writhed round and round, faster and faster, till she told them to go. And they all went away directly, back to their holes, and on the lady's breast there would be a most curious, beautiful stone, shaped something like an egg, and coloured dark blue and yellow, and red, and green, marked like a serpent's scales. It was called a glame stone, and with it one could do all sorts of wonderful things, and nurse said her great-grandmother had seen a glame stone with her own eyes, and it was for all the world shiny and scaly like a snake. And the lady could do a lot of other things as well, but she was quite fixed that she would not be married. And there were a great many gentlemen who wanted to marry her, but there were five of them who were chief, and their names were Sir Simon, Sir John, Sir Oliver, Sir Richard, and Sir Rowland. All the others believed she spoke the truth, and that she would choose one of them to be her man when a year and a day was done; it was only Sir Simon, who was very crafty, who thought she was deceiving them all, and he vowed he would watch and try if he could find out anything. And though he was very wise he was very young, and he had a smooth, soft face like a girl's, and he pretended, as the rest did, that he would not come to the castle for a year and a day, and he said he was going away beyond the sea to foreign parts. But he really only went a very little way, and came back dressed like a servant girl, and so he got a place in the castle to wash the dishes. And he waited and watched, and he listened and said nothing, and he hid in dark places, and woke up at night and looked out, and he heard things and he saw things that he thought were very strange. And he was so sly that he told the girl that waited on the lady that he was really a young man, and that he had dressed up as a girl because he loved her so very much and wanted to be in the same house with her, and the girl was so pleased that she told him many things, and he was more than ever certain that the Lady Avelin was deceiving him and the others. And he was so clever, and told the servant so many lies, that one night he managed to hide in the Lady Avelin's room behind the curtains. And he stayed quite still and never moved, and at last the lady came. And she bent down under the bed, and raised up a stone, and there was a hollow place underneath, and out of it she took a waxen image, just like the clay one that I and nurse had made in the brake. And all the time her eyes were burning like rubies. And she took the little wax doll up in her arms and held it to her breast, and she whispered and she murmured, and she took it up and she laid it down again, and she held it high, and she held it low, and she laid it down again. And she said, "Happy is he that begat the bishop, that ordered the clerk, that married the man, that had the wife, that fashioned the hive, that harboured the bee, that gathered the wax that my own true love was made of." And she brought out of an aumbry a great golden bowl, and she brought out of a closet a great jar of wine, and she poured some of the wine into the bowl, and she laid her mannikin very gently in the wine, and washed it in the wine all over. Then she went to a cupboard and took a small round cake and laid it on the image's mouth, and then she bore it softly and covered it up. And Sir Simon, who was watching all the time, though he was terribly frightened, saw the lady bend down and stretch out her arms and whisper and sing, and then Sir Simon saw beside her a handsome young man, who kissed her on the lips. And they drank wine out of the golden bowl together, and they ate the cake together. But when the sun rose there was only the little wax doll, and the lady hid it again under the bed in the hollow place. So Sir Simon knew quite well what the lady was, and he waited and he watched, till the time she had said was nearly over, and in a week the year and a day would be done. And one night, when he was watching behind the curtains in her room, he saw her making more wax dolls. And she made five, and hid them away. And the next night she took one out, and held it up, and filled the golden bowl with water, and took the doll by the neck and held it under the water. Then she said—

> Sir Dickon, Sir Dickon, your day is done,
> You shall be drowned in the water wan.

And the next day news came to the castle that Sir Richard had been drowned at the ford. And at night she took another doll and tied a violet cord round its neck and hung it up on a nail. Then she said—

> Sir Rowland, your life has ended its span,
> High on a tree I see you hang.

And the next day news came to the castle that Sir Rowland had been hanged by robbers in the wood. And at night she took another doll, and drove her bodkin right into its heart. Then she said—

> Sir Noll, Sir Noll, so cease your life,
> Your heart is piercèd with the knife.

And the next day news came to the castle that Sir Oliver had fought in a tavern, and a stranger had stabbed him to the heart. And at night she took another doll, and held it to a fire of charcoal till it was melted. Then she said—

> Sir John, return, and turn to clay,
> In fire of fever you waste away.

And the next day news came to the castle that Sir John had died in a burning fever. So then Sir Simon went out of the castle and mounted his horse and rode away to the bishop and told him everything. And the bishop sent his men, and they took the Lady Avelin, and everything she had done was found out. So on the day after the year and a day, when she was to have been married, they carried her through the town in her smock, and they tied her to a great stake in the market-place, and burned her alive before the bishop with her wax image hung round her neck. And people said the wax man screamed in the burning of the flames. And I thought of this story again and again as I was lying awake in my bed, and I seemed to see the Lady Avelin in the market-place, with the yellow flames eating up her beautiful white body. And I thought of it so much that I seemed to get into the story myself, and I fancied I was the lady, and that they were coming to take me to be burnt with fire, with all the people in the town looking at me. And I wondered whether she cared, after all the strange things she had done, and whether it hurt very much to be burned at the stake. I tried again and again to forget nurse's stories, and to remember the secret I had seen that afternoon, and what was in the secret wood, but I could only see the dark and a glimmering in the dark, and then it went away, and I only saw myself running, and then a great moon came up white over a dark round hill. Then all the old stories came back again, and the queer rhymes that nurse used to sing to me; and there was one beginning "Halsy cumsy Helen musty," that she used to sing very softly when she wanted me to go to sleep. And I began to sing it to myself inside of my head, and I went to sleep.

The next morning I was very tired and sleepy, and could hardly do my lessons, and I was very glad when they were over and I had had my dinner, as I wanted to go out and be alone. It was a warm day, and I went to a nice turfy hill by the river, and sat down on my mother's old shawl that I had brought with me on purpose. The sky was grey, like the day before, but there was a kind of white gleam behind it, and from where I was sitting I could look down on the town, and it was all still and quiet and white, like a picture. I remembered that it was on that hill that nurse taught me to play an old game called "Troy Town," in which one had to dance, and wind in and out on a pattern in the grass, and then when one had danced and turned long enough the other person asks you questions, and you

96

can't help answering whether you want to or not, and whatever you are told to do you feel you have to do it. Nurse said there used to be a lot of games like that that some people knew of, and there was one by which people could be turned into anything you liked, and an old man her great-grandmother had seen had known a girl who had been turned into a large snake. And there was another very ancient game of dancing and winding and turning, by which you could take a person out of himself and hide him away as long as you liked, and his body went walking about quite empty, without any sense in it. But I came to that hill because I wanted to think of what had happened the day before, and of the secret of the wood. From the place where I was sitting I could see beyond the town, into the opening I had found, where a little brook had led me into an unknown country. And I pretended I was following the brook over again, and I went all the way in my mind, and at last I found the wood, and crept into it under the bushes, and then in the dusk I saw something that made me feel as if I were filled with fire, as if I wanted to dance and sing and fly up into the air, because I was changed and wonderful. But what I saw was not changed at all, and had not grown old, and I wondered again and again how such things could happen, and whether nurse's stories were really true, because in the daytime in the open air everything seemed quite different from what it was at night, when I was frightened, and thought I was to be burned alive. I once told my father one of her little tales, which was about a ghost, and asked him if it was true, and he told me it was not true at all, and that only common, ignorant people believed in such rubbish. He was very angry with nurse for telling me the story, and scolded her, and after that I promised her I would never whisper a word of what she told me, and if I did I should be bitten by the great black snake that lived in the pool in the wood. And all alone on the hill I wondered what was true. I had seen something very amazing and very lovely, and I knew a story, and if I had really seen it, and not made it up out of the dark, and the black bough, and the bright shining that was mounting up to the sky from over the great round hill, but had really seen it in truth, then there were all kinds of wonderful and lovely and terrible things to think of, so I longed and trembled, and I burned and got cold. And I looked down on the town, so quiet and still, like a little white picture, and I thought over and over if it could be true. I was a long time before I could make up my mind to anything; there was such a strange fluttering at my heart that seemed to whisper to me all the time that I had not made it up out of my head, and yet it seemed quite impossible, and I knew my father and everybody would say it was dreadful rubbish. I never dreamed of telling him or anybody else a word about it, because I knew it would be of no use, and I should only get laughed at or scolded, so for a long time I was very quiet, and went about thinking and wondering; and at night I used to dream of amazing things, and sometimes I woke up in the early morning and held out my arms with a cry. And I was frightened, too, because there were dangers, and some awful thing would happen to me, unless I took great care, if the story were true. These old tales were always in my head, night and morning, and I went over them and told them to myself over and over again, and went for walks in the places where nurse had told them to me; and when I sat in the nursery by the fire in the evenings I used to fancy nurse was sitting in the other chair, and telling me some wonderful story in a low voice, for fear anybody should be listening. But she used to like best to tell me about things when we were right out in the country, far from the house, because she said she was telling me such secrets, and walls have ears. And if it was something more than ever secret, we had to hide in brakes or woods; and I used to think it was such fun creeping along a hedge, and going very softly, and then we would get behind the bushes or run into the wood all of a sudden, when we were sure that none was watching us; so we knew that we had our-secrets quite all to ourselves, and nobody else at all knew anything about them. Now and then, when we had hidden ourselves as I have described, she used to show me all sorts of odd things. One day, I remember, we were in a hazel brake, overlooking the brook, and we were so snug and warm, as though it was April; the sun was quite hot, and the leaves were just coming out. Nurse said she would show me something funny that would make me laugh, and then she showed me, as she said, how one could turn a whole house upside down, without anybody being able to find out, and the pots and pans would jump about, and the china would be broken, and the chairs would tumble over of themselves. I tried it one day in the kitchen, and I found I could do it quite well, and a whole row of plates on the dresser fell off it, and cook's little work-table tilted up and turned right over "before her eyes," as she said, but she was so frightened and turned so white that I didn't do it again, as I liked her. And afterwards, in the hazel copse, when she had shown me how to make things tumble about, she showed me how to make rapping noises, and I learnt how to do that, too. Then she taught me rhymes to say on certain occasions, and peculiar marks to make on other occasions, and other things that her great-grandmother had taught her when she was a little girl herself. And these were all the things I was thinking about in those days after the strange walk when I thought I had seen a great secret, and I wished nurse were there for me to ask her about it, but she had gone away more than two years before, and nobody seemed to know what had become of her, or where she had gone. But I shall always remember those days if I live to be quite old, because all the time I felt so strange, wondering and doubting, and feeling quite sure at one time, and making up my mind, and then I would feel quite sure that such things couldn't happen really, and it began all over again. But I took great care not to do certain things that might be very dangerous. So I waited and wondered for a long time, and though I was not sure at all, I never dared to try to find out. But one day I became sure that all that nurse said was quite true, and I was all alone when I found it out. I trembled all over with joy and terror, and as fast as I could I ran into one of the old brakes where we used to go—it was the one by the lane, where nurse made the little clay man—and I ran into it, and I crept into it; and when I came to the place where the elder was, I covered up my face with my hands and lay down flat on the grass, and I stayed there for two hours without moving, whispering to myself delicious, terrible things, and saying some words over and over again. It was all true and wonderful and splendid, and when I remembered the story I knew and thought of what I had really seen, I got hot and I got cold, and the air seemed full of scent, and flowers, and singing. And first I wanted to make a little clay man, like the one nurse had made so long ago, and I had to invent plans and stratagems, and to look about, and to think of things beforehand, because nobody must dream of anything that I was doing or going to do, and I was too old to carry clay about in a tin bucket. At last I thought of a plan, and I brought the wet clay to the brake, and did everything that nurse had done, only I made a much finer image than the one she had made; and when it was finished I did everything that I could imagine and much more than she did, because it was the likeness of something far better. And a few days later, when I had done my lessons early, I went for the second time by the way of the little brook that had led me into a strange country. And I followed the brook, and went through the bushes, and beneath the low branches of trees, and up thorny thickets on the hill, and by dark woods full of creeping thorns, a long, long way. Then I crept through the dark tunnel where the brook had been and the ground was stony, till at last I came to the thicket that climbed up the hill, and though the leaves were coming out upon the trees, everything looked almost as black as it was on the first day that I went there. And the thicket was just the same, and I went up slowly till I came out on the big bare hill, and began to walk among the wonderful rocks. I saw the terrible voor again on everything, for though the sky was brighter, the ring of wild hills all around was still dark, and the hanging woods looked dark and dreadful, and the strange rocks were as grey as ever; and when I looked down on them from the great mound, sitting on the stone, I saw all their amazing circles and rounds within rounds, and I had to sit quite still and watch them as they began to turn about me, and each stone danced in its place, and they seemed to go round and round in a great whirl, as if one were in the middle of all the stars and heard them rushing through the air. So I went down among the rocks to dance with them and to sing extraordinary songs; and I went down through the other thicket, and drank from the bright stream in the close and secret valley, putting my lips down to the bubbling water; and then I went on till I came to the deep, brimming well among the glittering moss, and I sat down. I looked before me into the secret darkness of the valley, and behind me was the great high wall of grass, and all around me there were the hanging woods that made the valley such a secret place. I knew there was nobody here at all besides myself, and that no one could see me. So I took off my boots and stockings, and let my feet down into the water, saying the words that I knew. And it was not cold at all, as I expected, but warm and very pleasant, and when my feet were in it I felt as if they were in silk, or as if the nymph were kissing them. So when I had done, I said the other words and made the signs, and then I dried my feet with a towel I had brought on purpose, and put on my stockings and boots. Then I climbed up the steep wall, and went into the place where there are the hollows, and the two beautiful mounds, and the round ridges of land, and all the strange shapes. I did not go down into the hollow this time, but I turned at the end, and made out the figures quite plainly, as it was lighter, and I had remembered the story I had quite forgotten before, and in the story the two figures are called Adam and Eve, and only those who know the story understand what they mean. So I went on and on till I came to the secret wood which must not be described, and I crept into it by the way I had found. And when I had gone about halfway I stopped, and turned round, and got ready, and I bound the handkerchief tightly round my eyes, and made quite sure that I could not see at all, not a twig, nor the end of a leaf, nor the light of the sky, as it was an old red silk handkerchief with large yellow spots, that went round twice and covered my eyes, so that I could see nothing. Then I began to go on, step by step, very slowly. My heart beat faster and faster, and something rose in my throat that choked me and made me want to cry out, but I shut my lips, and went on. Boughs caught in my hair as I went, and great thorns tore me; but I went on to the end of the path. Then I stopped, and held out my arms and bowed, and I went round the first time, feeling with my hands, and there was nothing. I went round the second time, feeling with my hands, and there was nothing. Then I went round the third time, feeling with my hands, and the story was all true, and I wished that the years were gone by, and that I had not so long a time to wait before I was happy for ever and ever.

Nurse must have been a prophet like those we read of in the Bible. Everything that she said began to come true, and since then other things that she told me of have happened. That was how I came to know that her stories were true and that I had not made up the secret myself out of my own head. But there was another thing that happened that day. I went a second time to the secret place. It was at the deep brimming well, and when I was standing on the moss I bent over and looked in, and then I knew who the white lady was that I had seen come out of the water in the wood long ago when I was quite little. And I trembled all over, because that told me other things. Then I remembered how sometime after I had seen the white people in the wood, nurse asked me more about them, and I told her all over again, and she listened, and said nothing for a long, long time, and at last she said, "You will see her again." So I understood what had happened and what was to happen. And I understood about the nymphs; how I might meet them in all kinds of places, and they would always help me, and I must always look for them, and find them in all sorts of strange shapes and appearances. And without the nymphs I could never have found the secret, and without them none of the other things could happen. Nurse had told me all about them long ago, but she called them by another name, and I did not know what she meant, or what her tales of them were about, only that they were very queer. And there were two kinds, the bright and the dark, and both were very lovely and very wonderful, and some people saw only one kind, and some only the other, but some saw them both. But usually the dark appeared first, and the bright ones came afterwards, and there were extraordinary tales about them. It was a day or two after I had come home from the secret place that I first really knew the nymphs. Nurse had shown me how to call them, and I had tried, but I did not know what she meant; and so I thought it was all nonsense. But I made up my mind I would try again, so I went to the wood where the pool was, where I saw the white people, and I tried again. The dark nymph, Alanna, came, and she turned the pool of water into a pool of fire...

EPILOGUE

"That's a very queer story," said Cotgrave, handing back the green book to the recluse, Ambrose. "I see the drift of a good deal, but there are many things that I do not grasp at all. On the last page, for example, what does she mean by 'nymphs'?"

"Well, I think there are references throughout the manuscript to certain "processes" which have been handed down by tradition from age to age. Some of these processes are just beginning to come within the purview of science, which has arrived at them—or rather at the steps which lead to them—by quite different paths. I have interpreted the reference to "nymphs" as a reference to one of these processes."

"And you believe that there are such things?"

"Oh, I think so. Yes, I believe I could give you convincing evidence on that point. I am afraid you have neglected the study of alchemy? It is a pity, for the symbolism, at all events, is very beautiful, and moreover if you were acquainted with certain books on the subject, I could recall to your mind phrases which might explain a good deal in the manuscript that you have been reading."

"Yes; but I want to know whether you seriously think that there is any foundation of fact beneath these fancies. Is it not all a department of poetry; a curious dream with which man has indulged himself?"

"I can only say that it is no doubt better for the great mass of people to dismiss it all as a dream. But if you ask my veritable belief—that goes quite the other way. No; I should not say belief, but rather knowledge. I may tell you that I have known cases in which men have stumbled quite by accident on certain of these 'processes,' and have been astonished by wholly unexpected results. In the cases I am thinking of there could have been no possibility of 'suggestion' or sub-conscious action of any kind. One might as well suppose a schoolboy 'suggesting' the existence of Æschylus to himself, while he plods mechanically through the declensions.

"But you have noticed the obscurity," Ambrose went on, "and in this particular case it must have been dictated by instinct, since the writer never thought that her manuscripts would fall into other hands. But the practice is universal, and for most excellent reasons. Powerful and sovereign medicines, which are, of necessity, virulent poisons also, are kept in a locked cabinet. The child may find the key by chance, and drink herself dead; but in most cases the search is educational, and the phials contain precious elixirs for him who has patiently fashioned the key for himself."

"You do not care to go into details?"

"No, frankly, I do not. No, you must remain unconvinced. But you saw how the manuscript illustrates the talk we had last week?"

"Is this girl still alive?"

"No. I was one of those who found her. I knew the father well; he was a lawyer, and had always left her very much to herself. He thought of nothing but deeds and leases, and the news came to him as an awful surprise. She was missing one morning; I suppose it was about a year after she had written what you have read. The servants were called, and they told things, and put the only natural interpretation on them—a perfectly erroneous one.

"They discovered that green book somewhere in her room, and I found her in the place that she described with so much dread, lying on the ground before the image."

"It was an image?"

"Yes, it was hidden by the thorns and the thick undergrowth that had surrounded it. It was a wild, lonely country; but you know what it was like by her description, though of course you will understand that the colours have been heightened. A child's imagination always makes the heights higher and the depths deeper than they really are; and she had, unfortunately for herself, something more than imagination. One might say, perhaps, that the picture in her mind which she succeeded in a measure in putting into words, was the scene as it would have appeared to an imaginative artist. But it is a strange, desolate land."

"And she was dead?"

"Yes. She had poisoned herself—in time. No; there was not a word to be said against her in the ordinary sense. You may recollect a story I told you the other night about a lady who saw her child's fingers crushed by a window?"

"And what was this statue?"

"Well, it was of Roman workmanship, of a stone that with the centuries had not blackened, but had become white and luminous. The thicket had grown up about it and concealed it, and in the Middle Ages the followers of a very old tradition had known how to use it for their own purposes. In fact it had been incorporated into the monstrous mythology of the Sabbath. You will have noted that those to whom a sight of that shining whiteness had been vouchsafed by chance, or rather, perhaps, by apparent chance, were required to blindfold themselves on their second approach. That is very significant."

"And is it there still?"

"I sent for tools, and we hammered it into dust and fragments."

"The persistence of tradition never surprises me," Ambrose went on after a pause. "I could name many an English parish where such traditions as that girl had listened to in her childhood are still existent in occult but unabated vigour. No, for me, it is the 'story' not the 'sequel,' which is strange and awful, for I have always believed that wonder is of the soul."

THE PRISM

Mary E. Wilkins (1852–1930)

Mary Eleanor Wilkins, or Wilkins Freeman as she became known after her marriage to Charles Freeman on New Year's Day 1902, was one of New England's best writers of both regional fiction and of ghost stories. Her career spanned nearly fifty years from selling her first stories in 1881 to her last in 1928. She was so prolific that despite having eight collections of her stories published during her life time, there remained many uncollected to be hunted down by devotees in the years since her death. Some of her ghost stories were collected in *The Wind in the Rose-Bush* in 1903, an essential volume for any library of the supernatural. This has since been augmented by the *Collected Ghost Stories of Mary E. Wilkins-Freeman* (1974) and even this missed a few of her haunting stories, including "The Prism". It was published just before her marriage and it may well be that those impending nuptials inspired this story about the loss of childhood innocence.

There had been much rain that season, and the vegetation was almost tropical. The wayside growths were jungles to birds and insects, and very near them to humans. All through the long afternoon of the hot August day, Diantha Fielding lay flat on her back under the lee of the stone wall which bordered her stepfather's, Zenas May's, south mowing-lot. It was pretty warm there, although she lay in a little strip of shade of the tangle of blackberry-vines, poison-ivy, and the grey pile of stones; but the girl loved the heat. She experienced the gentle languor which is its best effect, instead of the fierce unrest and irritation which is its worst. She left that to rattlesnakes and nervous women. As for her, in times of extreme heat, she hung over life with tremulous flutters, like a butterfly over a rose, moving only enough to preserve her poise in the scheme of things, and realizing to the full the sweetness of all about her.

She heard, as she lay there, the voice of a pine-tree not far away—a solitary pine which was full of gusty sweetness; she smelled the wild grapes, which were reluctantly ripening across the field over the wall that edged the lane; she smelled the blackberry-vines; she looked with indolent fascination at the virile sprays of poison-ivy. It was like innocence surveying sin, and wondering what it was like. Once her stepmother, Mrs. Zenas May, had been poisoned with ivy, and both eyes had been closed thereby. Diantha did not believe that the ivy would so serve her. She dared herself to touch it, then she looked away again.

She heard a far-carrying voice from the farm-house at the left calling her name. "Diantha! Diantha!" She lay so still that she scarcely breathed. The voice came again. She smiled triumphantly. She knew perfectly well what was wanted: that she should assist in preparing supper. Her stepmother's married daughter and her two children were visiting at the house. She preferred remaining where she was. Her sole fear of disturbance was from the children. They were like little ferrets. Diantha did not like them. She did not like children very well under any circumstances. To her they seemed always out of tune; the jar of heredity was in them, and she felt it, although she did not know enough to realize what she felt. She was only twelve years old, a child still, though tall for her age.

The voice came again. Diantha shifted her position a little; she stretched her slender length luxuriously; she felt for something which hung suspended around her neck under her gingham waist, but she did not then remove it. "Diantha! Diantha!" came the insistent voice.

Diantha lay as irresponsive as the blackberry-vine which trailed beside her like a snake. Then she heard the house door close with a bang; her ears were acute. She felt again of that which was suspended from her neck. A curious expression of daring, of exultation, of fear, was in her face. Presently she heard the shrill voices of children; then she lay so still that she seemed fairly to obliterate herself by silence and motionlessness.

Two little girls in pink frocks came racing past; their flying heels almost touched her, but they never saw her.

When they were well past, she drew a cautious breath, and felt again of the treasure around her neck.

After a while she heard the soft padding of many hoofs in the heavy dust of the road, a dog's shrill bark, the tinkle of a bell, the absent-minded shout of a weary man. The hired man was driving the cows home. The fragrance of milk-dripping udders, of breaths sweetened with clover and meadow-grass, came to her. Suddenly a cold nose rubbed against her face; the dog had found her out. But she was a friend of his. She patted him, then pushed him away gently, and he understood that she wished to remain concealed. He went barking back to the man. The cows broke into a clumsy gallop; the man shouted. Diantha smelled the dust of the road which flew over the field like smoke. She heard the children returning down the road behind the cows. When the cows galloped, they screamed with half fearful delight. Then it all passed by, and she heard the loud clang of a bell from the farm-house.

Then Diantha pulled out the treasure which was suspended from her neck by an old blue ribbon, and she held it up to the low western sun, and wonderful lights of red and blue and violet and green and orange danced over the shaven stubble of the field before her delighted eyes. It was a prism which she had stolen from the best-parlour lamp—from the lamp which had been her own mother's, bought by her with her school-teaching money before her marriage, and brought by her to grace her new home.

Diantha Fielding, as far as relatives went, was in a curious position. First her mother died when she was very young, only a few months old; then her father had married again, giving her a stepmother; then her father had died two years later, and her stepmother had married again, giving her a stepfather. Since then the stepmother had died, and the stepfather had married a widow with a married daughter, whose two children had raced down the road behind the cows. Diantha often felt in a sore bewilderment of relationships. She had not even a cousin of her own; the dearest relative she had was the daughter of a widow whom a cousin of her mother's had married for a second wife. The cousin was long since dead. The wife was living, and Diantha's little step second cousin, as she reckoned it, lived in the old homestead which had belonged to Diantha's grandfather, across the way from the May farm-house. It was a gambrel-roof, half-ruinous structure, well banked in front with a monstrous growth of lilacs, and overhung by a great butternut-tree.

Diantha knew well that she was heaping up vials of cold wrath upon her head by not obeying the supper-bell, but she lay still. Then Libby came—Libby, the little cousin, stepping very cautiously and daintily; for she wore slippers of her mother's, which hung from her small heels, and she had lost them twice already.

She stopped before Diantha. Her slender arms, terminating in hands too large for them, hung straight at her sides in the folds of her faded blue-flowered muslin. Her pretty little heat-flushed face had in it no more speculation than a flower, and no more changing. She was like a flower, which would blossom the same next year, and the next year after that, and the same until it died. There was no speculation in her face as she looked at Diantha dangling the prism in the sunlight, merely unimaginative wonder and admiration.

"It's a drop off your best-parlour lamp," said she, in her thin, sweet voice.

"Look over the field, Libby!" cried Diantha, excitedly.

Libby looked.

"Tell me what you see, quick!"

"What I see? Why, grass and things."

"No, I don't mean them; what you see from this."

Diantha shook the prism violently.

"I see a lot of different colours dancing," replied Libby, "same as you always see. Addie Green had an ear-drop that was broken off their best-parlour lamp. Her mother gave it to her."

"Don't you see anything but different lights?"

"Of course I don't. That's all there is to see."

Diantha sighed.

"That drop ain't broken," said the other little girl. "How did she happen to let you have it?" By "she" Libby meant Diantha's stepmother.

"I took it," replied Diantha. She was fastening the prism around her neck again.

Libby gasped and stared at her. "Didn't you ask her?"

"If I'd asked her, she'd said no, and it was my own mother's lamp. I had a right to it."

"What'll she do to you?"

"I don't know, if she finds out. I sha'n't tell her, if I can help it without lying."

Diantha fastened her gingham frock securely over the prism. Then she rose, and the two little girls went home across the dry stubble of the field.

"I didn't go when she called me, and I didn't go when the supper-bell rang," said Diantha.

Libby stared at her wonderingly. She had never felt an impulse to disobedience in her life; she could not understand this other child, who was a law unto herself. She walked very carefully in her large slippers.

"What'll she do to you?" she inquired.

Diantha tossed her head like a colt.

"She won't do anything, I guess, except make me go without my supper. If she does, I ain't afraid; but I guess she won't, and I'd a heap rather go without my supper than go to it when I don't want to."

Libby looked at her with admiring wonder. Diantha was neatly and rigorously, rather than tastefully, dressed. Her dark blue-and-white gingham frock was starched stiffly; it hung exactly at the proper height from her slender ankles; she wore a clean white collar; and her yellow hair was braided very tightly and smoothly, and tied with a punctilious blue bow. In strange contrast with the almost martial preciseness of her attire was the expression of her little face, flushed, eager to enthusiasm, almost wild, with a light in her blue eyes which did not belong there, according to the traditions concerning little New England maidens, with a feverish rose on her cheeks, which should have been cool and pale. However, that had all come since she had dangled the prism in the rays of the setting sun.

"What did you think you saw when you shook that ear-drop off the lamp?" asked Libby; but she asked without much curiosity.

"Red and green and yellow colours, of course," replied Diantha, shortly.

When they reached Diantha's door, Libby bade her good night, and sped across the road to her own house. She stood a little in fear of Diantha's stepmother, if Diantha did not. She knew just the sort of look which would be directed toward the other little girl, and she knew from experience that it might include her. From her Puritan ancestry she had a certain stubbornness when brought to bay, but no courage of aggression; so she ran.

Diantha marched in. She was utterly devoid of fear.

Her stepmother, Mrs. Zenas May, was washing the supper dishes at the kitchen sink. All through the house sounded a high sweet voice which was constantly off the key, singing a lullaby to the two little girls, who had to go to bed directly after they had finished their evening meal.

Mrs. Zenas May turned around and surveyed Diantha as she entered. There was nothing in the least unkind in her look; it was simply the gaze of one on a firm standpoint of existence upon another swaying on a precarious balance—the sort of look a woman seated in a car gives to one standing. It was irresponsible, while cognizant of the discomfort of the other person.

"Where were you when the supper-bell rang?" asked Mrs. Zenas May. She was rather a pretty woman, with an exquisitely cut profile. Her voice was very even, almost as devoid of inflections as a deaf-and-dumb person's. Her gingham gown was also rigorously starched. Her fair hair showed high lights of gloss from careful brushing; it was strained back from her blue-veined temples.

"Out in the field," replied Diantha.

"Then you heard it?"

"Yes, ma'am."

"The supper-table is cleared away," said Mrs. May. That was all she said. She went on polishing the tumblers, which she was rinsing in ammonia water.

Diantha glanced through the open door and saw the dining-room table with its chenille after-supper cloth on. She made no reply, but went up-stairs to her own chamber. That was very comfortable—the large south one back of her step-parents'. Not a speck of dust was to be seen in it; the feather-bed was an even mound of snow. Diantha sat down by the window, and gazed out at the deepening dusk. She felt at the prism around her neck, but she did not draw it out, for it was of no use in that low light. She could not invoke the colours which it held. Her chamber door was open. Presently she heard the best-parlour door open, and heard quite distinctly her stepmother's voice. She was speaking to her stepfather.

"There's a drop broken off the parlour lamp," said she.

There was an unintelligible masculine grunt of response.

"I wish you'd look while I hold the lamp, and see if you can find it on the floor anywhere," said her stepmother. Her voice was still even. The loss of a prism from the best-parlour lamp was not enough to ruffle her outward composure.

"Don't you see it?" she asked, after a little.

Again came the unintelligible masculine grunt.

"It is very strange," said Mrs. May. "Don't look any more."

She never inquired of Diantha concerning the prism. In truth, she believed one of her grandchildren, whom she adored, to be responsible for the loss of the glittering ornament, and was mindful of the fact that Diantha's mother had originally owned that lamp. So she said nothing, but as soon as might be purchased another, and Diantha kept her treasure quite unsuspected.

She did not, however, tremble in the least while the search was going on down-stairs. She had her defence quite ready. To her sense of justice it was unquestionable. She would simply say that the lamp had belonged to her own mother, consequently to her; that she had a right to do as she chose with it. She had not the slightest fear of any reproaches which Mrs. May would bring to bear upon her. She knew she would not use bodily punishment, as she never had; but she would have stood in no fear of that.

Diantha did not go to bed for a long time. There was a full moon, and she sat by the window, leaning her two elbows on the sill, making a cup of her hands, in which she rested her peaked chin, and peered out.

It was nearly nine o'clock when some one entered the room with heavy, soft movements, like a great tame dog. It was her stepfather, and he had in his hand a large wedge of apple-pie.

"Diantha," he said, in a loud whisper, "you gone to bed?"

"No, sir," replied Diantha. She liked her stepfather. She was always aware of a clumsy, covert partizanship from him.

"Well," said he, "here's a piece of pie. You hadn't ought to go to bed without any supper. You'd ought to come in when the bell rings another time, Diantha."

"Thank you, father," said Diantha, reaching out her hand for the pie.

Zenas May, who was large and shaggily blond, with a face like a great blank of good nature, placed a heavy hand on her little, tightly braided head, and patted it.

"Better eat your pie and go to bed," he said. Then he shambled down-stairs very softly, lest his wife hear him.

Diantha ate her pie obediently, and went to bed, and with the first morning sunlight she removed her prism from her neck, and flashed it across the room, and saw what she saw, or what she thought she saw.

Diantha kept the prism, and nobody except Libby knew it, and she was quite safe with a secret. While she did not in the least comprehend, she was stanch. Even when she grew older and had a lover, she did not tell him; she did not even tell him when she was married to him that Diantha Fielding always carried a drop off the best-parlour lamp, which belonged to her own mother, and when she flashed it in the sunlight she thought she saw things. She kept it all to herself. Libby married before Diantha, before Diantha had a lover even. Young men, for some reason, were rather shy of Diantha, although she had a little property in her own right, inherited from her own father and mother, and was, moreover, extremely pretty. However, her prettiness was not of a type to attract the village men as quickly as Libby's more material charms. Diantha was very thin and small, and her colour was as clear as porcelain, and she gave a curious impression of mystery, although there was apparently nothing whatever mysterious about her.

But her turn came. A graduate of a country college, a farmer's son, who had worked his own way through college, had now obtained the high school. He saw Diantha, and fell in love with her, although he struggled against it. He said to himself that she was too delicate, that he was a poor man, that he ought to have a more robust wife, who would stand a better chance of discharging her domestic and maternal duties without a breakdown. Reason and judgment were strongly developed in him. His passion for Diantha was entirely opposed to both, but it got the better of him. One afternoon in August when Diantha was almost twenty, he, passing by her house, saw her sitting on her front doorstep, stopped, and proposed a little stroll in the woods, and asked her to marry him.

"I never thought much about getting married," said Diantha. Then she leaned toward him as if impelled by some newly developed instinct. She spoke so low that he could not hear her, and he asked her over.

"I never thought much about getting married," repeated Diantha, and she leaned nearer him.

He laughed a great triumphant laugh, and caught her in his arms.

"Then it is high time you did, you darling," he said.

Diantha was very happy.

They lingered in the woods a long time, and when they went home, the young man, whose name was Robert Black, went in with her, and told her stepmother what had happened.

"I have asked your daughter to marry me, Mrs. May," he said, "and she has consented, and I hope you are willing."

Mrs. May replied that she had no objections, stiffly, without a smile. She never smiled. Instead of smiling, she always looked questioningly even at their beloved grandchildren. They had lived with her since their mother's death, two pretty, boisterous girls, pupils of Robert Black, who had had their own inevitable little dreams regarding him, as they had had regarding every man who came in their way.

When their grandmother told them that Diantha was to marry the hero who had dwelt in their own innocently bold air-castles of girlish dreams, they started at first as from a shock of falling imaginations; then they began to think of their attire as bridesmaids.

Mrs. Zenas May was firmly resolved that Diantha should have as grand a wedding as if she had been her own daughter.

"Folks sha'n't say that she didn't have as good an outfit and wedding as if her own mother had been alive to see to it," she said.

As for Diantha, she thought very little about her outfit or the wedding, but about Robert. All at once she was possessed by a strong angel of primal conditions of whose existence she had never dreamed. She poured out her very soul; she made revelations of the inmost innocences of her nature to this ambitious, faithful, unimaginative young man. She had been some two weeks betrothed, and they were walking together one afternoon, when she showed him her prism.

She no longer wore it about her neck as formerly. A dawning unbelief in it had seized her, and yet there were times when to doubt seemed to doubt the evidence of her own senses.

That afternoon, as they were walking together in the lonely country road, she stopped him in a sunny interval between the bordering woods, where the road stretched for some distance between fields foaming with wild carrot and mustard, and swarmed over with butterflies, and she took her prism out of her pocket and flashed it full before her wondering lover's eyes.

He looked astonished, even annoyed; then he laughed aloud with a sort of tender scorn.

"What a child you are, dear!" he said. "What are you doing with that thing?"

"What do you see, Robert?" the girl cried eagerly, and there was in her eyes a light not of her day and generation, maybe inherited from some far-off Celtic ancestor—a strain of imagination which had survived the glaring light of latter days of commonness.

He eyed her with amazement; then he looked at the gorgeous blots and banners of colour over the fields.

"See? Why, I see the prismatic colours, of course. What else should I see?" he asked.

"Nothing else?"

"No. Why, what else should I see? I see the prismatic colours from the refraction of the sunlight."

Diantha looked at the dancing tints, then at her lover, and spoke with a solemn candour, as if she were making confession of an alien faith. "Ever since I was a child, I have seen, or thought so—" she began.

"What, for heaven's sake?" he cried impatiently.

"You have read about—fairies and—such things?"

"Of course. What do you mean, Diantha?"

"I have seen, or thought so, beautiful little people moving and dancing in the broken lights across the fields."

"For heaven's sake, put up that thing, and don't talk such nonsense, Diantha!" cried Robert, almost brutally. He had paled a little.

"I have, Robert."

"Don't talk such nonsense. I thought you were a sensible girl," said the young man.

Diantha put the prism back in her pocket.

All the rest of the way Robert was silent and gloomy. His old doubts had revived. His judgment for the time being got the upper hand of his passion. He began to wonder if he ought to marry a girl with such preposterous fancies as those. He began to wonder if she were just right in her mind.

He parted from her coolly, and came the next evening, but remained only a short time. Then he stayed away several days. He called on Sunday, then did not come again for four days. On Friday Diantha grew desperate. She went by herself out in the sunny field, walking ankle-deep in flowers and weeds, until she reached the margin of a little pond on which the children skated in winter. Then she took her prism from her pocket and flashed it in the sunlight, and for the first time she failed to see what she had either seen, or imagined, for so many years.

She saw only the beautiful prismatic colours flashing across the field in bars and blots and streamers of rose and violet, of orange and green. That was all. She stooped, and dug in the oozy soil beside the pond with her bare white hands, and made, as it were, a little grave, and buried the prism out of sight. Then she washed her hands in the pond, and waved them about until they were dry. Afterward she went swiftly across the field to the road which her lover must pass on his way from school, and, when she saw him coming, met him, blushing and trembling.

"I have put it away, Robert," she said. "I saw nothing; it was only my imagination."

It was a lonely road. He looked at her doubtfully, then he laughed, and put an arm around her.

"It's all right, little girl," he replied; "but don't let such fancies dwell in your brain. This is a plain, common world, and it won't do."

"I saw nothing; it must have been my imagination," she repeated. Then she leaned her head against her lover's shoulder. Whether or not she had sold her birthright, she had got her full measure of the pottage of love which filled to an ecstasy of satisfaction her woman's heart.

She and Robert were married, and lived in a pretty new house, from the western windows of which she could see the pond on whose borders she had buried the prism. She was very happy. For the time being, at least, all the mysticism in her face had given place to an utter revelation of earthly bliss. People said how much Diantha had improved since her marriage, what a fine housekeeper she was, how much common sense she had, how she was such a fitting mate for her husband, whom she adored.

Sometimes Diantha, looking from a western window, used to see the pond across the field, reflecting the light of the setting sun, and looking like an eye of revelation of the earth; and she would remember that key of a lost radiance and a lost belief of her own life, which was buried beside it. Then she would go happily and prepare her husband's supper.

THE MYSTERIOUS CARD

and

THE MYSTERIOUS CARD UNVEILED

Cleveland Moffett (1863–1926)

A New York journalist and later newspaper editor, Moffett was also a frequent contributor to magazines, especially *McClure's*, in which he wrote many articles about developments in science, either new inventions or new discoveries. Amongst these was "Seeing by Wire" (1899) in which he described what would become television. His interest in science remained and during the First World War he wrote the future-war novel, *The Conquest of America* (1916), set five years hence, which speculated what might happen if Germany won the war in Europe and fixed her sights on the United States. *Possessed* (1920) is a novel of spiritualism and dual personality, based on events that Moffett had himself witnessed. Early in his career Moffett wrote "The Mysterious Card" for *The Black Cat*. It was such a perplexing story that the magazine's readers demanded a sequel and it is these two stories for which Moffett is now best remembered.

R ichard Burwell, of New York, will never cease to regret that the French language was not made a part of his education. This is why:

On the second evening after Burwell arrived in Paris, feeling lonely without his wife and daughter, who were still visiting a friend in London, his mind naturally turned to the theatre. So, after consulting the daily amusement calendar, he decided to visit the Folies Bergère, which he had heard of as one of the notable sights. During an intermission he went into the beautiful garden, where gay crowds were strolling among the flowers, and lights, and fountains. He had just seated himself at a little three-legged table, with a view to enjoying the novel scene, when his attention was attracted by a lovely woman, gowned strikingly, though in perfect taste, who passed near him, leaning on the arm of a gentleman. The only thing that he noticed about this gentleman was that he wore eye-glasses.

Now Burwell had never posed as a captivator of the fair sex, and could scarcely credit his eyes when the lady left the side of her escort and, turning back as if she had forgotten something, passed close by him, and deftly placed a card on his table. The card bore some French words written in purple ink, but, not knowing that language, he was unable to make out their meaning. The lady paid no further heed to him, but, rejoining the gentleman with the eye-glasses, swept out of the place with the grace and dignity of a princess. Burwell remained staring at the card.

Needless to say, he thought no more of the performance or of the other attractions about him. Everything seemed flat and tawdry compared with the radiant vision that had appeared and disappeared so mysteriously. His one desire now was to discover the meaning of the words written on the card.

Calling a fiacre, he drove to the Hotel Continental, where he was staying. Proceeding directly to the office and taking the manager aside, Burwell asked if he would be kind enough to translate a few words of French into English. There were no more than twenty words in all.

"Why, certainly," said the manager, with French politeness, and cast his eyes over the card. As he read, his face grew rigid with astonishment, and, looking at his questioner sharply, he exclaimed: "Where did you get this, monsieur?"

Burwell started to explain, but was interrupted by: "That will do, that will do. You must leave the hotel."

"What do you mean?" asked the man from New York, in amazement.

"You must leave the hotel now—tonight—without fail," commanded the manager excitedly.

Now it was Burwell's turn to grow angry, and he declared heatedly that if he wasn't wanted in this hotel there were plenty of others in Paris where he would be welcome. And, with an assumption of dignity, but piqued at heart, he settled his bill, sent for his belongings, and drove up the Rue de la Paix to the Hotel Bellevue, where he spent the night.

The next morning he met the proprietor, who seemed to be a good fellow, and, being inclined now to view the incident of the previous evening from its ridiculous side, Burwell explained what had befallen him, and was pleased to find a sympathetic listener.

"Why, the man was a fool," declared the proprietor. "Let me see the card; I will tell you what it means." But as he read, his face and manner changed instantly.

"This is a serious matter," he said sternly. "Now I understand why my confrère refused to entertain you. I regret, monsieur, but I shall be obliged to do as he did."

"What do you mean?"

"Simply that you cannot remain here."

With that he turned on his heel, and the indignant guest could not prevail upon him to give any explanation.

"We'll see about this," said Burwell, thoroughly angered.

It was now nearly noon, and the New Yorker remembered an engagement to lunch with a friend from Boston, who, with his family, was stopping at the Hotel de l'Alma. With his luggage on the carriage, he ordered the cocher to drive directly there, determined to take counsel with his countryman before selecting new quarters. His friend was highly indignant when he heard the story—a fact that gave Burwell no little comfort, knowing, as he did, that the man was accustomed to foreign ways from long residence abroad.

"It is some silly mistake, my dear fellow; I wouldn't pay any attention to it. Just have your luggage taken down and stay here. It is a nice, homelike place, and it will be very jolly, all being together. But, first, let me prepare a little 'nerve settler' for you."

After the two had lingered a moment over their Manhattan cocktails, Burwell's friend excused himself to call the ladies. He had proceeded only two or three steps when he turned, and said: "Let's see that mysterious card that has raised all this row."

He had scarcely withdrawn it from Burwell's hand when he started back, and exclaimed:—

"Great God, man! Do you mean to say—this is simply—"

Then, with a sudden movement of his hand to his head, he left the room.

He was gone perhaps five minutes, and when he returned his face was white.

"I am awfully sorry," he said nervously; "but the ladies tell me they—that is, my wife—she has a frightful headache. You will have to excuse us from the lunch."

Instantly realizing that this was only a flimsy pretence, and deeply hurt by his friend's behaviour, the mystified man arose at once and left without another word. He was now determined to solve this mystery at any cost. What could be the meaning of the words on that infernal piece of pasteboard?

Profiting by his humiliating experiences, he took good care not to show the card to any one at the hotel where he now established himself,—a comfortable little place near the Grand Opera House.

All through the afternoon he thought of nothing but the card, and turned over in his mind various ways of learning its meaning without getting himself into further trouble. That evening he went again to the Folies Bergère in the hope of finding the mysterious woman, for he was now more than ever anxious to discover who she was. It even occurred to him that she might be one of those beautiful Nihilist conspirators, or, perhaps, a Russian spy, such as he had read of in novels. But he failed to find her, either then or on the three subsequent evenings which he passed in the same place. Meanwhile the card was burning in his pocket like a hot coal. He dreaded the thought of meeting anyone that he knew, while this horrible cloud hung over him. He bought a French–English dictionary and tried to pick out the meaning word by word, but failed. It was all Greek to him. For the first time in his life, Burwell regretted that he had not studied French at college.

After various vain attempts to either solve or forget the torturing riddle, he saw no other course than to lay the problem before a detective agency. He accordingly put his case in the hands of an agent de la sureté who was recommended as a competent and trustworthy man. They had a talk together in a private room, and, of course, Burwell showed the card. To his relief, his adviser at least showed no sign of taking offence. Only he did not and would not explain what the words meant.

"It is better," he said, "that monsieur should not know the nature of this document for the present. I will do myself the honour to call upon monsieur tomorrow at his hotel, and then monsieur shall know everything."

"Then it is really serious?" asked the unfortunate man.

"Very serious," was the answer.

The next twenty-four hours Burwell passed in a fever of anxiety. As his mind conjured up one fearful possibility after another he deeply regretted that he had not torn up the miserable card at the start. He even seized it,—prepared to strip it into fragments, and so end the whole affair. And then his Yankee stubbornness again asserted itself, and he determined to see the thing out, come what might.

"After all," he reasoned, "it is no crime for a man to pick up a card that a lady drops on his table."

Crime or no crime, however, it looked very much as if he had committed some grave offence when, the next day, his detective drove up in a carriage, accompanied by a uniformed official, and requested the astounded American to accompany them to the police headquarters.

"What for?" he asked.

"It is only a formality," said the detective; and when Burwell still protested the man in uniform remarked: "You'd better come quietly, monsieur; you will have to come, anyway."

An hour later, after severe cross-examination by another official, who demanded many facts about the New Yorker's age, place of birth, residence, occupation, etc., the bewildered man found himself in the Conciergerie prison. Why he was there or what was about to befall him Burwell had no means of knowing; but before the day was over he succeeded in having a message sent to the American Legation, where he demanded immediate protection as a citizen of the United States. It was not until evening, however, that the Secretary of Legation, a consequential person, called at the prison. There followed a stormy interview, in which the prisoner used some strong language, the French officers gesticulated violently and talked very fast, and the Secretary calmly listened to both sides, said little, and smoked a good cigar.

"I will lay your case before the American minister," he said as he rose to go, "and let you know the result tomorrow."

"But this is an outrage. Do you mean to say—" Before he could finish, however, the Secretary, with a strangely suspicious glance, turned and left the room.

That night Burwell slept in a cell.

The next morning he received another visit from the non-committal Secretary, who informed him that matters had been arranged, and that he would be set at liberty forthwith.

"I must tell you, though," he said, "that I have had great difficulty in accomplishing this, and your liberty is granted only on condition that you leave the country within twenty-four hours, and never under any conditions return."

Burwell stormed, raged, and pleaded; but it availed nothing. The Secretary was inexorable, and yet he positively refused to throw any light upon the causes of this monstrous injustice.

"Here is your card," he said, handing him a large envelope closed with the seal of Legation. "I advise you to burn it and never refer to the matter again."

That night the ill-fated man took the train for London, his heart consumed by hatred for the whole French nation, together with a burning desire for vengeance. He wired his wife to meet him at the station, and for a long time debated with himself whether he should at once tell her the sickening truth. In the end he decided that it was better to keep silent. No sooner, however, had she seen him than her woman's instinct told her that he was labouring under some mental strain. And he saw in a moment that to withhold from her his burning secret was impossible, especially when she began to talk of the trip they had planned through France. Of course no trivial reason would satisfy her for his refusal to make this trip, since they had been looking forward to it for years; and yet it was impossible now for him to set foot on French soil.

So he finally told her the whole story, she laughing and weeping in turn. To her, as to him, it seemed incredible that such overwhelming disasters could have grown out of so small a cause, and, being a fluent French scholar, she demanded a sight of the fatal piece of pasteboard. In vain her husband tried to divert her by proposing a trip through Italy. She would consent to nothing until she had seen the mysterious card which Burwell was now convinced he ought long ago to have destroyed. After refusing for awhile to let her see it, he finally yielded. But, although he had learned to dread the consequences of showing that cursed card, he was little prepared for what followed. She read it turned pale, gasped for breath, and nearly fell to the floor.

"I told you not to read it," he said; and then, growing tender at the sight of her distress, he took her hand in his and begged her to be calm. "At least tell me what the thing means," he said. "We can bear it together; you surely can trust me."

But she, as if stung by rage, pushed him from her and declared, in a tone such as he had never heard from her before, that never, never again would she live with him. "You are a monster!" she exclaimed. And those were the last words he heard from her lips.

Failing utterly in all efforts at reconciliation, the half-crazed man took the first steamer for New York, having suffered in scarcely a fortnight more than in all his previous life. His whole pleasure trip had been ruined, he had failed to consummate important business arrangements, and now he saw his home broken up and his happiness ruined. During the voyage he scarcely left his stateroom, but lay there prostrated with agony. In this black despondency the one thing that sustained him was the thought of meeting his partner, Jack Evelyth, the friend of his boyhood, the sharer of his success, the bravest, most loyal fellow in the world. In the face of even the most damning circumstances, he felt that Evelyth's rugged common sense would evolve some way of escape from this hideous nightmare. Upon landing at New York he hardly waited for the gang-plank to be lowered before he rushed on shore and grasped the hand of his partner, who was waiting on the wharf.

"Jack," was his first word, "I am in dreadful trouble, and you are the only man in the world who can help me."

An hour later Burwell sat at his friend's dinner table, talking over the situation.

Evelyth was all kindness, and several times as he listened to Burwell's story his eyes filled with tears.

"It does not seem possible, Richard," he said, "that such things can be; but I will stand by you; we will fight it out together. But we cannot strike in the dark. Let me see this card."

"There is the damned thing," Burwell said, throwing it on the table.

Evelyth opened the envelope, took out the card, and fixed his eyes on the sprawling purple characters.

"Can you read it?" Burwell asked excitedly.

"Perfectly," his partner said. The next moment he turned pale, and his voice broke. Then he clasped the tortured man's hand in his with a strong grip. "Richard," he said slowly, "if my only child had been brought here dead it would not have caused me more sorrow than this does. You have brought me the worst news one man could bring another."

His agitation and genuine suffering affected Burwell like a death sentence.

"Speak, man," he cried; "do not spare me. I can bear anything rather than this awful uncertainty. Tell me what the card means."

Evelyth took a swallow of brandy and sat with head bent on his clasped hands.

"No, I can't do it; there are some things a man must not do."

Then he was silent again, his brows knitted. Finally he said solemnly:—

"No, I can't see any other way out of it. We have been true to each other all our lives; we have worked together and looked forward to never separating. I would rather fail and die than see this happen. But we have got to separate, old friend; we have got to separate."

They sat there talking until late into the night. But nothing that Burwell could do or say availed against his friend's decision. There was nothing for it but that Evelyth should buy his partner's share of the business or that Burwell buy out the other. The man was more than fair in the financial proposition he made; he was generous, as he always had been, but his determination was inflexible; the two must separate. And they did.

With his old partner's desertion, it seemed to Burwell that the world was leagued against him. It was only three weeks from the day on which he had received the mysterious card; yet in that time he had lost all that he valued in the world,—wife, friends, and business. What next to do with the fatal card was the sickening problem that now possessed him.

He dared not show it; yet he dared not destroy it. He loathed it; yet he could not let it go from his possession. Upon returning to his house he locked the accursed thing away in his safe as if it had been a package of dynamite or a bottle of deadly poison. Yet not a day passed that he did not open the drawer where the thing was kept and scan with loathing the mysterious purple scrawl.

In desperation he finally made up his mind to take up the study of the language in which the hateful thing was written. And still he dreaded the approach of the day when he should decipher its awful meaning.

One afternoon, less than a week after his arrival in New York, as he was crossing Twenty-third Street on the way to his French teacher, he saw a carriage rolling up Broadway. In the carriage was a face that caught his attention like a flash. As he looked again he recognized the woman who had been the cause of his undoing. Instantly he sprang into another cab and ordered the driver to follow after. He found the house where she was living. He called there several times; but always received the same reply, that she was too much engaged to see anyone. Next he was told that she was ill, and on the following day the servant said she was much worse. Three physicians had been summoned in consultation. He sought out one of these and told him it was a matter of life or death that he see this woman. The doctor was a kindly man and promised to assist him. Through his influence, it came about that on that very night Burwell stood by the bedside of this mysterious woman. She was beautiful still, though her face was worn with illness.

"Do you recognize me?" he asked tremblingly, as he leaned over the bed, clutching in one hand an envelope containing the mysterious card. "Do you remember seeing me at the Folies Bergère a month ago?"

"Yes," she murmured, after a moment's study of his face; and he noted with relief that she spoke English.

"Then, for God's sake, tell me, what does it all mean?" he gasped, quivering with excitement.

"I gave you the card because I wanted you to—to—"

Here a terrible spasm of coughing shook her whole body, and she fell back exhausted.

An agonizing despair tugged at Burwell's heart. Frantically snatching the card from its envelope, he held it close to the woman's face.

"Tell me! Tell me!"

With a supreme effort, the pale figure slowly raised itself on the pillow, its fingers clutching at the counterpane.

Then the sunken eyes fluttered—forced themselves open—and stared in stony amazement upon the fatal card, while the trembling lips moved noiselessly, as if in an attempt to speak. As Burwell, choking with eagerness, bent his head slowly to hers, a suggestion of a smile flickered across the woman's face. Again the mouth quivered, the man's head bent nearer and nearer to hers, his eyes riveted upon the lips. Then, as if to aid her in deciphering the mystery, he turned his eyes to the card.

With a cry of horror he sprang to his feet, his eyeballs starting from their sockets. Almost at the same moment the woman fell heavily upon the pillow.

Every vestige of the writing had faded! The card was blank!

The woman lay there dead.

No physician was ever more scrupulous than I have been, during my thirty years of practice, in observing the code of professional secrecy; and it is only for grave reasons, partly in the interests of medical science, largely as a warning to intelligent people, that I place upon record the following statements.

One morning a gentleman called at my offices to consult me about some nervous trouble. From the moment I saw him, the man made a deep impression on me, not so much by the pallor and worn look of his face as by a certain intense sadness in his eyes, as if all hope had gone out of his life. I wrote a prescription for him, and advised him to try the benefits of an ocean voyage. He seemed to shiver at the idea, and said that he had been abroad too much, already.

As he handed me my fee, my eye fell upon the palm of his hand, and I saw there, plainly marked on the Mount of Saturn, a cross surrounded by two circles. I should explain that for the greater part of my life I have been a constant and enthusiastic student of palmistry. During my travels in the Orient, after taking my degree, I spent months studying this fascinating art at the best sources of information in the world. I have read everything published on palmistry in every known language, and my library on the subject is perhaps the most complete in existence. In my time I have examined at least fourteen thousand palms, and taken casts of many of the more interesting of them. But I had never seen such a palm as this; at least, never but once, and the horror of the case was so great that I shudder even now when I call it to mind.

"Pardon me," I said, keeping the patient's hand in mine, "would you let me look at your palm?"

I tried to speak indifferently, as if the matter were of small consequence, and for some moments I bent over the hand in silence. Then, taking a magnifying glass from my desk, I looked at it still more closely. I was not mistaken; here was indeed the sinister double circle on Saturn's mount, with the cross inside,—a marking so rare as to portend some stupendous destiny of good or evil, more probably the latter.

I saw that the man was uneasy under my scrutiny, and, presently, with some hesitation, as if mustering courage, he asked: "Is there anything remarkable about my hand?"

"Yes," I said, "there is. Tell me, did not something very unusual, something very horrible, happen to you about ten or eleven years ago?"

I saw by the way the man started that I had struck near the mark, and, studying the stream of fine lines that crossed his lifeline from the Mount of Venus, I added: "Were you not in some foreign country at that time?"

The man's face blanched, but he only looked at me steadily out of those mournful eyes. Now I took his other hand, and compared the two, line by line, mount by mount, noting the short square fingers, the heavy thumb, with amazing willpower in its upper joint, and gazing again and again at that ominous sign on Saturn.

"Your life has been strangely unhappy, your years have been clouded by some evil influence."

"My God," he said weakly, sinking into a chair, "how can you know these things?"

"It is easy to know what one sees," I said, and tried to draw him out about his past, but the words seemed to stick in his throat.

"I will come back and talk to you again," he said, and he went away without giving me his name or any revelation of his life.

Several times he called during subsequent weeks, and gradually seemed to take on a measure of confidence in my presence. He would talk freely of his physical condition, which seemed to cause him much anxiety. He even insisted upon my making the most careful examination of all his organs, especially of his eyes, which, he said, had troubled him at various times. Upon making the usual tests, I found that he was suffering from a most uncommon form of colour blindness, that seemed to vary in its manifestations, and to be connected with certain hallucinations or abnormal mental states which recurred periodically, and about which I had great difficulty in persuading him to speak. At each visit I took occasion to study his hand anew, and each reading of the palm gave me stronger conviction that here was a life mystery that would abundantly repay any pains taken in unravelling it.

While I was in this state of mind, consumed with a desire to know more of my unhappy acquaintance and yet not daring to press him with questions, there came a tragic happening that revealed to me with startling suddenness the secret I was bent on knowing. One night, very late, in fact it was about four o'clock in the morning, I received an urgent summons to the bedside of a man who had been shot. As I bent over him I saw that it was my friend, and for the first time I realized that he was a man of wealth and position, for he lived in a beautifully furnished house filled with art treasures and looked after by a retinue of servants. From one of these I learned that he was Richard Burwell, one of New York's most respected citizens—in fact, one of her best-known philanthropists, a man who for years had devoted his life and fortune to good works among the poor.

But what most excited my surprise was the presence in the house of two officers, who informed me that Mr. Burwell was under arrest, charged with murder. The officers assured me that it was only out of deference to his well-known standing in the community that the prisoner had been allowed the privilege of receiving medical treatment in his own home; their orders were peremptory to keep him under close surveillance.

Giving no time to further questionings, I at once proceeded to examine the injured man, and found that he was suffering from a bullet wound in the back at about the height of the fifth rib. On probing for the bullet, I found that it had lodged near the heart, and decided that it would be exceedingly dangerous to try to remove it immediately. So I contented myself with administering a sleeping potion.

As soon as I was free to leave Burwell's bedside I returned to the officers and obtained from them details of what had happened. A woman's body had been found a few hours before, shockingly mutilated, on Water Street, one of the dark ways in the swarming region along the river front. It had been found at about two o'clock in the morning by some printers from the office of the *Courier des Etats Unis*, who, in coming from their work, had heard cries of distress and hurried to the rescue. As they drew near they saw a man spring away from something huddled on the sidewalk, and plunge into the shadows of the night, running from them at full speed.

Suspecting at once that here was the mysterious assassin so long vainly sought for many similar crimes, they dashed after the fleeing man, who darted right and left through the maze of dark streets, giving out little cries like a squirrel as he ran. Seeing that they were losing ground, one of the printers fired at the fleeing shadow, his shot being followed by a scream of pain, and hurrying up they found a man writhing on the ground. The man was Richard Burwell.

The news that my sad-faced friend had been implicated in such a revolting occurrence shocked me inexpressibly, and I was greatly relieved the next day to learn from the papers that a most unfortunate mistake had been made. The evidence given before the coroner's jury was such as to abundantly exonerate Burwell from all shadow of guilt. The man's own testimony, taken at his bedside, was in itself almost conclusive in his favour. When asked to explain his presence so late at night in such a part of the city, Burwell stated that he had spent the evening at the Florence Mission, where he had made an address to some unfortunates gathered there, and that later he had gone with a young missionary worker to visit a woman living on Frankfort Street, who was dying of consumption. This statement was borne out by the missionary worker himself, who testified that Burwell had been most tender in his ministrations to the poor woman and had not left her until death had relieved her sufferings.

Another point which made it plain that the printers had mistaken their man in the darkness, was the statement made by all of them that, as they came running up, they had overheard some words spoken by the murderer, and that these words were in their own language, French. Now it was shown conclusively that Burwell did not know the French language, that indeed he had not even an elementary knowledge of it.

Another point in his favour was a discovery made at the spot where the body was found. Some profane and ribald words, also in French, had been scrawled in chalk on the door and doorsill, being in the nature of a coarse defiance to the police to find the assassin, and experts in handwriting who were called testified unanimously that Burwell, who wrote a refined, scholarly hand, could never have formed those misshapen words.

Furthermore, at the time of his arrest no evidence was found on the clothes or person of Burwell, nothing in the nature of bruises or bloodstains that would tend to implicate him in the crime. The outcome of the matter was that he was honourably discharged by the coroner's jury, who were unanimous in declaring him innocent, and who brought in a verdict that the unfortunate woman had come to her death at the hand of some person or persons unknown.

On visiting my patient late on the afternoon of the second day I saw that his case was very grave, and I at once instructed the nurses and attendants to prepare for an operation. The man's life depended upon my being able to extract the bullet, and the chance of doing this was very small. Mr. Burwell realized that his condition was critical, and, beckoning me to him, told me that he wished to make a statement he felt might be his last. He spoke with agitation which was increased by an unforeseen happening. For just then a servant entered the room and whispered to me that there was a gentleman downstairs who insisted upon seeing me, and who urged business of great importance. This message the sick man overheard, and lifting himself with an effort, he said excitedly: "Tell me, is he a tall man with glasses?"

The servant hesitated.

"I knew it; you cannot deceive me; that man will haunt me to my grave. Send him away, doctor; I beg of you not to see him."

Humouring my patient, I sent word to the stranger that I could not see him, but, in an undertone, instructed the servant to say that the man might call at my office the next morning. Then, turning to Burwell, I begged him to compose himself and save his strength for the ordeal awaiting him.

"No, no," he said, "I need my strength now to tell you what you must know to find the truth. You are the only man who has understood that there has been some terrible influence at work in my life. You are the only man competent to study out what that influence is, and I have made provision in my will that you shall do so after I am gone. I know that you will heed my wishes?"

The intense sadness of his eyes made my heart sink; I could only grip his hand and remain silent.

"Thank you; I was sure I might count on your devotion. Now, tell me, doctor, you have examined me carefully, have you not?"

I nodded.

"In every way known to medical science?"

I nodded again.

"And have you found anything wrong with me,—I mean, besides this bullet, anything abnormal?"

"As I have told you, your eyesight is defective; I should like to examine your eyes more thoroughly when you are better."

"I shall never be better; besides it isn't my eyes; I mean myself, my soul,—you haven't found anything wrong there?"

"Certainly not; the whole city knows the beauty of your character and your life."

"Tut, tut; the city knows nothing. For ten years I have lived so much with the poor that people have almost forgotten my previous active life when I was busy with money-making and happy in my home. But there is a man out West, whose head is white and whose heart is heavy, who has not forgotten, and there is a woman in London, a silent, lonely woman, who has not forgotten. The man was my partner, poor Jack Evelyth; the woman was my wife. How can a man be so cursed, doctor, that his love and friendship bring only misery to those who share it? How can it be that one who has in his heart only good thoughts can be constantly under the shadow of evil? This charge of murder is only one of several cases in my life where, through no fault of mine, the shadow of guilt has been cast upon me.

"Years ago, when my wife and I were perfectly happy, a child was born to us, and a few months later, when it was only a tender, helpless little thing that its mother loved with all her heart, it was strangled in its cradle, and we never knew who strangled it, for the deed was done one night when there was absolutely no one in the house but my wife and myself. There was no doubt about the crime, for there on the tiny neck were the finger marks where some cruel hand had closed until life went.

"Then a few years later, when my partner and I were on the eve of fortune, our advance was set back by the robbery of our safe. Some one opened it in the night, someone who knew the combination, for it was the work of no burglar, and yet there were only two persons in the world who knew that combination, my partner and myself. I tried to be brave when these things happened, but as my life went on it seemed more and more as if some curse were on me.

"Eleven years ago I went abroad with my wife and daughter. Business took me to Paris, and I left the ladies in London, expecting to have them join me in a few days. But they never did join me, for the curse was on me still, and before I had been forty-eight hours in the French capital something happened that completed the wreck of my life. It doesn't seem possible, does it, that a simple white card with some words scrawled on it in purple ink could effect a man's undoing? And yet that was my fate. The card was given me by a beautiful woman with eyes like stars. She is dead long ago, and why she wished to harm me I never knew. You must find that out.

"You see I did not know the language of the country, and, wishing to have the words translated,—surely that was natural enough,—I showed the card to others. But no one would tell me what it meant. And, worse than that, wherever I showed it, and to whatever person, there evil came upon me quickly. I was driven from one hotel after another; an old acquaintance turned his back on me; I was arrested and thrown into prison; I was ordered to leave the country."

The sick man paused for a moment in his weakness, but with an effort forced himself to continue:—

"When I went back to London, sure of comfort in the love of my wife, she too, on seeing the card, drove me from her with cruel words. And when finally, in deepest despair, I returned to New York, dear old Jack, the friend of a life-time, broke with me when I showed him what was written. What the words were I do not know, and suppose no one will ever know, for the ink has faded these many years. You will find the card in my safe with other papers. But I want you, when I am gone, to find out the mystery of my life; and—and—about my fortune, that must be held until you have decided. There is no one who needs my money as much as the poor in this city, and I have bequeathed it to them unless—"

In an agony of mind, Mr. Burwell struggled to go on, I soothing and encouraging him.

"Unless you find what I am afraid to think, but—but—yes, I must say it,—that I have not been a good man, as the world thinks, but have—O doctor, if you find that I have unknowingly harmed any human being, I want that person, or these persons, to have my fortune. Promise that."

Seeing the wild light in Burwell's eyes, and the fever that was burning him, I gave the promise asked of me, and the sick man sank back calmer.

A little later, the nurse and attendants came for the operation. As they were about to administer the ether, Burwell pushed them from him, and insisted on having brought to his bedside an iron box from the safe.

"The card is here," he said, laying his trembling hand upon the box, "you will remember your promise!"

Those were his last words, for he did not survive the operation.

Early the next morning I received this message: "The stranger of yesterday begs to see you;" and presently a gentleman of fine presence and strength of face, a tall, dark-complexioned man wearing glasses, was shown into the room.

"Mr. Burwell is dead, is he not?" were his first words.

"Who told you?"

"No one told me, but I know it, and I thank God for it."

There was something in the stranger's intense earnestness that convinced me of his right to speak thus, and I listened attentively.

"That you may have confidence in the statement I am about to make, I will first tell you who I am;" and he handed me a card that caused me to lift my eyes in wonder, for it bore a very great name, that of one of Europe's most famous savants.

"You have done me much honour, sir," I said with respectful inclination.

"On the contrary you will oblige me by considering me in your debt, and by never revealing my connection with this wretched man. I am moved to speak partly from considerations of human justice, largely in the interest of medical science. It is right for me to tell you, doctor, that your patient was beyond question the Water Street assassin."

"Impossible!" I cried.

"You will not say so when I have finished my story, which takes me back to Paris, to the time, eleven years ago, when this man was making his first visit to the French capital."

"The mysterious card!" I exclaimed.

"Ah, he has told you of his experience, but not of what befell the night before, when he first met my sister."

"Your sister?"

"Yes, it was she who gave him the card, and, in trying to befriend him, made him suffer. She was in ill health at the time, so much so that we had left our native India for extended journeyings. Alas! we delayed too long, for my sister died in New York, only a few weeks later, and I honestly believe her taking off was hastened by anxiety inspired by this man."

"Strange," I murmured, "how the life of a simple New York merchant could become entangled with that of a great lady of the East."

"Yet so it was. You must know that my sister's condition was due mainly to an over fondness for certain occult investigations, from which I had vainly tried to dissuade her. She had once befriended some adepts, who, in return, had taught her things about the soul she had better have left unlearned. At various times while with her I had seen strange things happen, but I never realized what unearthly powers were in her until that night in Paris. We were returning from a drive in the Bois; it was about ten o'clock, and the city lay beautiful around us as Paris looks on a perfect summer's night. Suddenly my sister gave a cry of pain and put her hand to her heart. Then, changing from French to the language of our country, she explained to me quickly that something frightful was taking place there, where she pointed her finger across the river, that we must go to the place at once—the driver must lash his horses—every second was precious.

"So affected was I by her intense conviction, and such confidence had I in my sister's wisdom, that I did not oppose her, but told the man to drive as she directed. The carriage fairly flew across the bridge, down the Boulevard St. Germain, then to the left, threading its way through the narrow streets that lie along the Seine. This way and that, straight ahead here, a turn there, she directing our course, never hesitating, as if drawn by some unseen power, and always urging the driver on to greater speed. Finally, we came to a black-mouthed, evil-looking alley, so narrow and roughly paved that the carriage could scarcely advance.

"'Come on!' my sister cried, springing to the ground; 'we will go on foot, we are nearly there. Thank God, we may yet be in time.'

"No one was in sight as we hurried along the dark alley, and scarcely a light was visible, but presently a smothered scream broke the silence, and, touching my arm, my sister exclaimed:—

"'There, draw your weapon, quick, and take the man at any cost!'

"So swiftly did everything happen after that that I hardly know my actions, but a few minutes later I held pinioned in my arms a man whose blows and writhings had been all in vain; for you must know that much exercise in the jungle had made me strong of limb. As soon as I had made the fellow fast I looked down and found moaning on the ground a poor woman, who explained with tears and broken words that the man had been in the very act of strangling her. Searching him I found a long-bladed knife of curious shape, and keen as a razor, which had been brought for what horrible purpose you may perhaps divine.

"Imagine my surprise, on dragging the man back to the carriage, to find, instead of the ruffianly assassin I expected, a gentleman as far as could be judged from face and manner. Fine eyes, white hands, careful speech, all the signs of refinement and the dress of a man of means.

"'How can this be?' I said to my sister in our own tongue as we drove away, I holding my prisoner on the opposite seat where he sat silent.

"'It is a *kulos*-man,' she said, shivering, 'it is a fiend-soul. There are a few such in the whole world, perhaps two or three in all.'

"'But he has a good face.'

"'You have not seen his real face yet; I will show it to you, presently.'

"In the strangeness of these happenings and the still greater strangeness of my sister's words, I had all but lost the power of wonder. So we sat without further word until the carriage stopped at the little chateau we had taken near the Parc Monteau.

"I could never properly describe what happened that night; my knowledge of these things is too limited. I simply obeyed my sister in all that she directed, and kept my eyes on this man as no hawk ever watched its prey. She began by questioning him, speaking in a kindly tone which I could ill understand. He seemed embarrassed, dazed, and professed to have no knowledge of what had occurred, or how he had come where we found him. To all my inquiries as to the woman or the crime he shook his head blankly, and thus aroused my wrath.

"'Be not angry with him, brother; he is not lying, it is the other soul.'

"She asked him about his name and country, and he replied without hesitation that he was Richard Burwell, a merchant from New York, just arrived in Paris, travelling for pleasure in Europe with his wife and daughter. This seemed reasonable, for the man spoke English, and, strangely enough, seemed to have no knowledge of French, although we both remember hearing him speak French to the woman.

"'There is no doubt,' my sister said, 'It is indeed a *kulos*-man; It knows that I am here, that I am Its master. Look, look!' she cried sharply, at the same time putting her eyes so close to the man's face that their fierce light seemed to burn into him. What power she exercised I do not know, nor whether some words she spoke, unintelligible to me, had to do with what followed, but instantly there came over this man, this pleasant-looking, respectable American citizen, such a change as is not made by death worms gnawing in a grave. Now there was a fiend grovelling at her feet, a foul, sin-stained fiend.

"'Now you see the demon-soul,' said my sister. 'Watch It writhe and struggle; it has served me well, brother, sayest thou not so, the lore I gained from our wise men?'

"The horror of what followed chilled my blood; nor would I trust my memory were it not that there remained and still remains plain proof of all that I affirm. This hideous creature, dwarfed, crouching, devoid of all resemblance to the man we had but now beheld, chattering to us in curious old-time French, poured out such horrid blasphemy as would have blanched the cheek of Satan, and made recital of such evil deeds as never mortal ear gave heed to. And as she willed my sister checked It or allowed It to go on. What it all meant was more than I could tell. To me it seemed as if these tales of wickedness had no connection with our modern life, or with the world around us, and so I judged presently from what my sister said.

"'Speak of the later time, since thou wast in this clay.'

"Then I perceived that the creature came to things of which I knew: It spoke of New York, of a wife, a child, a friend. It told of strangling the child, of robbing the friend; and was going on to tell God knows what other horrid deeds when my sister stopped It.

"'Stand as thou didst in killing the little babe, stand, stand!' and once more she spoke some words unknown to me. Instantly the demon sprang forward, and, bending Its clawlike hands, clutched them around some little throat that was not there,—but I could see it in my mind. And the look on its face was a blackest glimpse of hell.

"'And now stand as thou didst in robbing the friend, stand, stand;' and again came the unknown words, and again the fiend obeyed.

"'These we will take for future use,' said my sister. And bidding me watch the creature carefully until she should return, she left the room, and, after none too short an absence, returned bearing a black box that was an apparatus for photography, and something more besides,—some newer, stranger kind of photography that she had learned. Then, on a strangely fashioned card, a transparent white card, composed of many layers of finest Oriental paper, she took the pictures of the creature in those two creeping poses. And when it all was done, the card seemed as white as before, and empty of all meaning until one held it up and examined it intently. Then the pictures showed. And between the two there was a third picture, which somehow seemed to show, at the same time, two faces in one, two souls, my sister said, the kindly visaged man we first had seen, and then the fiend.

"Now my sister asked for pen and ink and I gave her my pocket pen which was filled with purple ink. Handing this to the *kulos*-man she bade him write under the first picture: 'Thus I killed my babe.' And under the second picture: 'Thus I robbed my friend.' And under the third, the one that was between the other two: 'This is the soul of Richard Burwell.' An odd thing about this writing was that it was in the same old French the creature had used in speech, and yet Burwell knew no French.

"My sister was about to finish with the creature when a new idea took her, and she said, looking at It as before:—'Of all thy crimes which one is the worst? Speak, I command thee!'

"Then the fiend told how once It had killed every soul in a house of holy women and buried the bodies in a cellar under a heavy door.

"Where was the house?'

"'At No. 19 Rue Picpus, next to the old graveyard.'

"'And when was this?'

"Here the fiend seemed to break into fierce rebellion, writhing on the floor with hideous contortions, and pouring forth words that meant nothing to me, but seemed to reach my sister's understanding, for she interrupted from time to time, with quick, stern words that finally brought It to subjection.

"'Enough,' she said, 'I know all,' and then she spoke some words again, her eyes fixed as before, and the reverse change came. Before us stood once more the honest-looking, fine-appearing gentleman, Richard Burwell, of New York.

"'Excuse me, madame,' he said, awkwardly, but with deference; 'I must have dosed a little. I am not myself tonight.'

"'No,' said my sister, 'you have not been yourself tonight.'

"A little later I accompanied the man to the Continental Hotel, where he was stopping, and, returning to my sister, I talked with her until late into the night. I was alarmed to see that she was wrought to a nervous tension that augured ill for her health. I urged her to sleep, but she would not.

"'No,' she said, 'think of the awful responsibility that rests upon me.' And then she went on with her strange theories and explanations, of which I understood only that here was a power for evil more terrible than a pestilence, menacing all humanity.

"'Once in many cycles it happens,' she said, 'that a *kulos*-soul pushes itself within the body of a new-born child, when the pure soul waiting to enter is delayed. Then the two live together through that life, and this hideous principle of evil has a chance upon the earth. It is my will, as I feel it my duty, to see this poor man again. The chances are that he will never know us, for the shock of this night to his normal soul is so great as to wipe out memory.'

"The next evening, about the same hour, my sister insisted that I should go with her to the *Folies Bergère*, a concert garden, none too well frequented, and when I remonstrated, she said: 'I must go,—It is there,' and the words sent a shiver through me.

"We drove to this place, and passing into the garden, presently discovered Richard Burwell seated at a little table, enjoying the scene of pleasure, which was plainly new to him. My sister hesitated a moment what to do, and then, leaving my arm, she advanced to the table and dropped before Burwell's eyes the card she had prepared. A moment later, with a look of pity on her beautiful face, she rejoined me and we went away. It was plain he did not know us."

To so much of the savant's strange recital I had listened with absorbed interest, though without a word, but now I burst in with questions.

"What was your sister's idea in giving Burwell the card?" I asked.

"It was in the hope that she might make the man understand his terrible condition, that is, teach the pure soul to know its loathsome companion."

"And did her effort succeed?"

"Alas! it did not; my sister's purpose was defeated by the man's inability to see the pictures that were plain to every other eye. It is impossible for the *kulos*-man to know his own degradation."

"And yet this man has for years been leading a most exemplary life?"

My visitor shook his head. "I grant you there has been improvement, due largely to experiments I have conducted upon him according to my sister's wishes. But the fiend soul was never driven out. It grieves me to tell you, doctor, that not only was this man the Water Street assassin, but he was the mysterious murderer, the long-sought-for mutilator of women, whose red crimes have baffled the police of Europe and America for the past ten years."

"You know this," said I, starting up, "and yet did not denounce him?"

"It would have been impossible to prove such a charge, and besides, I had made oath to my sister that I would use the man only for these soul-experiments. What are his crimes compared with the great secret of knowledge I am now able to give the world?"

"A secret of knowledge?"

"Yes," said the savant, with intense earnestness, "I may tell you now, doctor, what the whole world will know, ere long, that it is possible to compel every living person to reveal the innermost secrets of his or her life, so long as memory remains, for memory is only the power of producing in the brain material pictures that may be projected externally by the thought rays and made to impress themselves upon the photographic plate, precisely as ordinary pictures do."

"You mean," I exclaimed, "that you can photograph the two principles of good and evil that exist in us?"

"Exactly that. The great truth of a dual soul existence, that was dimly apprehended by one of your Western novelists, has been demonstrated by me in the laboratory with my camera. It is my purpose, at the proper time, to entrust this precious knowledge to a chosen few who will perpetuate it and use it worthily."

"Wonderful, wonderful!" I cried, "and now tell me, if you will, about the house on the Rue Picpus. Did you ever visit the place?"

"We did, and found that no buildings had stood there for fifty years, so we did not pursue the search."

"And the writing on the card, have you any memory of it, for Burwell told me that the words have faded?"

"I have something better than that; I have a photograph of both card and writing, which my sister was careful to take. I had a notion that the ink in my pocket pen would fade, for it was a poor affair. This photograph I will bring you tomorrow."

"Bring it to Burwell's house," I said.

The next morning the stranger called as agreed upon.

"Here is the photograph of the card," he said.

"And here is the original card," I answered, breaking the seal of the envelope I had taken from Burwell's iron box. "I have waited for your arrival to look at it. Yes, the writing has indeed vanished; the card seems quite blank."

"Not when you hold it this way," said the stranger, and as he tipped the card I saw such a horrid revelation as I can never forget. In an instant I realized how the shock of seeing that card had been too great for the soul of wife or friend to bear. In these pictures was the secret of a cursed life. The resemblance to Burwell was unmistakable, the proof against him was overwhelming. In looking upon that piece of pasteboard the wife had seen a crime which the mother could never forgive, the partner had seen a crime which the friend could never forgive. Think of a loved face suddenly melting before your eyes into a grinning skull, then into a mass of putrefaction, then into the ugliest fiend of hell, leering at you, distorted with all the marks of vice and shame. That is what I saw, that is what they had seen!

"Let us lay these two cards in the coffin," said my companion impressively, "we have done what we could."

Eager to be rid of the hateful piece of pasteboard (for who could say that the curse was not still clinging about it?), I took the strange man's arm, and together we advanced into the adjoining room where the body lay. I had seen Burwell as he breathed his last, and knew that there had been a peaceful look on his face as he died. But now, as we laid the two white cards on the still, breast, the savant suddenly touched my arm, and pointing to the dead man's face, now frightfully distorted, whispered:—"See, even in death It followed him. Let us close the coffin quickly."

A MOONLIGHT FABLE

H. G. Wells (1866–1946)

Wells is remembered as the father of science fiction, a historian and
a social commentator, amongst many things, but he's seldom remembered as a writer of supernatural and weird fiction. Yet many of his
early stories leaned more towards the fantastic than the scientific,
a matter hinted at in the title of his collection *Twelve Stories and a
Dream* (1903). His fantasies, both light and dark, include "The Apple",
"The Red Room", "The Man Who Could Work Miracles", "The
Inexperienced Ghost", "The Door in the Wall", "The Magic Shop",
and the one included here, "A Moonlight Fable", also known as "The
Beautiful Suit". The beauty of these early stories is how Wells takes
the ordinary man in the street and sees how he reacts to something
strange. The result is always haunting.

There was once a little man whose mother made him a beautiful suit of clothes. It was green and gold and woven so that I can not describe how delicate and fine it was, and there was a tie of orange fluffiness that tied up under his chin. And the buttons in their newness shone like stars. He was proud and pleased by his suit beyond measure, and stood before the long looking-glass when first he put it on, so astonished and delighted with it that he could hardly turn himself away.

He wanted to wear it everywhere and show it to all sorts of people. He thought over all the places he had ever visited and all the scenes he had ever heard described, and tried to imagine what the feel of it would be if he were to go now to those scenes and places wearing his shining suit, and he wanted to go out forthwith into the long grass and the hot sunshine of the meadow wearing it. Just to wear it! But his mother told him, "No." She told him he must take great care of his suit, for never would he have another nearly so fine; he must save it and save it and only wear it on rare and great occasions. It was his wedding suit, she said. And she took his buttons and twisted them up with tissue paper for fear their bright newness should be tarnished, and she tacked little guards over the cuffs and elbows and wherever the suit was most likely to come to harm. He hated and resisted these things, but what could he do? And at last her warnings and persuasions had effect and he consented to take off his beautiful suit and fold it into its proper creases and put it away. It was almost as though he gave it up again. But he was always thinking of wearing it and of the supreme occasion when some day it might be worn without the guards, without the tissue paper on the buttons, utterly and delightfully, never caring, beautiful beyond measure.

One night when he was dreaming of it, after his habit, he dreamed he took the tissue paper from one of the buttons and found its brightness a little faded, and that distressed him mightily in his dream. He polished the poor faded button and polished it, and if anything it grew duller. He woke up and lay awake thinking of the brightness a little dulled and wondering how he would feel if perhaps when the great occasion (whatever it might be) should arrive, one button should chance to be ever so little short of its first glittering freshness, and for days and days that thought remained with him, distressingly. And when next his mother let him wear his suit, he was tempted and nearly gave way to the temptation just to fumble off one little bit of tissue paper and see if indeed the buttons were keeping as bright as ever.

He went trimly along on his way to church full of this wild desire. For you must know his mother did, with repeated and careful warnings, let him wear his suit at times, on Sundays, for example, to and fro from church, when there was no threatening of rain, no dust nor anything to injure it, with its buttons covered and its protections tacked upon it and a sunshade in his hand to shadow it if there seemed too strong a sunlight for its colours. And always, after such occasions, he brushed it over and folded it exquisitely as she had taught him, and put it away again.

Now all these restrictions his mother set to the wearing of his suit he obeyed, always he obeyed them, until one strange night he woke up and saw the moonlight shining outside his window. It seemed to him the moonlight was not common moonlight, nor the night a common night, and for a while he lay quite drowsily with this odd persuasion in his mind. Thought joined on to thought like things that whisper warmly in the shadows. Then he sat up in his little bed suddenly, very alert, with his heart beating very fast and a quiver in his body from top to toe. He had made up his mind. He knew now that he was going to wear his suit as it should be worn. He had no doubt in the matter. He was afraid, terribly afraid, but glad, glad.

He got out of his bed and stood a moment by the window looking at the moonshine-flooded garden and trembling at the thing he meant to do. The air was full of a minute clamour of crickets and murmurings, of the infinitesimal shouting of little living things. He went very gently across the creaking boards, for fear that he might wake the sleeping house, to the big dark clothes-press wherein his beautiful suit lay folded, and he took it out garment by garment and softly and very eagerly tore off its tissue-paper covering and its tacked protections, until there it was, perfect and delightful as he had seen it when first his mother had given it to him—a long time it seemed ago. Not a button had tarnished, not a thread had faded on this dear suit of his; he was glad enough for weeping as in a noiseless hurry he put it on. And then back he went, soft and quick, to the window and looked out upon the garden and stood there for a minute, shining in the moonlight, with his buttons twinkling like stars, before he got out on the sill and, making as little of a rustling as he could, clambered down to the garden path below. He stood before his mother's house, and it was white and nearly as plain as by day, with every window-blind but his own shut like an eye that sleeps. The trees cast still shadows like intricate black lace upon the wall.

The garden in the moonlight was very different from the garden by day; moonshine was tangled in the hedges and stretched in phantom cobwebs from spray to spray. Every flower was gleaming white or crimson black, and the air was aquiver with the thridding of small crickets and nightingales singing unseen in the depths of the trees.

There was no darkness in the world, but only warm, mysterious shadows, and all the leaves and spikes were edged and lined with iridescent jewels of dew. The night was warmer than any night had ever been, the heavens by some miracle at once vaster and nearer, and spite of the great ivory-tinted moon that ruled the world, the sky was full of stars.

The little man did not shout nor sing for all his infinite gladness. He stood for a time like one awe-stricken, and then, with a queer small cry and holding out his arms, he ran out as if he would embrace at once the whole warm round immensity of the world. He did not follow the neat set paths that cut the garden squarely, but thrust across the beds and through the wet, tall, scented herbs, through the night stock and the nicotine and the clusters of phantom white mallow flowers and through the thickets of southern-wood and lavender, and knee-deep across a wide space of mignonette. He came to the great hedge and he thrust his way through it, and though the thorns of the brambles scored him deeply and tore threads from his wonderful suit, and though burs and goosegrass and havers caught and clung to him, he did not care. He did not care, for he knew it was all part of the wearing for which he had longed. "I am glad I put on my suit," he said; "I am glad I wore my suit."

Beyond the hedge he came to the duck-pond, or at least to what was the duck-pond by day. But by night it was a great bowl of silver moonshine all noisy with singing frogs, of wonderful silver moon-shine twisted and clotted with strange patternings, and the little man ran down into its waters between the thin black rushes, knee-deep and waist-deep and to his shoulders, smiting the water to black and shining wavelets with either hand, swaying and shivering wavelets, amid which the stars were netted in the tangled reflections of the brooding trees upon the bank. He waded until he swam, and so he crossed the pond and came out upon the other side, trailing, as it seemed to him, not duckweed, but very silver in long, clinging, dripping masses. And up he went through the transfigured tangles of the willow-herb and the uncut seeding grasses of the farther bank. And so he came glad and breathless into the highroad. "I am glad," he said, "beyond measure, that I had clothes that fitted this occasion."

The highroad ran straight as an arrow flies, straight into the deep blue pit of sky beneath the moon, a white and shining road between the singing nightingales, and along it he went, running now and leaping, and now walking and rejoicing, in the clothes his mother had made for him with tireless, loving hands. The road was deep in dust, but that for him was only soft whiteness, and as he went a great dim moth came fluttering round his wet and shimmering and hastening figure. At first he did not heed the moth, and then he waved his hands at it and made a sort of dance with it as it circled round his head. "Soft moth!" he cried, "dear moth! And wonderful night, wonderful night of the world! Do you think my clothes are beautiful, dear moth? As beautiful as your scales and all this silver vesture of the earth and sky?"

And the moth circled closer and closer until at last its velvet wings just brushed his lips...

And next morning they found him dead with his neck broken in the bottom of the stone pit, with his beautiful clothes a little bloody and foul and stained with the duckweed from the pond. But his face was a face of such happiness that, had you seen it, you would have understood indeed how that he had died happy, never knowing that cool and streaming silver for the duckweed in the pond.

FEAR

Catherine Wells (1872–1927)

Born Amy Catherine Robbins, she married the author H. G. Wells
in 1895 after having lived with him for a year. She became Catherine
Wells, the name she kept for her writing life, but as a wife, mother and
friend, she was always Jane Wells. Despite her husband's promiscuity
they stayed married until her death from cancer aged only fifty-five.
She was the mother of two children, George and Frank. When she
turned to writing she wanted to be accepted for herself, not as her
husband's wife, and used to send the stories to magazines from a
different address and through a different agent. Her stories were
published for almost twenty years, her final piece, "The Last Fairy"
being finished as her final illness took hold and was completed with
the help of her son, Frank. After her death, her husband assembled
The Book of Catherine Wells (1928) which included other previously
unpublished material. Amongst them was the story reprinted here,
an emotional plea from the heart.

On the Kentish coast between Folkestone and Dover there is a stretch of stunted trees and thickly tangled bushes and undergrowth between the sea and the receded cliffs, a Strip of picturesque desolation some half mile broad and five miles long. In high summer the nearer end towards Folkestone is the resort of happy holiday parties, picnicking all about a tea and ginger beer shanty; further on its solitudes, wilder and more beautiful, are seldom disturbed. The high road to Dover lies distantly up and away over the top of the cliffs, and such few houses as there are on that road stand remotely back, as if they shrink from the approach of the treacherous cliff edge that creeps ever nearer to them. Here and there the sheer white fall of the cliff is broken by a weedy slope down which a scrambling path traces a thin line, and beneath comes that stretch of tumbled land-slidden ground, its little hills and valleys richly netted with rose briars and brambles, wayfaring tree and hawthorn, and carpeted with short grass all beset with yellow rock roses and violets and a hundred other flowers.

There, close to the sea, in a grassy hollow that spread itself to the hot summer sun, lay a woman face downward to the ground, and sobbed. Her expensive, pretty muslin dress showed little rents here and there where it had been caught by unheeded brambles. And she sobbed because she had come into that lonely and beautiful place to take her life into her hands and end it and die.

She had been sitting there on the grass a long while, it seemed to her, trying to think for the last of so many times, what other thing she could possibly do. But no new light came to her. Her life seemed all too tangled now for new beginnings, and she herself too weary to imagine any. Her husband would never forgive her when he knew, and so went her tired mind again over the old trodden track—nothing could stop his knowing, even if he did not know already. She thought it certain that he did know already. Why else should he have got leave and be coming home again so soon?

She stared upon the sea that lay before her, calm and flat like a lake surface, its edge slapping gently on the grey, clayish sand. Silvery pale blue with lights and shades like satin it was, and further out it was streaked with azure bands. Far on the horizon hung the sails of the fishing-fleet, and it was so still about her that there seemed no nearer living thing.

She could not meet her husband, passionate, noisy, raging with anger as he would be. It was the sick fear of him that had driven her away here. He must be already in their house. She could imagine, and it made her tremble, his heavy tread upstairs, the flung open doors, the harsh loud demands for her. Even if she had stayed to meet him and brave it out with what courage she could, what good would it have been? He would never have let her speak one word of excuse or explanation; he would shout at her and curse, and fling her at last out of his house as he would a dead flower from his coat. What could she be but helpless before a creature so fixed and immutable? Why was there never a human being who could understand the trouble and the unhappiness and the misery, and the muddle and the lies that had netted about her? She wanted to cry, cry to that wise and kindly soul like a child that is hurt and be comforted and loved and set on her feet to try again. And instead of that it seemed to her as

if an invisible hand had thrust her down a narrow passage of consequences, impelling her by the whispered fear of the terror behind,
till she had come at last to a door, a way out, the only way out, that
escape whose key was in the little chemist's bottle in her pocket. The
memory of it there stung her with fear; in it she saw the terror that
had followed her re-embodied before her now instead of behind
her, crouched to spring and grip and shake the pulsating life out of
her young and beautiful body.

She sat and gazed at the blue sea, and tried to make it seem
real to herself that she would presently lie there dead, growing
colder and stiff. In a few moments it might be, if she chose. In a
few hours it would have to be. She felt suddenly very lonely. For a
long time now she had sat there and seen no one. About an hour
since a straggling line of black dots had appeared over the headland
on the Folkestone side, schoolboys, they were, hunting the bay
for fossils under the energetic direction of an explanatory master.
They had come near enough for her to hear their shouts and the
deeper voice of their tutor, and then they had turned back again,
and disappeared at last in twos and threes beyond the headland.
They left her the lonelier for having come and gone. Indeed, she
felt a little frightened at seeing, so measured out to her eye by
those remote black dots, how much she was alone. A rustle in the
grass above, the dart of a bird back to its hidden nest, made her
start; and then she turned and watched for some time the business-
like coming and going of a pair of blue tits among the pale gold
dried grass stems that fringed against the sky; patiently and lovingly
attendant they were upon a faintly clamorous invisible cheeping.
It was their happy domesticity that struck to her heart and set her
sobbing, a sobbing that became violent and uncontrolled. And
afterwards she lay still.

She sat up at last, and then stood up with the thought of going down to the edge of the satin-surfaced sea. But as she turned she saw about a quarter of a mile away on a little hillock among the bushes, the slouching figure of a man who seemed to look at her.

Before she recognized its unlikeness she had an instant's panic fear that it might be her husband. She turned from the sea and walked on among the bushes, the softly bred woman's fear of tramps instinctively setting her to put distance between herself and that dubious figure. She walked on quickly for about half a mile, among the stunted trees and up and down slopes, having lost sight of the man almost at once, and then she stopped and sat again upon the grass.

She would have to do it soon; she would have to do it soon. That invisible hand was pressing her hardly now against the very door itself. The afternoon had grown late, and the shadows had lengthened till those of a gorse bush three yards away lay across her feet. The blue was paling out of the sea before a tinge of yellow that grew warmer. The sea was swelling up, and flowing silently nearer with the turned tide. A faint chill crept into the air. It would have to be done soon.

She slipped her hand into her pocket and felt the cool smooth glass of the little bottle there between her fingers. Slowly she drew it out and held it in her lap and looked at it. The thing she had to do became to her as queer and meaningless, as unreasonably stupid, as something that happens in a dream.

She turned as if to look once more upon all the beauty that was about her, and with a clutch of terror at her heart, saw the ill-conditioned figure she had seen before, looking at her and coming towards her, less than a hundred yards away.

With a rush came Fear upon her, and possessed her. She had a watch upon her breast that glittered, shining trinkets on her wrists. She got up hastily, turned some high bushes, and frankly began to run, running into the thicker undergrowth and bending where the trees fell away, lest her head should show. She ran inland towards the cliff and doubled back, her heart thumping heavily with fear, threading through a maze of little tracks, through tiny woods, by a deep-lying pool of black and green stagnant water, struggling with brambles that caught and tore at her, pressed by one thought, to escape the horror of that stealthy pursuer. Thicker grew the trees, and thicker.

She stopped at last in a little opening among them, a circle of thin grass and bracken surrounded so completely by high bushes and small trees that she could hardly see from where she had stepped into the place. She was hot and panting and the noisy beating of her heart against her breast left her breathless. But here was safe hiding. She sank down upon the grass.

Her hand still clutched upon the little bottle. As her breath grew quiet she saw it there and sat and gazed at it, helplessly, in a curious state of mind that was not thought, but only a dull pain. Twilight grew upon her. A light wind stirred; she shivered. Ah! night was coming and the cold, cold and solitude and the dark; presently she would grow hungry, and the world that had ever held her so caressingly in its lap would lash her with the whip of elementary human needs. That waited for her here, and over there waited her home—her home and her husband. With a low shuddering cry she pulled the stopper from the little bottle, shut her eyes in anguish, and pushed it against her mouth and swallowed.

It dropped out of her hand. For an instant that seemed long she thought that nothing was going to happen to her. Everything was suddenly without sound. Then came a spasm at her heart more terrible in its instant pain than anything she had ever imagined. Without knowing it she fell back upon the ground, and the bushes and patch of sky before her grew small in her vision and very distant, then rushed back upon her and swayed and swayed.

Then she saw, and the sight glazed her eyes in horror, the bushes part before her, and from among them looked out a cunning, evil face.

THE LITTLE ROOM

and

THE SEQUEL TO
THE LITTLE ROOM

Madeline Yale Wynne (1847–1918)

Wynne's father, Linus Yale, was the founder of the Yale Lock Manu-facturing Company and it is from him that she inherited her gift as a metal smith, designer and artist. With her friend Annie Putnam she established an Arts and Crafts society in Deerfield, Massachusetts, promoting jewellery, rugs, baskets and other products. The novelist George Washington Cable said of her that "She was one of the most joyous souls I ever came in touch with..." She was not a prolific story writer but whatever she turned her hand to was always polished and unique. That was especially true of "The Little Room" and its sequel, one of those puzzling stories that once read will never be forgotten.

"How would it do for a smoking-room?"

"Just the very place! only, you know, Roger, you must not think of smoking in the house. I am almost afraid that having just a plain, common man around, let alone a smoking man, will upset Aunt Hannah. She is New England—Vermont New England—boiled down."

"You leave Aunt Hannah to me; I'll find her tender side. I'm going to ask her about the old sea-captain and the yellow calico."

"Not yellow calico—blue chintz."

"Well, yellow *shell* then."

"No, no! don't mix it up so; you won't know yourself what to expect, and that's half the fun."

"Now you tell me again exactly what to expect; to tell the truth, I didn't half hear about it the other day; I was wool-gathering. It was something queer that happened when you were a child, wasn't it?"

"Something that began to happen long before that, and kept happening, and may happen again; but I hope not."

"What was it?"

"I wonder if the other people in the car can hear us?"

"I fancy not; we don't hear them—not consecutively, at least."

"Well, mother was born in Vermont, you know; she was the only child by a second marriage. Aunt Hannah and Aunt Maria are only half-aunts to me, you know."

"I hope they are half as nice as you are."

"Roger, be still; they certainly will hear us."

"Well, don't you want them to know we are married?"

"Yes, but not just married. There's all the difference in the world."

"You are afraid we look too happy!"

"No; only I want my happiness all to myself."

"Well, the little room?"

"My aunts brought mother up; they were nearly twenty years older than she. I might say Hiram and they brought her up. You see, Hiram was bound out to my grandfather when he was a boy, and when grandfather died Hiram said he 's'posed he went with the farm, 'long o' the critters,' and he has been there ever since. He was my mother's only refuge from the decorum of my aunts. They are simply workers. They make me think of the Maine woman who wanted her epitaph to be: 'She was a *hard* working woman.'"

"They must be almost beyond their working-days. How old are they?"

"Seventy, or thereabouts; but they will die standing; or, at least, on a Saturday night, after all the house-work is done up. They were rather strict with mother, and I think she had a lonely childhood. The house is almost a mile away from any neighbours, and off on top of what they call Stony Hill. It is bleak enough up there, even in summer.

"When mamma was about ten years old they sent her to cousins in Brooklyn, who had children of their own, and knew more about bringing them up. She stayed there till she was married; she didn't go to Vermont in all that time, and of course hadn't seen her sisters, for they never would leave home for a day. They couldn't even be induced to go to Brooklyn to her wedding, so she and father took their wedding trip up there."

"And that's why we are going up there on our own?"

"Don't, Roger; you have no idea how loud you speak."

"You never say so except when I am going to say that one little word."

"Well, don't say it, then, or say it very, very quietly."

"Well, what was the queer thing?"

"When they got to the house, mother wanted to take father right off into the little room; she had been telling him about it, just as I am going to tell you, and she had said that of all the rooms, that one was the only one that seemed pleasant to her. She described the furniture and the books and paper and everything, and said it was on the north side, between the front and back room. Well, when they went to look for it, there was no little room there; there was only a shallow china-closet. She asked her sisters when the house had been altered and a closet made of the room that used to be there. They both said the house was exactly as it had been built—that they had never made any changes, except to tear down the old wood-shed and build a smaller one.

"Father and mother laughed a good deal over it, and when anything was lost they would always say it must be in the little room, and any exaggerated statement was called 'little-roomy.' When I was a child I thought that was a regular English phrase, I heard it so often.

"Well, they talked it over, and finally they concluded that my mother had been a very imaginative sort of a child, and had read in some book about such a little room, or perhaps even dreamed it, and then had 'made believe,' as children do, till she herself had really thought the room was there."

"Why, of course, that might easily happen."

"Yes, but you haven't heard the queer part yet; you wait and see if you can explain the rest as easily.

"They staid at the farm two weeks, and then went to New York to live. When I was eight years old my father was killed in the war, and mother was broken-hearted. She never was quite strong afterwards, and that summer we decided to go up to the farm for three months.

"I was a restless sort of a child, and the journey seemed very long to me; and finally, to pass the time, mamma told me the story of the little room, and how it was all in her own imagination, and how there really was only a china-closet there.

"She told it with all the particulars; and even to me, who knew beforehand that the room wasn't there, it seemed just as real as could be. She said it was on the north side, between the front and back rooms; that it was very small, and they sometimes called it an entry. There was a door also that opened out-of-doors, and that one was painted green, and was cut in the middle like the old Dutch doors, so that it could be used for a window by opening the top part only. Directly opposite the door was a lounge or couch; it was covered with blue chintz—India chintz—some that had been brought over by an old Salem sea-captain as a 'venture.' He had given it to Hannah when she was a young girl. She was sent to Salem for two years to school. Grandfather originally came from Salem."

"I thought there wasn't any room or chintz."

"*That is just it.* They had decided that mother had imagined it all, and yet you see how exactly everything was painted in her mind, for she had even remembered that Hiram had told her that Hannah could have married the sea-captain if she had wanted to!

"The India cotton was the regular blue stamped chintz, with the peacock figure on it. The head and body of the bird were in profile, while the tail was full front view behind it. It had seemed to take mamma's fancy, and she drew it for me on a piece of paper as she talked. Doesn't it seem strange to you that she could have made all that up, or even dreamed it?

"At the foot of the lounge were some hanging shelves with some old books on them. All the books were leather-coloured except one; that was bright red, and was called the *Ladies' Album*. It made a bright break between the other thicker books.

"On the lower shelf was a beautiful pink sea-shell, lying on a mat made of balls of red shaded worsted. This shell was greatly coveted by mother, but she was only allowed to play with it when she had been particularly good. Hiram had shown her how to hold it close to her ear and hear the roar of the sea in it.

"I know you will like Hiram, Roger; he is quite a character in his way.

"Mamma said she remembered, or *thought* she remembered, having been sick once, and she had to lie quietly for some days on the lounge; then was the time she had become so familiar with everything in the room, and she had been allowed to have the shell to play with all the time. She had had her toast brought to her in there, with make-believe tea. It was one of her pleasant memories of her childhood; it was the first time she had been of any importance to anybody, even herself.

"Right at the head of the lounge was a light-stand, as they called it, and on it was a very brightly polished brass candlestick and a brass tray, with snuffers. That is all I remember of her describing, except that there was a braided rag rug on the floor, and on the wall was a beautiful flowered paper—roses and morning-glories in a wreath on a light blue ground. The same paper was in the front room."

"And all this never existed except in her imagination?"

"She said that when she and father went up there, there wasn't any little room at all like it anywhere in the house; there was a china-closet where she had believed the room to be."

"And your aunts said there had never been any such room."

"That is what they said."

"Wasn't there any blue chintz in the house with a peacock figure?"

"Not a scrap, and Aunt Hannah said there had never been any that she could remember; and Aunt Maria just echoed her—she always does that. You see, Aunt Hannah is an up-and-down New England woman. She looks just like herself; I mean, just like her character. Her joints move up and down or backward and forward in a plain square fashion. I don't believe she ever leaned on anything in her life, or sat in an easy-chair. But Maria is different; she is rounder and softer; she hasn't any ideas of her own; she never had any. I don't believe she would think it right or becoming to have one that differed from Aunt Hannah's, so what would be the use of having any? She is an echo, that's all.

"When mamma and I got there, of course I was all excitement to see the china-closet, and I had a sort of feeling that it would be the little room after all. So I ran ahead and threw open the door, crying, 'Come and see the little room.'

"And Roger," said Mrs. Grant, laying her hand in his, "there really was a little room there, exactly as mother had remembered it. There was the lounge, the peacock chintz, the green door, the shell, the morning-glory, and rose paper, *everything exactly as she had described it to me.*"

"What in the world did the sisters say about it?"

"Wait a minute and I will tell you. My mother was in the front hall still talking with Aunt Hannah. She didn't hear me at first, but I ran out there and dragged her through the front room, saying, 'The room *is* here—it is all right.'

"It seemed for a minute as if my mother would faint. She clung to me in terror. I can remember now how strained her eyes looked and how pale she was.

"I called out to Aunt Hannah and asked her when they had had the closet taken away and the little room built; for in my excitement I thought that that was what had been done.

"'That little room has always been there,' said Aunt Hannah, 'ever since the house was built.'

"'But mamma said there wasn't any little room here, only a china-closet, when she was here with papa,' said I.

"'No, there has never been any china-closet there; it has always been just as it is now,' said Aunt Hannah.

"Then mother spoke; her voice sounded weak and far off. She said, slowly, and with an effort, 'Maria, don't you remember that you told me that there had *never been any little room here?* and Hannah said so too, and then I said I must have dreamed it?'

"'No, I don't remember anything of the kind,' said Maria, without the slightest emotion. 'I don't remember you ever said anything about any china-closet. The house has never been altered; you used to play in this room when you were a child, don't you remember?'

"'I know it,' said mother, in that queer slow voice that made me feel frightened. 'Hannah, don't you remember my finding the china-closet here, with the gilt-edged china on the shelves, and then *you* said that the *china-closet* had always been here?'

"'No,' said Hannah, pleasantly but unemotionally—'no, I don't think you ever asked me about any china-closet, and we haven't any gilt-edged china that I know of.'

"And that was the strangest thing about it. We never could make them remember that there had ever been any question about it. You would think they could remember how surprised mother had been before, unless she had imagined the whole thing. Oh, it was so queer! They were always pleasant about it, but they didn't seem to feel any interest or curiosity. It was always this answer: 'The house is just as it was built; there have never been any changes, so far as we know.'

"And my mother was in an agony of perplexity. How cold their grey eyes looked to me! There was no reading anything in them. It just seemed to break my mother down, this queer thing. Many times that summer, in the middle of the night, I have seen her get up and take a candle and creep softly down-stairs. I could hear the steps creak under her weight. Then she would go through the front room and peer into the darkness, holding her thin hand between the candle and her eyes. She seemed to think the little room might vanish. Then she would come back to bed and toss about all night, or lie still and shiver; it used to frighten me.

"She grew pale and thin, and she had a little cough; then she did not like to be left alone. Sometimes she would make errands in order to send me to the little room for something—a book, or her fan, or her handkerchief; but she would never sit there or let me stay in there long, and sometimes she wouldn't let me go in there for days together. Oh, it was pitiful!"

"Well, don't talk any more about it, Margaret, if it makes you feel so," said Mr. Grant.

"Oh yes, I want you to know all about it, and there isn't much more—no more about the room.

"Mother never got well, and she died that autumn. She used often to sigh, and say, with a wan little laugh, 'There is one thing I am glad of, Margaret: your father knows now all about the little room.' I think she was afraid I distrusted her. Of course, in a child's way, I thought there was something queer about it, but I did not brood over it. I was too young then, and took it as a part of her illness. But, Roger, do you know, it really did affect me. I almost hate to go there after talking about it; I somehow feel as if it might, you know, be a china-closet again."

"That's an absurd idea."

"I know it; of course it can't be. I saw the room, and there isn't any china-closet there, and no gilt-edged china in the house, either."

And then she whispered: "But, Roger, you may hold my hand as you do now, if you will, when we go to look for the little room."

"And you won't mind Aunt Hannah's grey eyes?"

"I won't mind *anything.*"

It was dusk when Mr. and Mrs. Grant went into the gate under the two old Lombardy poplars and walked up the narrow path to the door, where they were met by the two aunts.

Hannah gave Mrs. Grant a frigid but not unfriendly kiss; and Maria seemed for a moment to tremble on the verge of an emotion, but she glanced at Hannah, and then gave her greeting in exactly the same repressed and noncommittal way.

Supper was waiting for them. On the table was the *gilt-edged china.* Mrs. Grant didn't notice it immediately, till she saw her husband smiling at her over his teacup; then she felt fidgety, and couldn't eat. She was nervous, and kept wondering what was behind her, whether it would be a little room or a closet.

After supper she offered to help about the dishes, but, mercy! she might as well have offered to help bring the seasons round; Maria and Hannah couldn't be helped.

So she and her husband went to find the little room, or closet, or whatever was to be there.

Aunt Maria followed them, carrying the lamp, which she set down, and then went back to the dish-washing.

Margaret looked at her husband. He kissed her, for she seemed troubled; and then, hand in hand, they opened the door. It opened into a *china-closet.* The shelves were neatly draped with scalloped paper; on them was the gilt-edged china, with the dishes missing that had been used at the supper, and which at that moment were being carefully washed and wiped by the two aunts.

Margaret's husband dropped her hand and looked at her. She was trembling a little, and turned to him for help, for some explanation, but in an instant she knew that something was wrong. A cloud had come between them; he was hurt; he was antagonized.

He paused for an appreciable instant, and then said, kindly enough, but in a voice that cut her deeply:

"I am glad this ridiculous thing is ended; don't let us speak of it again."

"Ended!" said she. "How ended?" And somehow her voice sounded to her as her mother's voice had when she stood there and questioned her sisters about the little room. She seemed to have to drag her words out. She spoke slowly: "It seems to me to have only just begun in my case. It was just so with mother when she—"

"I really wish, Margaret, you would let it drop. I don't like to hear you speak of your mother in connection with it. It—" He hesitated, for was not this their wedding-day? "It doesn't seem quite the thing, quite delicate, you know, to use her name in the matter."

She saw it all now: *he didn't believe her*. She felt a chill sense of withering under his glance.

"Come," he added, "let us go out, or into the dining-room, some-where, anywhere, only drop this nonsense."

He went out; he did not take her hand now—he was vexed, baffled, hurt. Had he not given her his sympathy, his attention, his belief—and his hand?—and she was fooling him. What did it mean?—she so truthful, so free from morbidness—a thing he hated. He walked up and down under the poplars, trying to get into the mood to go and join her in the house.

Margaret heard him go out; then she turned and shook the shelves; she reached her hand behind them and tried to push the boards away; she ran out of the house on to the north side and tried to find in the darkness, with her hands, a door, or some steps leading to one. She tore her dress on the old rose-trees, she fell and rose and stumbled; then she sat down on the ground and tried to think. What could she think—was she dreaming?

She went into the house and out into the kitchen, and begged Aunt Maria to tell her about the little room—what had become of it, when had they built the closet, when had they bought the gilt-edged china?

They went on washing dishes and drying them on the spotless towels with methodical exactness; and as they worked they said that there had never been any little room, so far as they knew; the china-closet had always been there, and the gilt-edged china had belonged to their mother, it had always been in the house.

"No, I don't remember that your mother ever asked about any little room," said Hannah. "She didn't seem very well that summer, but she never asked about any changes in the house; there hadn't ever been any changes."

There it was again: not a sign of interest, curiosity, or annoyance, not a spark of memory.

She went out to Hiram. He was telling Mr. Grant about the farm. She had meant to ask him about the room, but her lips were sealed before her husband.

Months afterwards, when time had lessened the sharpness of their feelings, they learned to speculate reasonably about the phenomenon, which Mr. Grant had accepted as something not to be scoffed away, not to be treated as a poor joke, but to be put aside as something inexplicable on any ordinary theory.

Margaret alone in her heart knew that her mother's words carried a deeper significance than she had dreamed of at the time. "One thing I am glad of, your father knows now," and she wondered if Roger or she would ever know.

Five years later they were going to Europe. The packing was done; the children were lying asleep, with their travelling things ready to be slipped on for an early start.

Roger had a foreign appointment. They were not to be back in America for some years. She had meant to go up to say good-by to her aunts; but a mother of three children intends to do a great many things that never get done. One thing she had done that very day, and as she paused for a moment between the writing of two notes that must be posted before she went to bed, she said:

"Roger, you remember Rita Lash? Well, she and Cousin Nan go up to the Adirondacks every autumn. They are clever girls, and I have intrusted to them something I want done very much."

"They are the girls to do it, then, every inch of them."

"I know it, and they are going to."

"Well?"

"Why, you see, Roger, that little room—"

"Oh—"

"Yes, I was a coward not to go myself, but I didn't find time, because I hadn't the courage."

"Oh! *that* was it, was it?"

"Yes, just that. They are going, and they will write us about it."

"Want to bet?"

"No; I only want to know."

Rita Lash and Cousin Nan planned to go to Vermont on their way to the Adirondacks. They found they would have three hours between trains, which would give them time to drive up to the Keys farm, and they could still get to the camp that night. But, at the last minute, Rita was prevented from going. Nan had to go to meet the Adirondack party, and she promised to telegraph her when she arrived at the camp. Imagine Rita's amusement when she received this message: "Safely arrived; went to the Keys farm; it is a little room."

Rita was amused, because she did not in the least think Nan had been there. She thought it was a hoax; but it put it into her mind to carry the joke further by really stopping herself when she went up, as she meant to do the next week.

She did stop over. She introduced herself to the two maiden ladies, who seemed familiar, as they had been described by Mrs. Grant.

They were, if not cordial, at least not disconcerted at her visit, and willingly showed her over the house. As they did not speak of any other stranger's having been to see them lately, she became confirmed in her belief that Nan had not been there.

In the north room she saw the roses and morning-glory paper on the wall, and also the door that should open into—what?

She asked if she might open it.

"Certainly," said Hannah; and Maria echoed, "Certainly."

She opened it, and found the china-closet. She experienced a certain relief; she at least was not under any spell. Mrs. Grant left it a china-closet; she found it the same. Good.

But she tried to induce the old sisters to remember that there had at various times been certain questions relating to a confusion as to whether the closet had always been a closet. It was no use; their stony eyes gave no sign.

Then she thought of the story of the sea-captain, and said, "Miss Keys, did you ever have a lounge covered with India chintz, with a figure of a peacock on it, given to you in Salem by a sea-captain, who brought it from India?"

"I dun'no as I ever did," said Hannah. That was all. She thought Maria's cheeks were a little flushed, but her eyes were like a stone wall.

She went on that night to the Adirondacks. When Nan and she were alone in their room she said, "By-the-way, Nan, what did you see at the farm-house? and how did you like Maria and Hannah?"

Nan didn't mistrust that Rita had been there, and she began excitedly to tell her all about her visit. Rita could almost have believed Nan had been there if she hadn't known it was not so. She let her go on for some time, enjoying her enthusiasm, and the impressive way in which she described her opening the door and finding the "little room." Then Rita said: "Now, Nan, that is enough fibbing. I went to the farm myself on my way up yesterday, and there is *no* little room, and there *never* has been any; it is a china-closet, just as Mrs. Grant saw it last."

She was pretending to be busy unpacking her trunk, and did not look up for a moment; but as Nan did not say anything, she glanced at her over her shoulder. Nan was actually pale, and it was hard to say whether she was most angry or frightened. There was something of both in her look. And then Rita began to explain how her telegram had put her in the spirit of going up there alone. She hadn't meant to cut Nan out. She only thought—Then Nan broke in: "It isn't that; I am sure you can't think it is that. But I went myself, and you did not go; you can't have been there, for *it is a little room.*"

Oh, what a night they had! They couldn't sleep. They talked and argued, and then kept still for a while, only to break out again, it was so absurd. They both maintained that they had been there, but both felt sure the other one was either crazy or obstinate beyond reason. They were wretched; it was perfectly ridiculous, two friends at odds

over such a thing; but there it was—"little room," "china-closet,"—
"china-closet," "little room."

The next morning Nan was tacking up some tarlatan at a window
to keep the midges out. Rita offered to help her, as she had done for
the past ten years. Nan's "No, thanks," cut her to the heart.

"Nan," said she, "come right down from that step-ladder and pack
your satchel. The stage leaves in just twenty minutes. We can catch
the afternoon express train, and we will go together to the farm. I am
either going there or going home. You better go with me."

Nan didn't say a word. She gathered up the hammer and tacks,
and was ready to start when the stage came round.

It meant for them thirty miles of staging and six hours of train,
besides crossing the lake; but what of that, compared with having a
lie lying round loose between them! Europe would have seemed easy
to accomplish, if it would settle the question.

At the little junction in Vermont they found a farmer with a wagon
full of meal-bags. They asked him if he could not take them up to
the old Keys farm and bring them back in time for the return train,
due in two hours.

They had planned to call it a sketching trip, so they said, "We have
been there before, we are artists, and we might find some views worth
taking; and we want also to make a short call upon the Misses Keys."

"Did ye calculate to paint the old *house* in the picture?"

They said it was possible they might do so. They wanted to see
it, anyway.

"Waal, I guess you are too late. The *house* burnt down last night,
and everything in it."

"For the land's sake! What'll Maria do now!"

"That's just what Hiram said—'What'll Maria do now!' It aint as if she had folks belongin' to her, and now the house is burnt, and Hannah is *as* she is, it does seem as if Maria'd find it hard git-tin' on alone and doin' her own thinkin'."

"There wan't nothin' saved, I s'pose."

"Next door to nothin'; one washtub, I believe, and the old grey horse that was out to pasture, that's about all; I did hear, though, something about the men-folks' having saved a blue-chintz sofy—'t was the only thing they could get out of the house before the roof fell in; they couldn't seem to get a holt of anythin' else, 't was so hot, and the old house burnt like tinder; Hannah she was that scairt she seemed dazed, and this mornin' Miss Fife, she that married Ben Fife down on the Edge farm, at the foot of the hill, they took 'em in and did for 'em; and when Lucindy Fife went to call 'em to breakfast at five o'clock, there was Maria cryin' like a baby, and Hannah lyin', like an image, with her eyes starin' wide open; she must a had a shock in the night."

"Fur the land's sake!" said the other woman again.

"Yes, and Miss Fife she tried to get Maria to eat somethin', but she wouldn't eat a thing; she just sat and cried; you know she was always sort of a shadder to Hannah, and now she's just like a baby."

"I declair! I believe I'll go up to Miss Fife's; I hate to lose the time, I ought to stir butter today; but just as likely as not lots of folks'll drop in, and I sort of want to hear it all at first hand."

"I believe you're right, and if you'll set a while, I'll hurry up these doughnuts and be ready in no time; it's a sort of lonesome walk up there."

The Widder Luke turned the light side of a doughnut under, the fat sizzled, and Jane Peebles said: "Did you hear what sofy 't was that they saved?"

"I don't rightly know myself which one 't was. Miss Culver she said it was the blue chintz one, but I don't recollect as they had no blue sofy; I don't seem to know exactly what they did have. Hannah never was just the same to me after we had that tiff over the raspberry jam she and I made for the church sale; but I aint goin' to bring that up agin her, now she's laid low; I shall go up there just the same in their time of trouble."

"I s'pose the sofy must have been a new one, or they wouldn't have been so keen to save it."

"I guess 't was;—seems as if these doughnuts wouldn't never brown; it's always so when you're in a hurry."

"I guess I'll ask Maria about that sofy," said Jane; "it's likely that she'll tell all she knows when she gets used to the situation; I always thought Maria was a sight nicer than she seemed. I know once she came near tellin' me how they made that soft soap, that special kind you know, so white, and it keeps like jell, year after year; 't was at a sewin'-bee, and Maria she warmed up and was just goin' to tell me, when Hannah she came in, and Maria she shet up as quick as anythin'. It was sort of curious how she knuckled down to Hannah. Did you ever think Hannah was sort of set?" added Jane, in a low, mysterious tone.

"Hannah *set!* She was sotter'n a meetin'-house, and you know it, Jane Peebles, for all you sided with her about that raspberry jam."

Widder Luke's eyes flashed as she lifted the kettle of hot fat. She got in a good stroke on an old score, and Jane did not dare to retort. Soon after twelve she and Jane Peebles were walking through the lane towards the Fifes'—there was a Sunday air about their dresses, but a Monday decision in their faces; the reporting in hill towns is done mostly by such volunteers, and one must "git up airly" for the first news.

Widder Luke carried a plate of doughnuts as a neighbourly tribute to the occasion.

At the Corners the women paused a moment; they could see from where they stood the black skeleton of the burned barn silhouetted against the sky, beyond "Huckleberry Hill."

Just then Si Briggs came along in his spring wagon, with two strange ladies on the back seat. They took the right-hand road that led to the old Keys place, and as they passed, Mr. Briggs drew his reins with an osh-sh-sh to his horse.

"Won't you get in and ride up the hill?"

Widder Luke and Miss Peebles decorously hesitated a moment, and then climbed over the wheel and sat on either side of Mr. Briggs, who settled himself leisurely between the two women with neighbourly familiarity. Then pointing backward with the butt-end of his whip to indicate and introduce his passengers, he said: "These ladies were pretty well disappointed to find the Keys house burnt up; they come all the way from—where did you say 't was you come from?"

"We came down from the Adirondacks," said Rita. "We wanted to call on Miss Hannah and Maria, and if possible to get a sketch of the house, to paint a picture of it."

"You don't say so! well I declair for it, it's too bad!" said the Widder Luke; "but there's sights of houses older'n that one you might paint; there's the Fife house, where they are stoppin' now; that's as old agin and more tumble-down, if that's what you want. I read a piece in the 'Greentown Gazette' about artists; it said they always took the worst-lookin' houses to paint, though it does seem queer to me."

"Did you know the Keys house very well, and can you tell us how the rooms were built?"

"Why, certain!" said Mr. Briggs. "I've been in it a hundred times if I have once."

Rita and Nan bent forward to listen; the horse jogged slowly up the hill, Mr. Briggs flicking his whip from side to side to encourage the steady walk.

"There was a hall a-runnin' right through the middle, from front to back—an awful waste of space to my thinkin'; when my brother Joel built his house he sot out to have just such a hall, and I said to him, sez I: 'While you're about it why don't you build a house, or else build a hall and let it out for dancin'?' Joel was dead set agin dancin' and it kind of stuck in his mind, so he built his'n without any hall; you jest step right out of doors into the settin'-room; it's nice in summer, but a *leetle* cold in winter."

"Yes, I should think it might be. What were the other rooms in the Keys house?"

"Wall, there was the family settin'-room, on the right-hand side of the hall, and back of that the bed-room for the old folks; Hannah she's slep' there for some years now; on the north side there was the keepin'-room, and back of that the dinin'-room, though I'll be blessed if I know why it wasn't a kitchen, that is, if a kitchen is where folks cook. Them Keyses, way back to Jonathan Keys, was always folks for high-flyin' names, 'specially Hannah."

"Was that all the rooms there were in the lower part?"

"Pretty much all, except a shed they used for a kitchen in old times."

"Wasn't there a little room between the front and back rooms on the north side?" asked Nan, a little hesitatingly, while Rita gave her a pinch of excitement.

"I don'no' as there was," said Mr. Briggs.

Jane Peebles spoke up:

"I believe there was some sort of a room there. I remember once Maria said she kept that north door a leetle crack open in fly-time, and it did seem to rid the little room of flies considerble."

"I don't recollect," said Mr. Briggs, "as there was a door on the north side, but I aint sure; them pine-trees was so dark and the rose-bushes so thick; I can't remember as I've been round there lately; it didn't seem any special place to go to."

"Well!" said Jane Peebles, decisively, "I guess there aint nobody in Titusville that knows any more about that house than I do, unless it's the Keyses themselves; and I *know* there was a little room."

"Now Jane!" said Widder Luke (Jane wilted a little); "if there was a little room there, where was the door to it—on the inside I mean? I guess I haven't been to the Baptist Sewing Circle for forty years for nothin', and the Keyses have had it once every year, in January; and I venture to say I've set and sewed in that front room scores of times, and the only door in the front room was the door into the china-closet, except, of course, the door into the hall-way; and as to the dinin'-room, as they called it" (Si Briggs was a widower, and this was a subtle compliment to him), "there wan't no door at all on that side of the room, just blank wall, with them black pictures of the family done in ink, under glass. I always was struck with that one of Jonathan Keys, it did look exactly like Hannah—just so set and stubborn about the mouth. Poor Hannah, she has had her day though. I have often heard my mother say that Hannah was the prettiest girl in Titusville when she was sixteen, though she was always that stiff. She was sixteen just before she went down to Salem."

Here was an opening, and Nan plunged in.

"I heard something about that: didn't she meet an old sea-captain down there and come near marrying him?"

"I don't know how near she came to marrying him, I know he never came to Titusville. Now I wonder how you ever came to hear that old story; it seems a hundred years ago since my mother told me."

"Here we be!" called out Mr. Briggs, as he stopped his horse with the soothing down-east osh-sh-sh.

Beyond them yawned the black pit where the cellar of the Keys house had been; the ashes still guarded the mystery of the Little Room.

"My! but don't it look mournful!" ejaculated Widder Luke, and then she continued: "My mother said 't was rumoured round Titusville that Hannah had caught a beau down to Salem. Of course that made a stir and folks wanted to know all the particulars, but all they could find out by hook or by crook was that 't was a sea-captain, and that he was after his third wife, having buried his two others, and that he had asked Hannah to marry him; he gave her lots of heathenish stuff that he had brought from India for his first wife. They couldn't seem to find out much more than that, when suddenly Hannah came home, without any warnin'; she brought an extry trunk back with her, but she did look dreadful peakid; she was sort of pale, and her eyes had a look just like her Grandfather Keys'; she hadn't never looked like any of the Keyses before. She didn't let on that anything had happened, and she went everywhere just the same, and nobody knew what she had brought home in that extry trunk, till one day, when the family had all gone to meetin', Nancy Stack—she was Hannah's mother's sister—she went and peeked in the trunk and she saw a lot of trash, sea-shells and queer sorts of calico; but just as she went to lift the tray to see what else there was, she heard the folks comin', so she shut it up quicker'n lightnin'; 't was a snap-lock and her apron got caught; she couldn't take time to open it, so she just tore off a piece of the hem to get away, meanin' to go and get the scrap out some other time; but Hannah must have been in the habit of goin' to that trunk, and before night she found the checked gingham caught in the lid, and Nancy Stark she left very sudden that afternoon and didn't never set foot in the house again. It's queer how it all comes back to me. I s'pose it's seein' the house gone and knowin' how Hannah was took last night."

"Oh, do tell us more," said Rita, breathlessly. "We know Mrs. Grant, their niece, and it is all so interesting."

"Wall, folks *is* generally interested in what they are interested in, but I don't know that there's much more to tell. The captain he never turned up to get his third wife. Nancy Stark she died, and Hannah and Maria here always lived up there alone since the old folks died, and a pretty lonesome spot it was, to be sure."

"Did anybody ever dare to ask Miss Hannah about the captain?"

"No, I guess not; folks up nere mind their own business pretty much."

There was a silence after this rebuke; but Nan, who always began to hold on when other people let go, said:

"I heard once that they had some beautiful china in the china-closet, some that had belonged to their grandmother."

Nobody volunteered any remark about this. Mr. Briggs had got out and was poking round with a stick in the ashes.

Nan persisted:

"Did you ever see the china?"

"*I* did," said Jane Peebles, "sights of times."

"What kind was it?"

"Oh, just blue willer pattern,—but there was sights of it."

"Then they didn't have any other kind, white with a gilt edge, for instance?"

"Wall, up *here*, blue willer, *if* it's the real old kind, is considered good 'nough for most folks."

"Why, of course; I only wish I had any half so nice," said Rita, politely.

"Be you a chaney collector?" asked Widder Luke, with a defiant note.

"Not at all, oh no; but I do wish we could find out whether they ever did have a gilt-edged set."

"Sakes alive! if you really want to know particular, I shouldn't make any bones myself about asking Maria. I should like her to know I don't bear any grudge against 'em, though we did have a fallin'-out about that jam, Hannah and me, come ten years ago next August. I shouldn't mind showin' I had friendly interest in them—now, they're in trouble."

The ruins of the old house looked small and insignificant in the broad sunshine. The poplars were shrivelled by the fire, and the thicket of roses was blackened and trampled; it was as dehumanized as if no one had lived there for a century.

Mr. Briggs came back to the wagon and said, briskly:

"Wall! where'll you go next?"

Rita and Nan hesitated; then Rita said:

"Do you suppose Miss Maria would like to see us? We met her niece just before she sailed for Europe. She asked us to call and give her aunts some messages, but if you think they are too much broken down by the fire and all—"

"Oh, no; it will do Maria good—it's no use cryin' over spilt milk, or burnt houses for that matter, and I guess you could look at Hannah too; she can't speak, I hear it said, but she lies right in the bed off of the livin'-room, and most everybody goes in to look at her."

"The theatre is nowhere," whispered Nan to Rita; "but isn't it ghastly!"

Miss Maria sat in state in the front room at the Fifes'; her black dress, borrowed from a neighbour, was large for even her plump figure, and it had a tendency to make her look as if she had been ill for a long time and had grown thin; her face was pale with the recent excitement, and wore the air of one who was waiting; she sat quite erect in the rocking-chair, with her plump hands folded on her lap; there was an appealing look in her eyes—she missed Hannah; there was no one to give her a pattern for thought or act. Neighbours passed in and out, and there was something so passive in Maria's look that they talked of her freely as *she* as if she were not there. There was plenty of sympathy for her, but it was swept out of sight by the tide of curiosity and detail,—how the house had caught fire; who had seen it first; how Hannah slept so heavily she could not be roused for a long time; how it happened that the well was so low; how the pump-handle broke; how the men tried to save something, but how little had been got out! and then, "how bad Hannah looks," and how old Simeon Bissell lived ten years after his stroke, and Hannah was younger than he, and the Keyses were a long-lived family.

They passed in and out of Hannah's room, Lucinda Fife asking each newcomer to "just step in and look at Hannah!"

Borne along by their sympathy and curiosity, Rita and Nan went in and looked on poor Hannah, stiff and uncompromising as of old, lying in her unwonted bed. She eyed them with her impenetrable grey gaze, and it was evident that the mystery of the Little Room would never be revealed by her, even if one could be bold enough to storm that granite citadel. They talked with Maria. She heard the messages from her niece in gentle silence. Rita took her passive hand and tried to tell her how they sympathized with her in her troubles, and to explain how it was they had happened to come at this time, but it evidently did not get below the surface of Maria's consciousness. She seemed most taken with Nan, however, and to like to have her near her. Just before they left her, Rita ventured to ask if any of their gilt-edged china was saved.

"No, I guess not," said Maria.

"Did they save the blue-chintz sofa?" impetuously asked Nan.

"No, I didn't hear as they did."

"You *did* have a gilt-edged china set, didn't you?" said Nan.

"And a blue sofa?" persuaded Rita.

"I don't seem to remember anything much," said Maria, with an appealing glance towards the room where Hannah lay. It would be barbarity to press her further just then.

Rita and Nan went away—not to the Adirondacks, however, but to spend a few days with Jane Peebles, who gladly acceded to their petition to be boarded there for a time.

"Miss Peebles, where is that man Hiram who always lived at the Keys'?" asked Rita, as Jane helped them to apple-sauce and ginger-bread at supper.

"Hiram? I guess he's pretty well tuckered out, what with the fire and Hannah's stroke; he come over here this mornin' and wanted a piece of my huckleberry pie; he said he couldn't seem to relish any other food; he always did set a great store by my pie; it wan't any better than what Hannah made, so far as I could see, but he always 'lotted on havin' the corner-piece when he brought me eggs from the farm.'

Miss Jane's secret was not so hard to discover as was the secret of the Little Room.

"I would like to talk with Hiram," said Nan.

"Oh, Hiram he'll talk till doomsday, once set him goin', and say pretty smart things too, for a man."

"Hiram, can't you tell us something about the old house?" asked Nan the next morning, as Hiram rose from the kitchen table where he had been taking the solace of a corner-piece of Jane's huckleberry pie.

"That depends," said Hiram, "upon what you want to know. I s'pose I can tell as much as anybody."

"What we really want to know," said Rita, candidly, "is whether there was a closet or a little room on the north side of the Keys house, between the front and the back rooms."

Hiram rubbed his ear carefully and began in a judicial way:

"When Jonathan Keys first built that house, some time way back in 1700, he planned to have—"

"Jane Peebles! Jane Peebles! you're wanted right off, up to the Fifes', and Hiram too; Hannah she's took worse, and Maria she's no more use than a babe unborn. I'm on my way up there now," concluded the Widder Luke, as she hurried up the hill.

When Rita and Nan went to say good-bye to Maria, a few days later, Maria clung to them. She had begun to like these new friends who had taken it upon themselves to try and do for her what Mrs. Grant would have done had she been there. She followed them to the door, and said, in a whisper:

"I asked Hannah, only the day before her last shock, whether she *did* have any gilt-edged china, and she sort of nodded. Then I asked her if we had a blue sofy, and she nodded again; but come to think it over by myself, I don't think it really meant anything, because you know Hannah couldn't do anything else but nod after she had that first stroke; she couldn't shake her head; but I thought I would tell you, you have been so kind and you seemed so interested."

Out on the stone wall at the Corners Nan and Rita sat and laughed and cried; the tragedy and the comedy appealed to them, and not even when Nan said, as they walked down to Jane Peebles' house, "All the same, *I saw the Little Room*," and Rita said, "*I saw the china-closet*," did they feel any bitterness.

"Good-bye," said Hiram; "I'm real glad you came, and I want you to tell Miss Grant, when you write to her, that Hiram—she'll remember Hiram fast enough—Hiram is going to marry Jane Peebles, and that Maria shan't never want for a home so long as Jane can make huckleberry pies."

"Oh, we are so glad; and you will send us a piece of wedding-cake, won't you?"

"I shouldn't wonder," said Hiram.

"Won't you please tell us what you started to that time when Miss Hannah was taken worse so suddenly? we do so want to know whether there was a room or a china-closet there on the north side."

"I do remember now that I started in to tell you that; it wan't much anyhow, only when their Grandfather Keys built the house he boasted that he intended to build the *entire* house of timber that hadn't a knot in it. He spent ten years a-gettin' the timber ready, and when it was done he found that right in the front-room closet they had put a piece of board with a great knot in it. He was dreadful mad, but he kept it there all the same—on purpose, he said, to show folks it wan't no use to set out to do anythin' perfect in this world."

"Then there was a china-closet—"

"Wall, yes, there certainly was a closet there."

"Oh, Nan!" said Rita, as the cars moved away from where Hiram stood, "he didn't say exactly what kind of a closet even then."

"No; but we can write to Jane and ask her to answer our questions with just yes or no. When she is Mrs. Hiram (I wonder if he ever had a last name) she will get it out of him if we can only interest her."

"Jane," said Hiram that evening, "if you could manage to wash on Saturday, so as to have an off-day on Monday, I don'no but we might as well be married then as any other time. I should feel sort of easier in my mind if Maria came down to live with us before they think her room is better than her company up to the Fifes', if Hannah should die."

"That's so, Hiram. I'll hurry round and fix things, and you better stop tonight and tell Maria that I'll be real glad to have her come and live with us; and Hiram, I've been thinking that if the men folks did save that blue-chintz sofy—"

"Wait a minute, Jane, I sort of want to tell you somethin'; 't aint anythin' I should want you to repeat, but it's somethin' that sort of troubles me some. You see, Miss Hannah she's always been good to me, and I shouldn't want to say anythin' to set folks a-talkin'; but Miss Hannah haint been exactly well for some weeks, and only the day before the fire she came to me and she says she thought 't was about time she put that old trunk full of duds, the one she's always kept in her closet, out of the way, and she guessed she'd have me burn it up. I thought 't was most a pity to destroy the trunk—it was a real good one, and hadn't never seen no travel to speak of—and so I said I'd take the things out and burn 'em; that seemed to trouble her, and she was real short with me. She said I was no better than all the other folks, that I was pryin' round to see what she kep' in it. I sort of soothed her, and then she said she'd been pestered most to death by folks always askin' her about some old blue chintz, and about a little room; and she guessed that if she could put that trunk out of sight, mebby folks would mind their own business and let her have some peace. So when Maria was out to the garden for some stuff for dinner, Miss Hannah she got me to help her carry the trunk out of her room and put it in the hall-closet; it wan't no kind of a place to keep it, but I thought it was better to humour her a mite, seein' she was out of sorts.

"In the middle of the night," continued Hiram, dropping his voice and looking round to see that nobody was coming up the walk, "in the middle of the night I smelt smoke, and thought right off that the barn must be a-burn-in', but I couldn't see no light; then I heard a sort of smothered noise, and I suspicioned right off what was the matter. I run to Maria's room and found her stumblin' round in the dark—her room bein' full of smoke she was sort of confused—and there was a turrible glare out in the hall. We found Miss Hannah out there wringin' her hands and callin' out: 'Oh, the trunk will be burnt up, the trunk will be burnt up!' We couldn't coax her to go away, and it did seem as she'd burn up in her tracks if I hadn't just took her and carried her out. By that time the house was all blazin', and, though the folks began to come, it wan't no use—it had to go. Hannah she was all dressed, and I don't believe she had been to bed."

"You don't think she *set* the house afire, Hiram?"

"No, not a-meanin' to; but what I think is that she felt lonesome without that trunk, and so she went down to the hall-closet when she thought we was asleep, and either she dropped her candle or else the things that hung in the closet caught fire, and she didn't see it till 't was too late, and then she was so fearful that the trunk would burn she wouldn't go away."

"What was in the trunk?"

Hiram shuffled from one foot to the other, then hesitated a little, and said:

"Jane, I've been comin' to see you a good many years, most ever since we was young, and yet we haint never exactly spoke of gittin' married till lately; but they aint so slow down in the city, and I guess Hannah sort of expected to git married to that sea-captain down to Salem. Anyways, whatever she kept in that trunk it came from Salem, and I *guess* 't was some stuff he gave her."

"You don't say so, all these years!"

In Paris, Mrs. Grant, with her husband, sat over the breakfast coffee in their little parlour in the Hotel St. Romain. The window opened on the balcony overhanging the Rue St. Roch. From the narrow street below floated the cry, "*Les moules, les moules?*" mingled with the clap, clap of the horses' hoofs on the asphalt below. The *concierge* sang as he swept the sidewalk before the door, and the newsboys cried, with their plaintive intonation, "*Le Figaro, Le Fig-aro! Le P'tit Journal!*"

"Roger," said Mrs. Grant, "I had such a curious dream last night. I suppose I must have been asleep, but I seemed to be awake, when suddenly I saw Aunt Hannah standing at the foot of my bed, just between the two posts. She stood quite still, and her eyes were fixed on me with her peculiar expression of reserve, but also as if she had an intense desire to speak. I was just going to cry out, 'Why, Aunt Hannah, is that you?' when suddenly I felt very passive, and as if a change was going on. The curtains of my bed moved back slowly, and I was again in that mysterious little room. I seemed to see either myself or my mother, I could not tell which it was, as a little girl, lying on the sofa; it was that same blue-chintz sofa I told you about; everything in the room was exactly as I remember seeing it when I was a child, even to the shell and the book on the shelf.

"I can't express to you how it was that I saw the little girl lying there; it was as if my mind was compelled by some other mind to see the little girl and the little room; and all the time I did not know whether it was my mother or myself as a child that I was looking at, and I could feel all the time my Aunt Hannah's grey eyes, though I could not see her while the vision of the little room lasted.

"It was some minutes before the scene began to fade, and it did so very gradually, just as it came: first, the roses and blue morning-glories on the paper began to waver and grow indistinct; then one object after another trembled and faded. It was exactly as if something outside of myself compelled me to see these things; and then, as the pressure of that other will was removed, the impression gradually disappeared. The last to go was the figure of the little girl, but she too faded; the bed-curtains seemed to evolve out of the walls of the room, and I was lying on my bed; but Aunt Hannah still stood between the foot-posts, with her eyes fixed on mine. Then came the impression that she could not speak, but that she wanted to convey some thought to me; and then these words came to me—not as if a voice spoke them, but as if they were being printed on my mind or consciousness:

"'Margaret, you must not worry any more about the Little Room, it has no connection with you or your mother, and it never had any: it all belongs to me. I am sorry that my secret ever troubled anyone else; I tried to keep it to myself, but sometimes it would get out. There'll never be any Little Room to trouble anybody else any more.'

"All the time I was hearing these words I felt Aunt Hannah's eyes; and then she began to move backward, slowly, and she seemed to vanish down a long, long distance, till I lost sight of her. The last thing I saw was her grey eyes fastened on my face. I awoke, and found myself sitting up, with my head bent forward, looking right between the foot-posts of the bed."

"Your Aunt Hannah seems to be more fond of travelling than she used to be. Paris is further from Titusville than Brooklyn," said Mr. Grant, lightly.

"Oh, don't, Roger, don't! I think Aunt Hannah must be dead."

THE THING IN
THE CELLAR

David H. Keller (1880–1966)

Keller is remembered today, when he's remembered at all, as a pioneer contributor to the early science-fiction magazines where he first appeared with "The Revolt of the Pedestrians" in 1928. For a quarter-of-a-century before that Keller had served first as a country doctor, in the horse-and-buggy days in Pennsylvania, and then as a junior physician at a mental institution in Illinois. He developed a profound knowledge of psychiatry and, with the entry of the United States into the First World War he was assigned to help soldiers suffering from what was then called "shell shock". He remained working in a mental institution until 1924 when he turned to writing. He used his knowledge of the deep workings and traumas of the mind in many of his stories such as "Unlocking the Past" (1928) about attempts to tap into ancestral memory; "The Inferiority Complex" (1930) about micromania; "No More Tomorrows" (1932) in which a psychologist removes an individual's understanding of the future and, especially "The Thing in the Cellar" (1932) which explores the power of imagination and fear.

I t was a large cellar, entirely out of proportion to the house above
it. The owner admitted that it was probably built for a distinctly
different kind of structure from the one which rose above it.
Probably the first house had been burned, and poverty had caused a
diminution of the dwelling erected to take its place.

A winding stone stairway connected the cellar with the kitchen.
Around the base of this series of steps successive owners of the house
had placed their firewood, winter vegetables and junk. The junk had
gradually been pushed back till it rose, head high, in a barricade of
uselessness. What was back of that barricade no one knew and no one
cared. For some hundreds of years no one had crossed it to penetrate
to the black reaches of the cellar behind it.

At the top of the steps, separating the kitchen from the cellar,
was a stout oaken door. This door was, in a way, as peculiar and
out of relation to the rest of the house as the cellar. It was a strange
kind of door to find in a modern house, and certainly a most
unusual door to find in the inside of the house—thick, stoutly
built, dexterously rabbeted together with huge wrought-iron hinges,
and a lock that looked as though it came from Castle Despair.
Separating a house from the outside world, such a door would be
excusable; swinging between kitchen and cellar it seemed peculiarly inappropriate.

DAVID H. KELLER

From the earliest months of his life Tommy Tucker seemed unhappy in the kitchen. In the front parlour, in the formal dining-room, and especially on the second floor of the house he acted like a normal, healthy child; but carry him to the kitchen, he at once began to cry. His parents, being plain people, ate in the kitchen save when they had company. Being poor, Mrs. Tucker did most of her work, though occasionally she had a charwoman in to do the extra Saturday cleaning, and thus much of her time was spent in the kitchen. And Tommy stayed with her, at least as long as he was unable to walk. Much of the time he was decidedly unhappy.

When Tommy learned to creep, he lost no time in leaving the kitchen. No sooner was his mother's back turned than the little fellow crawled as fast as he could for the doorway opening into the front of the house, the dining-room and the front parlour. Once away from the kitchen, he seemed happy; at least, he ceased to cry. On being returned to the kitchen his howls so thoroughly convinced the neighbours that he had colic that more than one bowl of catnip and sage tea was brought to his assistance.

It was not until the boy learned to talk that the Tuckers had any idea as to what made the boy cry so hard when he was in the kitchen. In other words, the baby had to suffer for many months till he obtained at least a little relief, and even when he told his parents what was the matter, they were absolutely unable to comprehend. This is not to be wondered at because they were both hard-working, rather simple-minded persons.

What they finally learned from their little son was this: that if the cellar door was shut and securely fastened with the heavy iron Tommy could at least eat a meal in peace; if the door was simply closed and not locked, he shivered with fear, but kept quiet; but if the door was open, if even the slightest streak of black showed that it was not

208

tightly shut, then the little three-year-old would scream himself to the point of exhaustion, especially if his tired father would refuse him permission to leave the kitchen.

Playing in the kitchen, the child developed two interesting habits. Rags, scraps of paper and splinters of wood were continually being shoved under the thick oak door to fill the space between the door and the sill. Whenever Mrs. Tucker opened the door there was always some trash there, placed by her son. It annoyed her, and more than once the little fellow was thrashed for this conduct, but punishment acted in no way as a deterrent. The other habit was as singular. Once the door was closed and locked, he would rather boldly walk over to it and caress the old lock. Even when he was so small that he had to stand on tiptoe to touch it with the tips of his fingers he would touch it with slow caressing strokes; later on, as he grew, he used to kiss it.

His father, who only saw the boy at the end of the day, decided that there was no sense in such conduct, and in his masculine way tried to break the lad of his foolishness. There was, of necessity, no effort on the part of the hard-working man to understand the psychology back of his son's conduct. All that the man knew was that his little son was acting in a way that was decidedly queer.

Tommy loved his mother and was willing to do anything he could to help her in the household chores, but one thing he would not do, and never did do, and that was to fetch and carry between the house and the cellar. If his mother opened the door, he would run screaming from the room, and he never returned voluntarily till he was assured that the door was closed.

He never explained just why he acted as he did. In fact, he refused to talk about it, at least to his parents, and that was just as well, because had he done so, they would simply have been more positive than ever that there was something wrong with their only child. They tried, in their own ways, to break the child of his unusual habits; failing to change him at all, they decided to ignore his peculiarities.

That is, they ignored them till he became six years old and the time came for him to go to school. He was a sturdy little chap by that time, and more intelligent than the usual boys beginning in the primer class. Mr. Tucker was, at times, proud of him; the child's attitude toward the cellar door was the one thing most disturbing to the father's pride. Finally nothing would do but that the Tucker family call on the neighbourhood physician. It was an important event in the life of the Tuckers, so important that it demanded the wearing of Sunday clothes, and all that sort of thing.

"The matter is just this, Doctor Hawthorn," said Mr. Tucker, in a somewhat embarrassed manner. "Our little Tommy is old enough to start to school, but he behaves childish in regard to our cellar, and the missus and I thought you could tell us what to do about it. It must be his nerves."

"Ever since he was a baby," continued Mrs. Tucker, taking up the thread of conversation where her husband had paused, "Tommy has had a great fear of the cellar. Even now, big boy that he is, he does not love me enough to fetch and carry for me through that door and down those steps. It is not natural for a child to act like he does, and what with chinking the cracks with rags and kissing the lock, he drives me to the point where I fear he may become daft-like as he grows older."

The doctor, eager to satisfy new customers, and dimly remembering some lectures on the nervous system received when he was a medical student, asked some general questions, listened to the boy's heart, examined his lungs and looked at his eyes and fingernails. At last he commented:

"Looks like a fine, healthy boy to me."

"Yes, all except the cellar door," replied the father.

"Has he ever been sick?"

"Naught but fits once or twice when he cried himself blue in the face," answered the mother.

"Frightened?"

"Perhaps. It was always in the kitchen."

"Suppose you go out and let me talk to Tommy by myself?"

And there sat the doctor very much at his ease and the little six-year-old boy very uneasy.

"Tommy, what is there in the cellar you are afraid of?"

"I don't know."

"Have you ever seen it?"

"No, sir."

"Ever heard it? smelt it?"

"No, sir."

"Then how do you know there is something there?"

"Because."

"Because what?"

"Because there is."

That was as far as Tommy would go, and at last his seeming obstinacy annoyed the physician even as it had for several years annoyed Mr. Tucker. He went to the door and called the parents into the office.

"He thinks there is something down in the cellar," he stated.

The Tuckers simply looked at each other.

"That's foolish," commented Mr. Tucker.

"'Tis just a plain cellar with junk and firewood and cider barrels in it," added Mrs. Tucker. "Since we moved into that house, I have not missed a day without going down those stone steps and I know there is nothing there. But the lad has always screamed when the door was open. I recall now that since he was a child in arms he has always screamed when the door was open."

"He thinks there is something there," said the doctor.

"That is why we brought him to you," replied the father. "It's the child's nerves. Perhaps fœtida, or something, will calm him."

"I tell you what to do," advised the doctor. "He thinks there is something there. Just as soon as he finds that he is wrong and that there is nothing there, he will forget about it. He has been humoured too much. What you want to do is to open that cellar door and make him stay by himself in the kitchen. Nail the door open so he can not close it. Leave him alone there for an hour and then go and laugh at him and show him how silly it was for him to be afraid of an empty cellar. I will give you some nerve and blood tonic and that will help, but the big thing is to show him that there is nothing to be afraid of."

On the way back to the Tucker home Tommy broke away from his parents. They caught him after an exciting chase and kept him between them the rest of the way home. Once in the house he disappeared and was found in the guest room under the bed. The afternoon being already spoiled for Mr. Tucker, he determined to keep the child under observation for the rest of the day. Tommy ate no supper, in spite of the urgings of the unhappy mother. The dishes were washed, the evening paper read, the evening pipe smoked; and then, and only then, did Mr. Tucker take down his tool box and get out a hammer and some long nails.

"And I am going to nail the door open, Tommy, so you can not close it, as that was what the doctor said, Tommy, and you are to be a man and stay here in the kitchen alone for an hour, and we will leave the lamp a-burning, and then when you find there is naught to be afraid of, you will be well and a real man and not something for a man to be ashamed of being the father of."

But at the last Mrs. Tucker kissed Tommy and cried and whispered to her husband not to do it, and to wait till the boy was larger; but nothing was to do except to nail the thick door open so it could not be shut and leave the boy there alone with the lamp burning and the dark open space of the doorway to look at with eyes that grew as hot and burning as the flame of the lamp.

That same day Doctor Hawthorn took supper with a classmate of his, a man who specialized in psychiatry and who was particularly interested in children. Hawthorn told Johnson about his newest case, the little Tucker boy, and asked him for his opinion. Johnson frowned.

"Children are odd, Hawthorn. Perhaps they are like dogs. It may be their nervous system is more acute than in the adult. We know that our eyesight is limited, also our hearing and smell. I firmly believe that there are forms of life which exist in such a form that we can neither see, hear nor smell them. Fondly we delude ourselves into the fallacy of believing that they do not exist because we can not prove their existence. This Tucker lad may have a nervous system that is peculiarly acute. He may dimly appreciate the existence of something in the cellar which is unappreciable to his parents. Evidently there is some basis to this fear of his. Now, I am not saying that there is anything in the cellar. In fact, I suppose that it is just an ordinary cellar, but this boy, since he was a baby, has thought that there was something there, and that is just as bad as though there actually were. What I would like to know is what makes him think so. Give me the address, and I will call tomorrow and have a talk with the little fellow."

"What do you think of my advice?"

"Sorry, old man, but I think it was perfectly rotten. If I were you, I would stop around there on my way home and prevent them from following it. The little fellow may be badly frightened. You see, he evidently thinks there is something there."

"But there isn't."

"Perhaps not. No doubt, he is wrong, but he thinks so."

It all worried Doctor Hawthorn so much that he decided to take his friend's advice. It was a cold night, a foggy night, and the physician felt cold as he tramped along the London streets. At last he came to the Tucker house. He remembered now that he had been there once before, long ago, when little Tommy Tucker came into the world. There was a light in the front window, and in no time at all Mr. Tucker came to the door.

"I have come to see Tommy," said the doctor.

"He is back in the kitchen," replied the father.

"He gave one cry, but since then he has been quiet," sobbed the wife.

"If I had let her have her way, she would have opened the door, but I said to her, 'Mother, now is the time to make a man out of our Tommy.' And I guess he knows by now that there was naught to be afraid of. Well, the hour is up. Suppose we go and get him and put him to bed?"

"It has been a hard time for the little child," whispered the wife.

Carrying the candle, the man walked ahead of the woman and the doctor, and at last opened the kitchen door. The room was dark.

"Lamp has gone out," said the man. "Wait till I light it."

"Tommy! Tommy!" called Mrs. Tucker.

But the doctor ran to where a white form was stretched on the floor. Sharply he called for more light. Trembling, he examined all that was left of little Tommy. Twitching, he looked into the open space down into the cellar. At last he looked at Tucker and Tucker's wife.

"Tommy—Tommy has been hurt—I guess he is dead!" he stammered.

The mother threw herself on the floor and picked up the torn, mutilated thing that had been, only a little while ago, her little Tommy.

The man took his hammer and drew out the nails and closed the door and locked it and then drove in a long spike to reinforce the lock. Then he took hold of the doctor's shoulders and shook him.

"What killed him, Doctor? What killed him?" he shouted into Hawthorn's ear.

The doctor looked at him bravely in spite of the fear in his throat.

"How do I know, Tucker?" he replied. "How do I know? Didn't you tell me that there was nothing there? Nothing down there? In the cellar?"

JOHNSON LOOKED BACK

Thomas Burke (1886–1945)

It is difficult to disentangle Burke's real life from the one he invented
about himself and yet there is probably more truth about his life
and thoughts in his fiction than in his autobiography. Burke became
known as the "laureate of London's Chinatown" through his many
stories and books set in London's East End and particularly in the
Limehouse region around the docks. He had been writing for fifteen
years before his volume *Limehouse Nights* (1916) made his name but
even then, when Burke revisited this area of his youth, he discovered
it had already changed beyond his memories. In effect Burke created
a life and a London of his own imaginings and it was so real that no
one argued with it. His books of engulfing storytelling include *The
Pleasantries of Old Quong* (1931) and the definitive *Night-Pieces* (1935),
which features the best of his unsettling stories, including the one
reprinted here.

Don't look behind you, Johnson. There's a man following you, but don't look behind. Go on just as you are going, down that brown-foggy street where the lamps make diffuse and feeble splashes on the brown. Go straight on and don't look behind, or you might be sorry. You might see something that you'll wish you hadn't seen.

He's a blind man, Johnson, but that makes little difference to him, and is of no use to you. You can't hear the tapping of his stick because he hasn't got a stick. He can't carry a stick. He hasn't any hands. But he's been blind so long that he can walk the streets of this district without a stick. He can smell his way about, and he can feel traffic and other dangers through his skin.

You can turn and twist as you like, and use your mortal eyes as much as you like, but that man without eyes will be close on your trail. He's faster than you. He's not impeded by perception of the objects that reach you through the eyes. You are not used to the uncertain cloud of fog and blears of light; you have to pick your steps. He can march boldly, for he marches always in clear, certain darkness. If you use cunning he can meet all your cunning. Without seeing you, or hearing you, he will know just where you go, and he will be close behind you. He will know what you are going to do the moment you have decided to do it; and he will be at your heels.

No; it won't help you at all to look behind you. It will only sicken you. It's not a pleasant spectacle—this man, blind and without hands, silently and steadfastly dogging you through the curling vapour. It's much better for you not to know that you are being pursued by this creature. The result will be the same anyway; you won't escape him, and it may save you a few minutes of misery not to know what is coming.

But why is he pursuing you? Why did he wait so long at the entrance to that dim street, whose very lamps seem to be ghosts of its darkness, to pick out your step from many others, and to follow you with this wolf-stride? You will not know that until you see him face to face. You have forgotten so many things; things that the strongest effort of memory will not recall; but your pursuer hasn't. He remembers; and all these years he has been seeking you, smelling about the streets of London, knowing that some day he is certain to strike the forbidding street down which you went when you first shook him off, and that he will find you there. And tonight he has found it and has smelt your presence there, and is with you once again.

Purpose is pursuing impulse. You are idle and at ease. He is in ferment. You are going to visit that abandoned house because it occurred to you to visit that abandoned house. He is following you because he has been waiting for nothing else. So there you go—he patient and intent; you, with free mind, picking your steps through the fog-smeared street. You have nothing to worry about. You walk through the fog with care, but with that sense of security which even the darkest streets of London cannot shake in Londoners familiar with them and with their people. You don't know what is catching up with you, and so long as you go straight ahead and don't look—

*

Oh, you fool! Johnson—you fool! I said—"*Don't* look behind you."

And now you've looked. And now you've seen. And now you know.

If you hadn't looked behind you would have escaped all the years of pain that are now coming upon you. It would have been all over in a few seconds. Now you've made it more dreadful. You've filled your mind with knowledge of it, and you're going to increase your torment by trying to get away. And above those two pains will come the pain of a struggle.

You won't get away. You have no chance at all. The man behind you is blind, and has no hands; but he has arms and he has feet, and he can use them. Don't think you can escape by dodging down that alley... That was a silly thing to do. Alleys hold fear more firmly than open streets. Fear gets clotted in their recesses and hangs there like cobwebs. You thought you were doing something clever which would perplex him, but you won't perplex him. He is driving you where he wants you. You thought that if you could get into the alleys, and twist and turn and double along the deserted wharves, you could shake him off. But you can't. It's just in the alleys that he wants to have you, and you went there under his direction.

Already you're helping him because you're feeling the clotted fear which has been hanging in these alleys through the centuries. You're getting muddled. You've lost count of the turns you've taken, and you're not sure whether you're going away from him or fleeing breast to breast upon him. You saw him in all his maimed ugliness, and you see him now in every moving heap of fog that loiters at the mouth of each new alley. Long before he is upon you, he has got you.

If you hadn't looked back, doom would have fallen upon you out of nothing. But you looked back, and now you know the source of that doom.

You might as well give up padding through the alleys. Their universe of yellow-spotted blackness is only deluding you with hope of refuge. No corner is dark enough to hide you from eyes that live in darkness. No doors can cover you from senses as keen as air. No turn that you take will carry you farther from him; you are taking the turns he wants you to take.

There! You've turned into a little square which has no opening save that by which you entered. You're done. You can't hear him coming because he's wearing thin list slippers; but he's very near you. He's very near that entry. You've no hope of getting out. When he seizes you it would be better to yield everything, cat-like, and go with his desire and his attack. Better that than to fight. Only fools fight the invincible. But of course you *will* fight.

Hush—he's here. He's at the entry. He's in the square. You know that he's moving towards you; you know it as certainly as steel knows magnet. And then, though the fog-filled square gives you no more sight than your enemy, you know that he has halted; and you feel the silence dripping about your ears, spot by spot.

And now he has made his spring. He is upon you, and your fists fly against him. But you cannot beat him back. His blows fall upon you, and they wound and sting. You cannot fight him as you would fight another man. Your blood is cold but your brain is hot, and your nerves and muscles receive confused commands. They begin to act by themselves, automatically and without force. Your brain is pre-occupied by this man.

It's no good, Johnson. Better to give in. You're only prolonging it. Your fists are useless against handless arms, or against feet. The fight is unequal. You have fists to fight with. He has none. And this lack of his puts all the advantage on his side. For a blow with the fist is painful and damaging; on the right point it may be fatal. But a blow with a stump, while equally painful and damaging, is something more. You're realizing that. It stains honest combat with something anomalous. Its impact on the face is not only a blow: it is an innuendo. It makes you think when you ought to be fighting.

And with the blows from those handless arms there are the blows from what seems to be an open hand. They tear along your face and about your neck, and each blow brings nausea. Not because it's a blow from an open hand, but because you know that this man has no hands, and because the feel of it is too long for a hand. And then you know what it is. The man with no hands is fighting you with his feet. You could put up with that if he were using feet as men do use them; if he were kicking you. What sucks the strength from your knees is that his feet are behaving like hands. You feel as a dreamer feels when fighting the dead. You are already beaten, not by superior strength, but by blows from handless arms and from feet behaving as hands. And you know that it was your work that robbed him of his hands and left him to use his feet as hands.

And now you're down. And now one of those feet, more flexible and more full of life than any common hand, is on your neck. And the fog in this little derelict square deepens from brown to black. The foot presses and presses, very softly and very heavily; and your eyes become black fog and your mind becomes black fog. Black upon black, increasingly, until with the last rush of breath you are swallowed into a black void and a black silence and a black cessation of being.

And so, Johnson, you destroyed yourself, and because you looked back you had the full bitterness of knowing that you destroyed yourself. For this blind and maimed and ferocious creature of the velvet steps was, of course, yourself. This creature without sight and without hands was your other self, your innermost guide, whom you so constantly thwarted and denied and broke. It was you who blinded him that he might not see your deeds, and it was the things you did with *your* hands which corrupted his, until he was left with none, and at last turned upon you. And then you looked back, and you saw yourself stalking yourself to destruction; and in the last blackness of terror you understood.

Happier for you if you had not looked back, and had not understood. For then, after a sojourn in the still dusk of Devachan, you would have returned to amend a wasted life by another pilgrimage. You would have returned blind and maimed to a life of struggle and frustration, poverty and contumely and pain. And you would have called it, with a shrug, what most men call it—Luck.

But you looked back. You are one of the few who die with full knowledge of their pursuer. So, with the blindness and mutilation, and the poverty and the pain, you will carry yet another tribulation. You will carry the tribulation of remembering *why* you are suffering.

THE WOMAN IN RED

and

UNMASKED

Muriel Campbell Dyar (1875–1963)

Born and raised in Ohio, Muriel Campbell Dyar was a regular contributor to the leading American magazines, especially *Harper's*, which published many of her stories in the years up to and during the First World War. It was in *Harper's* that her first story about Elizabeth and David appeared, a New England couple which eventually developed into her sentimental episodic novel of married life, *Davie and Elizabeth, Wonderful Adventures* (1908). But she made her reputation in *The Black Cat*, a magazine which thrived on publishing stories of the unusual and in which she appeared with the mysterious "The Woman in Red" and its much-demanded sequel.

Winter reigned throughout Europe, but on the Riviera spring and summer bloomed together. Overhead the sky was infinitely blue, below the sea was green and purple and amethyst. Everywhere the sun, everywhere the scent of geranium and mimosa, the fragrance of rose and violet. Always the deep boom, boom of the waves thundering against the tall cliffs of Monaco, always the cry of the sea gull, forever the chimes from the church of Sainte Dévote.

At Monte Carlo, that paradise of the gamester, the season was at its height. The Hôtels de Paris and Beau-Rivage were crowded, those of the quarter La Condamine were full, and well-dressed people, finding shelter in some cheap lodging house over in Monaco, gave the name of some more fashionable resort when applying for a *carte d'admission* to the "Cercle des Étrangeres," the euphemistic title of that institution which draws hither the avid and the inquisitive of all the nations. Day after day, night after night, the Casino overflowed with those who came to tempt Fortune. Every one laughed and sang and was gay. Heavy hearts are hidden at Monte Carlo.

It was at a concert that she first appeared—the Woman in Red. The French tenor was just beginning his number when the doors of the middle box of the right hand tier swung slowly open and closed behind her. She stood for just a moment outlined against the ivory background. Very tall she seemed, dressed from head to foot in red—not cardinal, nor crimson—but the most intense and glowing scarlet. From out this mass of colour her bare throat rose vividly white, and down the satin of her skirt her ungloved arms hung, soft and round as those of a child. Her hair, too, fine and fair, gave her head a rather childish look. And then—no wonder fans stopped fluttering and silks began to rustle—her face was entirely concealed by a mask of dark red velvet!

The lady seated herself quickly, with a curious grace in every movement, and the red of her dress spreading out around her, stained as with blood the whiteness of the box. She raised her glass and insolently swept the house, moving her head so that the jewels in her hair blazed and flamed into the faces turned in her direction. A laugh floated from above as a woman in the gallery, with her programme twisted into a little roll, mocked the motion. The Woman in Red turned away her face with a shrug of her white shoulders, and sat through the performance quite still and indifferent. At the beginning of the last number she rose slowly, and gathering together her shimmering scarlet left the box. That was the introduction to the world of Monte Carlo of the Woman in Red.

After that, interest centred about her, increasing as her peculiarities became known. She never wore a suggestion of any colour but red, and that alone was enough to make her conspicuous. Then the mask, thought to have been merely a caprice on the night of the concert, was never removed. That rendered her mysterious. She talked but little, going about silently, with a soft, light step. One might be quite alone, and the next moment suddenly aware of the Red Woman's presence. When the tall young Englishman who lost everything at a turn of the wheel went out into the Casino garden and, cocking his pistol in the shadow of the cacti, muttered, "I'll end the whole cursed business!" the Woman in Red murmured persuasively beside him, "Oh, I wouldn't—"and he didn't, and when a lady knelt one evening before the image of the Virgin in the church of Sainte Dévote, and whispered wildly, "O Blessed Mother, forgive me my sins!" it was the Woman in Red who finished softly for her, "and those who sin against me." This made her something more than conspicuous and mysterious—it made her awesome.

No one ever saw her smoke, but her scarlet garments always exhaled a faint odour of cigarettes. Every night she came into the roulette room and sat there in her scarlet dress, with a red flower in her hair, and put down her stakes with as much emotion as though the gold and notes were worthless. Consistent in her colour scheme, she invariably placed her money on the red, and nine times out of ten she won.

To make her a trifle more conspicuous, mysterious and eerie, she had for a chaperone a woman so thin and wrinkled and old as to seem hardly capable of life. When some one ventured to ask her a question about the Woman in Red the creature cackled, "Oh, the devil, the devil, the devil. How should I know?"

"No wonder the men like her," chattered a lively little Frenchwoman. "They'd like us if we muffled our faces and wore clothes like that. I'll wager she has the face of a *blanchisseuse*—any one could be fascinating behind a velvet mask!"

"She is, certainly," said a bystander, drily.

"*Peste!*" exclaimed the sallow critic angrily. "No one wants that old count or that stupid baron or that pink-cheeked English boy, anyway!"

It is true that the Woman in Red had found ardent admirers in the old count and the stupid baron and the English boy—the one to whom she had whispered that night behind the cacti—and the rivalry between them increased as the season passed. Today one was in favour, tomorrow another, and the frequenters of the Casino got to betting on the chances of the several suitors till it became almost as exciting as a game at one of the tables.

But throughout it all the woman remained calm, inscrutable, mysterious. Neither of the three could persuade her to tell her name or take off her mask.

"I answer to any name," she said. "I have forgotten my own, and as for my face, what makes you think it beautiful?"

"Oh, *you*," said the courtly old count.

"Your hands," said the stupid baron.

"Your hair," said the blond young Englishman, with British egotism.

In answer to each she only laughed a hard little laugh, not altogether pleasant to hear.

To be much talked about and to say little appeared to suit her. A month after her advent no one in Monte Carlo or Monaco knew a whit more about her than at first, and no one would have hesitated to give half his fortune—had he had one—to know everything. The mystery of the masked woman was exasperating—the theories concerning her innumerable. Perhaps the majority of the women believed that, being very ugly, she had adopted this means of attracting the attention rightfully belonging to beauty. She was a problem which might be studied for weeks without arriving at a solution.

The warm southern days crept lazily along, and as sometimes happens even in that sheltered paradise, began to grow oppressively hot. It was on the languid evening of one of these scorching days that the Woman in Red and the young Englishman were gaming side by side at the roulette table. The air of the Casino was heavy and scented, there was a murmur of laughter and talk, and the frequent click-clack of the roulette balls. The woman pushed back her chair impatiently and said to the man:

"Do come out into the garden—it is insufferably hot in here!"

"I should think," said the young man at length, as they strolled through the shrubbery, "that your mask would be unbearable!"

"It is."

"Then why not take it off?"

"I did not come out to talk of that."

"But perhaps I did!" The British shoulders squared themselves aggressively.

The woman made no reply, but continued her occupation of listlessly slipping a ring up and down her finger.

"Oh, I have dropped it!" she suddenly cried, and stooped quickly to search for it. The low branch of a tree caught in the coils of her yellow hair. To free it she impatiently drew up her head. There was a sharp click, as of the release of a metal catch, and the velvet mask, loosened, fell softly to the ground. She made an inarticulate noise in her throat, and her hands were thrown upward in an ineffectual attempt to conceal her face, but the young man was too quick for her; There, in the bright white moonlight, he looked full at the face of the Woman in Red and, with a terrible cry of horror, fell like one dead upon the grass.

It was a long time before he opened his eyes and felt the touch of the woman's hand upon his brow and the cool trickle of water over his face. He lay passive, thinking of nothing. Then suddenly it all came back.

"Oh, don't, don't, *don't* touch me!" he gasped. "Keep away from me!"

He staggered to his feet, and pressed his hands to his eyes to shut out the vision that would return. His knees trembled and his teeth chattered. Something as white as the moonlight gathered at his lips.

The woman made an imploring gesture. "Oh, see, I have put it on again," and she turned her head that he might behold the velvet mask.

At the sound of her voice he shivered in terror and, without a word, but making a strange moaning noise, he ran, like one demented, in the direction of the lighted Casino. And in the still, white moonlight the Woman in Red stood like one of the statues of the terraced garden, its marble purity turned to scarlet.

The next night she was at her usual place at the roulette table, but it was the stupid baron who sat beside her.

"Why don't you play?" he asked, as she sat motionless and indifferent, eyed curiously by the spectators of the game. She sat up wearily and pushed a pile of gold and notes upon the red, No. 12. The croupier started the wheel revolving rapidly in one direction and sent the ball deftly rolling in the other, and there was a little buzz of conversation. Tongues wagged briskly while eyes were fastened on the whirling wheel.

"What has become of our English friend?" asked one.

"Gone home," was the answer from another across the table. "Perhaps the heat went to his head!" He tapped his forehead significantly.

Gradually the wheel slowed down, and the ball was about to settle with its customary click. Gamblers leaned over the table to see the result of their bets. The slowly rolling sphere was just dropping into No. 12! No, it has settled into the adjoining compartment.

"*Vingt-huit, noir gagne!*" calls out the croupier with shrill monotony, and the shining heaps are distributed to the winners.

"And Madame has lost!" exclaimed the stupid baron, in surprise.

The Woman in Red made no reply, but stood up and, with an imperious motion not to follow, walked steadily from the *salle de jeu*, a vivid bit of colour under the glittering lights of the splendid apartment.

Early the next morning she was found lying on the marble steps of the Casino, dead in her scarlet dress. The stain trailing along the snowy marble had been scarlet, too, but was now turning to a reddish brown. In one fine, strong hand was tightly clutched a folded note. The servants and people who gathered in trembling awe sent for the priest of the church of Sainte Dévote to read it. He came quickly, panting a little for breath. Taking the paper from the fingers of the dead woman, he glanced over it nervously, while the people looked on in breathless silence. It was written in French.

"I will read it," the priest said slowly, and he translated the writing in trembling tones:

"'I have taken my own life—let that pass. Let no one lift the mask from my face but the priest of the church of Sainte Dévote, and I pray him, when he knows my secret, to say mass for my soul. By all that is holy, respect these words.'"

As his solemn voice ceased, those crowding about shuddered and fell back in nameless fear. They at once carried the body of the woman to where she had lodged, the early morning sun gleaming strangely on her scarlet garments and yellow hair. The priest entered the house and closed the door upon the crowd.

When he again emerged, he was hardly recognizable. His face, deadly white, twitched and quivered spasmodically, his eyes protruded and rolled wildly from side to side, and his lips were parted in an awful, unholy smile. His trembling hands could scarcely hold the crucifix. To those who spoke to him he made no answer—he did not seem to hear.

They buried the woman that evening at sunset, among the nameless graves on the hill behind Monte Carlo, as speedily as possible. When the grim, grotesque companion of the dead was asked if any one should be sent for, the only answer she would give was:

"Oh, the devil, the devil, the devil. How should I know?"

The priest from the church of Sainte Dévote mumbled the service rapidly and indistinctly over the grave, with one shaking hand raised in a defensive attitude, as though to banish something or still the quaking terror that shook him from head to foot. When the ritual was ended he turned to the dense crowd which no secrecy or word of authority had been able to keep away, and said so sternly and distinctly that his voice echoed in the silence:

"Whosoever as much as dares to touch this grave, upon him I pronounce the everlasting curse of the Holy Church of Rome!"

Down the sloping hillside, back to the town he led the procession, all the way shaking like a leaf. When they came again to the narrow streets he suddenly stopped trembling and began to laugh, and at the sound of such laughter the people stumbled over each other in their anxiety to get away.

The Commissaire Spécial and the Administration acted promptly and with energy. There was an extra concert that very night, a grand ball on that succeeding, followed by a comic opera. At Monte Carlo it will not do to encourage reminiscence. And so, by and by, people stopped thinking, and began to talk of other things. The old count and the stupid baron were among the first to drop the subject. But when to the mad priest in his cell there came continually the deep boom, boom of the sea, the cry of the gull and the chimes of the church where he should never more say mass, he laughed, and laughed, and laughed—though he could not remember why!

By a strange twist of circumstances—call them coincidences if you will, or by another name if you can see relentless Purpose working through all things—I have lately, and almost simultaneously, come into possession of two remarkable revelations concerning the mystery of the Woman in Red—the heroine of that most astounding tragedy of Monte Carlo—and they supply the threads to lead a thoughtful mind either to its complete solution or, perhaps, to a still mistier labyrinth within the borderland between flesh and spirit.

My friend Dawson, going up and down the earth in search of health, had been induced to try the healing summer air of southern Arizona and thither we went. The day after our arrival at our destination it rained, with all the discomfort to tourists of wetness in a climate warranted dry. Dawson, in his querulous, invalid's humour, railed at the unpleasant weather as we paced back and forth on the sheltered veranda of the hotel, his fretful eyes on the muddy street and the drift of the fine, white rain.

"Always rain," he grumbled, "rain in London, rain in Paris, rain on the Rhine, rain in Rome, rain here, rain everywhere!"

"You forget," I said, "the Riviera."

"Ye-es," he admitted, "but that was two winters ago."

A girl passed by on the street just then, erect and graceful under her dripping umbrella. A gust of wind, blowing back the cape from her shoulders exposed its scarlet lining, which made a quick flash of colour, in the dull, grey morning.

"Monte Carlo!" exclaimed Dawson, with a sudden, backward leap of memory.

"Mystery and masks, and the Scarlet Lady," I said in return.

It had come back to us both, at that flash of scarlet and my careless mention of the Riviera—the awful tragedy of the Woman in Red and the mystery surrounding it and her. We had worn the subject to threads in talking it over the first few months after we had left Monte Carlo, though it was certainly a fruitful subject: The strange appearance of the woman at the gambling resort; her caprice of colour and her invariable mask; her success at the gambling table; the sudden disappearance of her young English lover and the well-authenticated rumour that he had lost his reason over the accidental sight of her face one night in the Casino gardens; her suicide immediately after; and, finally, the madness which had come upon the priest of Sainte Dévote, who had lifted the mask from her dead face at her request. But gradually the mystery had been crowded out of our minds by the new scenes and events of our travels and by the ever present anxiety for my friend's health, so that for over a year the subject had not been mentioned.

Now, in an instant, the old horror and fascination of it was upon me once more and I saw by the look in Dawson's eyes that it was so with him. I saw again the tall cliffs of Monaco, with the restless amethyst sea at their feet; the slender, curiously graceful figure in scarlet as it moved before us at Monte Carlo, in the flower-crowded streets and in the brilliant *salle de jeu* of the Casino, and I saw again the ugly stain darkening in the sun on the marble steps.

Without preface, Dawson took up the subject we had dropped so long ago.

"Jack, what in creation was behind that woman's mask?" he began argumentatively and with irritation.

"My dear Dawson," I answered wearily, "how should I know! Perhaps something outside the bounds of creation."

"I am sure she was the Devil," he said, after a pause, but without that emphasis which springs from conviction.

Then we took up the old theories about the matter, over which we had argued so often before. With a sick man's nervous fancy, Dawson insisted that a terrible deformity, or a disfiguring birthmark, or the signs of leprosy, if suddenly and unexpectedly revealed in the face of a human being, might, under certain conditions, cause insanity. But I, arguing the question from the standpoint of vigorous health, was positive that, while such a revelation would undoubtedly be a shock, it could not, under any conditions, have so serious an effect on a sound mind. There were no special reasons for us to doubt the mental strength of the Englishman or of the priest, two men who had drifted together into the tragedy, apparently by the merest chance. Dawson grew cross over the puzzle and puffed his cigar vindictively.

"I wish I could get hold of that infernal old woman," he growled. "I'd get the truth out of her somehow."

A man with whom we had formed a slight acquaintance at the hotel now joined us, and the matter of the Woman in Red was dropped. I could see, however, by the wrathful crease in Dawson's forehead that he was thinking of it still.

His ill-humour over it lasted all day, even until the early dusk, and we went down to dinner. As he was then still taciturn, I amused myself by staring covertly at the people about me. There were the usual semi-invalids at a health resort and the usual curious tourists, eager over everything, from the February almond blossoms on the tables to the Arizona olives on the bill of fare. A little bored by the scene and not over-pleased with my dinner, I was about to rouse Dawson, when I noticed at the farther end of the table opposite us a big, fair, youngish man, half hidden from my view by a huge palm. His face was turned from me and I caught only the ruddy outline of its profile, shaded by abundant, light hair, noticeably grey. Then he turned and I saw his face.

"Dawson," I said, as quietly as I could, "Look!"

He glanced up in the direction I indicated.

"Oh, by jove, by jove!" he said softly under his breath.

It was the young Englishman of Monte Carlo!

I know that my face was flushed with excitement, and I heard the fork in Dawson's hand clatter sharply against his plate. Afterwards, in our room, we talked it over. Upon one thing we were agreed; we would ask the Englishman, point blank if need be, *what* was behind the mask of the Woman in Red. That he was the same boy, grown older more in looks than in years, whom we had seen at Monte Carlo was certain; that he was again in his right mind the circumstances attested, and that we must learn what he saw that night in the gardens was, perhaps, the most absolutely certain thing in the world. We must know, even at the risk of unsettling his reason again by recalling the frightful incident. Dawson remarked grimly that it would be better to unsettle his than to lose ours, and delegated to me the task of bringing about an interview.

I bungled badly, but I managed it. Meeting him in the hotel lobby I claimed a previous acquaintance with him on the Continent, using glibly enough his name, which I had ascertained from the clerk. Being a gentleman and a slow-minded subject of Her Majesty, he did not disclaim me, and a quarter of an hour later he and Dawson and I sat together in our room, talking genially between the puffs of our cigars. We found topics of common interest in plenty and spent a pleasant hour chatting over our travels and the ranching possibilities of Arizona, in which the Englishman was evidently interested. Dawson began to grow uneasy and signalled to me to play trumps. Before I could think how to begin, the Englishman asked suddenly: "By the way, where did you say you ran across me?"

I had not said, but I did now, looking at him squarely:

"At Monte Carlo, two winters ago." The fine colour left his face.

"You remember," I continued cruelly, "it was the winter of the Woman in Red sensation." He put up his hand to hide his trembling ashen lips.

"For heaven's sake, don't!" he cried. But there was no thought of *finesse* on our part. Dawson leaned forward, his eyes big with eagerness.

"*What*," he fairly shouted, "was behind that woman's mask?"

And this is the story we persuaded the Englishman to tell. He drew farther back into the shadows of the room as he told it, his hand going up now and then to cover his lips, which trembled in spite of him.

"You know the whole wretched affair, of course," he said, "if you were in Monte Carlo at the time. I wish I had not been! You saw how the Count and the Baron and I made fools of ourselves over the woman, I the most blatantly, without doubt. Heaven knows I could not help it, and I doubt if any man of my years and temperament could have done so. Whether it was partly the baffling mystery of her mask I do not know, but there was a fascination about her that was irresistible. I begged her on my knees to let me see her face, begged her a dozen times a day, but she would only turn away with a bitter little laugh. The more she refused my request, the more convinced I became that she was beautiful and that her mask was only a caprice. I formed in my mind a face to fit her hair and her white hands and her charm altogether—a face so clear to me that, had I been an artist,

I could have painted it. I was madly jealous of the suave old Count and the witless Baron, and they of me, but gradually I gained favour with her, until it was she and I who, as a rule, walked together and talked together and gamed together, I following her scarlet gown as if bewitched.

One night we left the Casino, where we had been playing, and went out into the gardens, away from the heat of the crowded rooms. Outside the moon made it as light as day. She was restless and nervous and would not sit down, so we walked to and fro on the terraces. The air was heavy with the scent of roses, and the moonlight was like wine. Half drunk with it and the gleam of her scarlet, I—oh, well, never mind what. I begged her again to take off her mask, and she answered lightly that she had not come out to talk of that. Angry at her refusal, I sulked like a child. She began listlessly slipping her ring up and down on her finger, and presently it slipped off and dropped to the ground. Before I could prevent her, she stooped to find it. A branch of a shrub caught in her hair and she drew back her head with a quick, nervous start to free it. I heard a little click, and her mask fell upon the gravel walk. Then I saw what I had longed so much to see."

Dawson sat up straight in his chair and my own pulse leaped.

"She was deformed, birth-marked, leprous—or the Devil!" broke in my friend.

The young Englishman drew farther back into the shadows.

"No," he answered nervelessly.

Dawson and I stared at each other, but something in the man's attitude kept us silent.

"There was a girl once at home in England," the shaking voice went on after a pause, "Margaret Allison, the daughter of a glover. I thought I loved her; at any rate, I told her so, for she was pretty, confoundedly so, and I was a young fool. Then I found out my mistake.

I remember—I shall never forget—how she looked and smiled at me when I told her I could not marry her. She—she killed herself, and I went to Monte Carlo and lost money to forget about it. Now, you may believe this or not, as you can, but when that woman's mask fell, I saw at first a Thing—not a human face, but a terrible white blur—and out of this came Margaret's face, which looked at me with awful, hurt eyes, and with that smile—O God, that smile! And Margaret lay dead in England. You know the rest. I believe I was crazed for a time, winding up with a fever. Not till long, long after did I learn the final tragedy in the 'Woman in Red' sensation, coming across it one day, while searching for something else in a file of old papers. There! you have my story."

He rose then and leaned against the mantel for a moment.

"Do you wonder," he asked simply, "that my hair is getting grey?"

Dawson's thin hands were twitching nervously.

"But what do you think—" he began.

The Englishmen stopped him authoritatively and turned to go.

"I do not think," he said, "if I can help it—not of that!"

When we were alone we could only sit and look at each other.

"Dawson," I asked finally, "what do *you* think?"

And Dawson smiled a very ghastly smile.

"I do not think," he answered. "I cannot."

We did not have much time to think after that, for the state of Dawson's health became so alarming that I had to telegraph for his mother and sister. Together we pulled him up again, and I, called home by business, left him convalescing in the sunshine.

I had been home barely a month when I received a letter from an old French physician, a resident of Monte Carlo, who had won a pile of bright twenty-franc pieces from me that eventful winter. This is an English version of his letter:

MY DEAR K.:—Do you remember the Woman in Red and her career that winter you were here? Do you remember the priest who went mad? Do you remember our interest in it all? Mon Dieu! A few days ago I was called to attend that priest, because I have some skill and am very cheap. I found him horribly ill; no hope, but perfectly sane—he had been that way for some days they told me—only not so ill. You know the mind sometimes comes back to a madman shortly before death. His face was yellow, like parchment, and shrivelled like a shrunk olive, with eyes—ah, Diable, what eyes! He tried all the time to speak, but could not. Finally he signed to me, then fell back, dying miserably. Afterwards, I found this paper be-neath his pillow, written by him apparently in his lucid interval. What do you think of it? Mon Dieu, I do not know what to think! Read for yourself.

The paper enclosed, in a pitifully weak hand, read as follows:

Has it been years, or months, or days that I have been here? They will not tell me. I swear that my mind again is clear as I write this—swear it by the Sacred Host and the blessed Mother of Heaven. Yesterday I heard them whisper among themselves that I must die, and I feel that it is so. Before I die I must confess what I saw behind the mask of the Woman in Red, since that was the sight which made me mad, and has kept me here these years, or months or weeks. Perhaps some one coming after me can explain it—some one more versed in the riddles of a weary world.

Before I lifted the mask from the face of this Scarlet Woman that day—whenever it was—I prayed, kneeling on the floor beside her, as one would for the soul of a sinner. I expected to see some disfigurement, hideous enough to be concealed, but nothing more. So it was with comparative calmness that I passed my hand under her bright hair, loosened the metal catch and raised the fatal velvet. Oh, that I could blot out what I saw! That it might not come before my eyes again! At first a white and fearful and shapeless Thing, not human. Then, though the creature was dead before me, there struggled into this a face, so faint I could barely see it, but, have mercy upon me, Merciful One! it was the face of my old mother, with livid, purple lips, looking at me as she did when I, with my boy's hands, crushed out her life, maddened by her cursed tongue. For long years I had kept my deed a secret, but now it cried up to me from this woman—how I know not. The face stayed only long enough to stare at me and burn itself into my brain forever—then it faded away. All this time, how long it is I do not know, I have had before me that fearful, unheard of Thing, through which something has tried to struggle, but, when I have nearly been able to see it, it has turned to a terrible scarlet, and I have laughed and laughed and laughed, I knew not why. With the scarlet stain on my hands and in my brain I make this statement—

Here the writing became illegible and finally stopped abruptly. Below, the doctor had written: "Sacré Bleu! it is enough to make lunatics of us all."

Was the Woman in Red a key-board, played upon by the spirits of the dead—helpless clay, moulded by unseen forces? Had each one who had lifted her mask beheld beneath it the most awful vision of which he could conceive? Would the old Count have seen the face of the little vaudeville artist—bah! you know the story. What would the Baron, what would I, what would *you* have seen?

THE NEW MOTHER

Lucy Clifford (1846–1929)

The true talent of Lucy Clifford has only recently been rediscovered
with a modern appreciation of her in depth studies of childhood such
as "The New Mother" and "Wooden Tony", the latter believed to
be a representation of a child with what is now called autism. Born
Sophia Lucy Lane, she married the mathematician and philosopher
William Kingdon Clifford in 1875. Alas he died only four years later of
consumption leaving Lucy alone to raise their children. However, she
developed a circle of literary friends and was able to support herself
by writing. Her breakthrough collection was *Anyhow Stories* in 1882
though some reviewers were horrified at what she would subject her
children to, as "The New Mother" shows.

The children were always called Blue-Eyes and the Turkey, and they came by the names in this manner. The elder one was like her dear father who was far away at sea, and when the mother looked up she would often say, "Child, you have taken the pattern of your father's eyes;" for the father had the bluest of blue eyes, and so gradually his little girl came to be called after them. The younger one had once, while she was still almost a baby, cried bitterly because a turkey that lived near to the cottage, and sometimes wandered into the forest, suddenly vanished in the middle of the winter; and to console her she had been called by its name.

Now the mother and Blue-Eyes and the Turkey and the baby all lived in a lonely cottage on the edge of the forest. The forest was so near that the garden at the back seemed a part of it, and the tall fir-trees were so close that their big black arms stretched over the little thatched roof, and when the moon shone upon them their tangled shadows were all over the white-washed walls.

It was a long way to the village, nearly a mile and a half, and the mother had to work hard and had not time to go often herself to see if there was a letter at the post-office from the dear father, and so very often in the afternoon she used to send the two children. They were very proud of being able to go alone, and often ran half the way to the post-office. When they came back tired with the long walk, there would be the mother waiting and watching for them, and the tea would be ready, and the baby crowing with delight; and if by any chance there was a letter from the sea, then they were happy indeed. The cottage room was so cosy: the walls were as white as snow inside as well as out, and against them hung the cake-tin and the baking-dish, and the lid of a large saucepan that had been worn out long before the children could remember, and the fish-slice, all polished and shining as bright as silver. On one side of the fireplace, above the bellows hung the almanac, and on the other the clock that always struck the wrong hour and was always running down too soon, but it was a good clock, with a little picture on its face and sometimes ticked away for nearly a week without stopping. The baby's high chair stood in one corner, and in another there was a cupboard hung up high against the wall, in which the mother kept all manner of little surprises. The children often wondered how the things that came out of that cupboard had got into it, for they seldom saw them put there.

"Dear children," the mother said one afternoon late in the autumn, "it is very chilly for you to go to the village, but you must walk quickly, and who knows but what you may bring back a letter saying that dear father is already on his way to England." Then Blue-Eyes and the Turkey made haste and were soon ready to go. "Don't be long," the mother said, as she always did before they started. "Go the nearest way and don't look at any strangers you meet, and be sure you do not talk with them."

"No, mother," they answered; and then she kissed them and called them dear good children, and they joyfully started on their way.

The village was gayer than usual, for there had been a fair the day before, and the people who had made merry still hung about the street as if reluctant to own that their holiday was over.

"I wish we had come yesterday," Blue-Eyes said to the Turkey; "then we might have seen something."

"Look there," said the Turkey, and she pointed to a stall covered with gingerbread; but the children had no money. At the end of the street, close to the Blue Lion where the coaches stopped, an old man sat on the ground with his back resting against the wall of a house, and by him, with smart collars round their necks, were two dogs. Evidently they were dancing dogs, the children thought, and longed to see them perform, but they seemed as tired as their master, and sat quite still beside him, looking as if they had not even a single wag left in their tails.

"Oh, I *do* wish we had been here yesterday," Blue-Eyes said again as they went on to the grocer's, which was also the post-office. The post-mistress was very busy weighing out half-pounds of coffee, and when she had time to attend to the children she only just said "No letter for you today," and went on with what she was doing. Then Blue-Eyes and the Turkey turned away to go home. They went back slowly down the village street, past the man with the dogs again. One dog had roused himself and sat up rather crookedly with his head a good deal on one side, looking very melancholy and rather ridiculous; but on the children went towards the bridge and the fields that led to the forest.

They had left the village and walked some way, and then, just before they reached the bridge, they noticed, resting against a pile of stones by the way-side, a strange dark figure. At first they thought it was some one asleep, then they thought it was a poor woman ill and hungry, and then they saw that it was a strange wild-looking girl, who seemed very unhappy, and they felt sure that something was the matter. So they went and looked at her, and thought they would ask her if they could do anything to help her, for they were kind children and sorry indeed for any one in distress.

The girl seemed to be tall, and was about fifteen years old. She was dressed in very ragged clothes. Round her shoulders there was an old brown shawl, which was torn at the corner that hung down the middle of her back. She wore no bonnet, and an old yellow handkerchief which she had tied round her head had fallen backwards and was all huddled up round her neck. Her hair was coal black and hung down uncombed and unfastened, just anyhow. It was not very long, but it was very shiny, and it seemed to match her bright black eyes and dark freckled skin. On her feet were coarse grey stockings and thick shabby boots, which she had evidently forgotten to lace up. She had something hidden away under her shawl, but the children did not know what it was. At first they thought it was a baby, but when, on seeing them coming towards her, she carefully put it under her and sat upon it, they thought they must be mistaken. She sat watching the children approach, and did not move or stir till they were within a yard of her; then she wiped her eyes just as if she had been crying bitterly, and looked up.

The children stood still in front of her for a moment, staring at her and wondering what they ought to do.

"Are you crying?" they asked shyly.

To their surprise she said in a most cheerful voice,

"Oh dear, no! quite the contrary. Are you?"

They thought it rather rude of her to reply in this way, for any one could see that they were not crying. They felt half in mind to walk away; but the girl looked at them so hard with her big black eyes, they did not like to do so till they had said something else.

"Perhaps you have lost yourself?" they said gently.

But the girl answered promptly, "Certainly not. Why, you have just found me. Besides," she added, "I live in the village."

The children were surprised at this, for they had never seen her before, and yet they thought they knew all the village folk by sight.

"We often go to the village," they said, thinking it might interest her.

"Indeed," she answered. That was all; and again they wondered what to do.

Then the Turkey, who had an inquiring mind, put a good straight-forward question. "What are you sitting on?" she asked.

"On a peardrum," the girl answered, still speaking in a most cheerful voice, at which the children wondered, for she looked very cold and uncomfortable.

"What is a peardrum?" they asked.

"I am surprised at your not knowing," the girl answered. "Most people in good society have one." And then she pulled it out and showed it to them. It was a curious instrument, a good deal like a guitar in shape; it had three strings, but only two pegs by which to tune them. The third string was never tuned at all, and thus added to the singular effect produced by the village girl's music. And yet, oddly, the peardrum was not played by touching its strings, but by turning a little handle cunningly hidden on one side.

But the strange thing about the peardrum was not the music it made, or the strings, or the handle, but a little square box attached to one side. The box had a little flat lid that appeared to open by a spring. That was all the children could make out at first. They were most anxious to see inside the box, or to know what it contained, but they thought it might look curious to say so.

"It really is a most beautiful thing, is a peardrum," the girl said, looking at it, and speaking in a voice that was almost affectionate.

"Where did you get it?" the children asked.

"I bought it," the girl answered.

"Didn't it cost a great deal of money?" they asked.

"Yes," answered the girl slowly, nodding her head, "it cost a great deal of money. I am very rich," she added.

And this the children thought a really remarkable statement, for they had not supposed that rich people dressed in old clothes, or went about without bonnets. She might at least have done her hair, they thought; but they did not like to say so.

"You don't look rich," they said slowly, and in as polite a voice as possible.

"Perhaps not," the girl answered cheerfully.

At this the children gathered courage, and ventured to remark, "You look rather shabby"—they did not like to say ragged.

"Indeed?" said the girl in the voice of one who had heard a pleasant but surprising statement. "A little shabbiness is very respectable," she added in a satisfied voice. "I must really tell them this," she continued. And the children wondered what she meant. She opened the little box by the side of the peardrum, and said, just as if she were speaking to some one who could hear her, "They say I look rather shabby; it is quite lucky; isn't it?"

"Why, you are not speaking to any one!" they said, more surprised than ever.

"Oh dear, yes! I am speaking to them both."

"Both?" they said, wondering.

"Yes. I have here a little man dressed as a peasant, and wearing a wide slouch hat with a large feather, and a little woman to match, dressed in a red petticoat, and a white handkerchief pinned across her bosom. I put them on the lid of the box, and when I play they dance most beautifully. The little man takes off his hat and waves it in the air, and the little woman holds up her petticoat a little bit on one side with one hand, and with the other sends forward a kiss."

"Oh! let us see; do let us see!" the children cried, both at once.

Then the village girl looked at them doubtfully.

"Let you see!" she said slowly. "Well, I am not sure that I can. Tell me, are you good?"

"Yes, yes," they answered eagerly, "we are very good!"

"Then it's quite impossible," she answered, and resolutely closed the lid of the box.

They stared at her in astonishment.

"But we are good," they cried, thinking she must have misunderstood them. "We are very good. Mother always says we are."

"So you remarked before," the girl said, speaking in a tone of decision.

Still the children did not understand.

"Then can't you let us see the little man and woman?" they asked.

"Oh dear, no!" the girl answered. "I only show them to naughty children."

"To naughty children!" they exclaimed.

"Yes, to naughty children," she answered; "and the worse the children the better do the man and woman dance."

She put the peardrum carefully under her ragged cloak, and prepared to go on her way.

"I really could not have believed that you were good," she said, reproachfully, as if they had accused themselves of some great crime. "Well, good day."

"Oh, but do show us the little man and woman," they cried.

"Certainly not. Good day," she said again.

"Oh, but we will be naughty," they said in despair.

"I am afraid you couldn't," she answered, shaking her head. "It requires a great deal of skill, especially to be naughty well. Good day," she said for the third time. "Perhaps I shall see you in the village tomorrow."

And swiftly she walked away, while the children felt their eyes fill with tears, and their hearts ache with disappointment.

"If we had only been naughty," they said, "we should have seen them dance; we should have seen the little woman holding her red petticoat in her hand, and the little man waving his hat. Oh, what shall we do to make her let us see them?"

"Suppose," said the Turkey, "we try to be naughty today; perhaps she would let us see them tomorrow."

"But, oh!" said Blue-Eyes, "I don't know how to be naughty; no one ever taught me."

The Turkey thought for a few minutes in silence. "I think I can be naughty if I try," she said. "I'll try tonight."

And then poor Blue-Eyes burst into tears.

"Oh, don't be naughty without me!" she cried. "It would be so unkind of you. You know I want to see the little man and woman just as much as you do. You are very, very unkind." And she sobbed bitterly.

And so, quarrelling and crying, they reached their home.

Now, when their mother saw them, she was greatly astonished, and, fearing they were hurt, ran to meet them.

"Oh, my children, oh, my dear, dear children," she said; "what is the matter?"

But they did not dare tell their mother about the village girl and the little man and woman, so they answered, "Nothing is the matter; nothing at all is the matter," and cried all the more.

"But why are you crying?" she asked in surprise.

"Surely we may cry if we like," they sobbed. "We are very fond of crying."

"Poor children!" the mother said to herself. "They are tired, and perhaps they are hungry; after tea they will be better." And she went back to the cottage, and made the fire blaze, until its reflection danced about on the tin lids upon the wall; and she put the kettle on to boil, and set the tea-things on the table, and opened the window to let in the sweet fresh air, and made all things look bright. Then she went to the little cupboard, hung up high against the wall, and took out some bread and put it on the table, and said in a loving voice, "Dear little children, come and have your tea; it is all quite ready for you. And see, there is the baby waking up from her sleep; we will put her in the high chair, and she will crow at us while we eat."

But the children made no answer to the dear mother; they only stood still by the window and said nothing.

"Come, children," the mother said again. "Come, Blue-Eyes, and come, my Turkey; here is nice sweet bread for tea."

Then Blue-Eyes and the Turkey looked round, and when they saw the tall loaf, baked crisp and brown, and the cups all in a row, and the jug of milk, all waiting for them, they went to the table and sat down and felt a little happier; and the mother did not put the baby in the high chair after all, but took it on her knee, and danced it up and down, and sang little snatches of songs to it, and laughed, and looked content, and thought of the father far away at sea, and wondered what he would say to them all when he came home again. Then suddenly she looked up and saw that the Turkey's eyes were full of tears.

"Turkey!" she exclaimed, "my dear little Turkey! what is the matter? Come to mother, my sweet; come to own mother." And putting the baby down on the rug, she held out her arms, and the Turkey, getting up from her chair, ran swiftly into them.

"Oh, mother," she sobbed, "oh, dear mother! I do so want to be naughty."

"My dear child!" the mother exclaimed.

"Yes, mother," the child sobbed, more and more bitterly. "I do so want to be very, very naughty."

And then Blue-Eyes left her chair also, and, rubbing her face against the mother's shoulder, cried sadly. "And so do I, mother. Oh, I'd give anything to be very, very naughty."

"But, my dear children," said the mother, in astonishment, "why do you want to be naughty?"

"Because we do; oh, what shall we do?" they cried together.

"I should be very angry if you were naughty. But you could not be, for you love me," the mother answered.

"Why couldn't we be naughty because we love you?" they asked.

"Because it would make me very unhappy; and if you love me you couldn't make me unhappy."

"Why couldn't we?" they asked.

Then the mother thought a while before she answered; and when she did so they hardly understood, perhaps because she seemed to be speaking rather to herself than to them.

"Because if one loves well," she said gently, "one's love is stronger than all bad feelings in one, and conquers them. And this is the test whether love be real or false, unkindness and wickedness have no power over it."

"We don't know what you mean," they cried; "and we do love you; but we want to be naughty."

"Then I should know you did not love me," the mother said.

"And what should you do?" asked Blue-Eyes.

"I cannot tell. I should try to make you better."

"But if you couldn't? If we were very, very, very naughty, and wouldn't be good, what then?"

"Then," said the mother sadly—and while she spoke her eyes filled with tears, and a sob almost choked her—"then," she said, "I should have to go away and leave you, and to send home a new mother, with glass eyes and wooden tail."

"You couldn't," they cried.

"Yes, I could," she answered in a low voice; "but it would make me very unhappy, and I will never do it unless you are very, very naughty, and I am obliged."

"We won't be naughty," they cried; "we will be good. We should hate a new mother; and she shall never come here." And they clung to their own mother, and kissed her fondly.

But when they went to bed they sobbed bitterly, for they remembered the little man and woman, and longed more than ever to see them; but how could they bear to let their own mother go away, and a new one take her place?

II

"Good-day," said the village girl, when she saw Blue-Eyes and the Turkey approach. She was again sitting by the heap of stones, and under her shawl the peardrum was hidden. She looked just as if she had not moved since the day before. "Good day," she said, in the same cheerful voice in which she had spoken yesterday; "the weather is really charming."

"Are the little man and woman there?" the children asked, taking no notice of her remark.

"Yes; thank you for inquiring after them," the girl answered; "they are both here and quite well. The little man is learning how to rattle the money in his pocket, and the little woman has heard a secret—she tells it while she dances."

"Oh, do let us see," they entreated.

"Quite impossible, I assure you," the girl answered promptly. "You see, you are good."

"Oh!" said-Blue Eyes, sadly; "but mother says if we are naughty she will go away and send home a new mother, with glass eyes and a wooden tail."

"Indeed," said the girl, still speaking in the same unconcerned voice, "that is what they all say."

"What do you mean?" asked the Turkey.

"They all threaten that kind of thing. Of course really there are no mothers with glass eyes and wooden tails; they would be much too expensive to make." And the common sense of this remark the children, especially the Turkey, saw at once, but they merely said, half crying—

"We think you might let us see the little man and woman dance."

"The kind of thing you would think," remarked the village girl.

"But will you if we are naughty?" they asked in despair.

"I fear you could not be naughty—that is, really—even if you tried," she said scornfully.

"Oh, but we will try; we will indeed," they cried; "so do show them to us."

"Certainly not beforehand," answered the girl, getting up and preparing to walk away.

"But if we are very naughty tonight, will you let us see them tomorrow?"

"Questions asked today are always best answered tomorrow," the girl said, and turned round as if to walk on. "Good day," she said blithely; "I must really go and play a little to myself; good day," she repeated, and then suddenly she began to sing—

"Oh, sweet and fair's the lady-bird,
     And so's the bumble-bee,

But I myself have long preferred
   The gentle chimpanzee,
   The gentle chimpanzee-e-e,
   The gentle chim—"

"I beg your pardon," she said, stopping, and looking over her shoulder; "it's very rude to sing without leave before company. I won't do it again."

"Oh, do go on," the children said.

"I'm going," she said, and walked away.

"No, we meant go on singing," they explained, "and do let us just hear you play," they entreated, remembering that as yet they had not heard a single sound from the peardrum.

"Quite impossible," she called out as she went along. "You are good, as I remarked before. The pleasure of goodness centres in itself; the pleasures of naughtiness are many and varied. Good day," she shouted, for she was almost out of hearing.

For a few minutes the children stood still looking after her, then they broke down and cried.

"She might have let us see them," they sobbed.

The Turkey was the first to wipe away her tears.

"Let us go home and be very naughty," she said; "then perhaps she will let us see them tomorrow."

"But what shall we do?" asked Blue-Eyes, looking up. Then together all the way home they planned how to begin being naughty. And that afternoon the dear mother was sorely distressed, for, instead of sitting at their tea as usual with smiling happy faces, and then helping her to clear away and doing all she told them, they broke their mugs and threw their bread and butter on the floor, and when the mother told them to do one thing they carefully went and did another, and as for helping her to put away, they left her to do it all by herself, and only stamped their feet with rage when she told them to go upstairs until they were good.

"We won't be good," they cried. "We hate being good, and we always mean to be naughty. We like being naughty very much."

"Do you remember what I told you I should do if you were very very naughty?" she asked sadly.

"Yes, we know, but it isn't true," they cried.

"There is no mother with a wooden tail and glass eyes, and if there were we should just stick pins into her and send her away; but there is none."

Then the mother became really angry at last, and sent them off to bed, but instead of crying and being sorry at her anger they laughed for joy, and when they were in bed they sat up and sang merry songs at the top of their voices.

The next morning quite early, without asking leave from the mother, the children got up and ran off as fast as they could over the fields towards the bridge to look for the village girl. She was sitting as usual by the heap of stones with the peardrum under her shawl.

"Now please show us the little man and woman," they cried, "and let us hear the peardrum. We were very naughty last night." But the girl kept the peardrum carefully hidden. "We were very naughty," the children cried again.

"Indeed," she said in precisely the same tone in which she had spoken yesterday.

"But we were," they repeated; "we were indeed."

"So you say," she answered. "You were not half naughty enough."

"Why, we were sent to bed!"

"Just so," said the girl, putting the other corner of the shawl over the peardrum. "If you had been really naughty you wouldn't have gone; but you can't help it, you see. As I remarked before, it requires a great deal of skill to be naughty well."

"But we broke our mugs, we threw our bread and butter on the floor, we did everything we could to be tiresome."

"Mere trifles," answered the village girl scornfully. "Did you throw cold water on the fire, did you break the clock, did you pull all the tins down from the walls, and throw them on the floor?"

"No!" exclaimed the children, aghast, "we did not do that."

"I thought not," the girl answered. "So many people mistake a little noise and foolishness for real naughtiness; but, as I remarked before, it wants skill to do the thing properly. Well, good day," and before they could say another word she had vanished.

"We'll be much worse," the children cried, in despair. "We'll go and do all the things she says;" and then they went home and did all these things. They threw water on the fire; they pulled down the baking-dish and the cake-tin, the fish-slice and the lid of the saucepan they had never seen, and banged them on the floor; they broke the clock and danced on the butter; they turned everything upside down; and then they sat still and wondered if they were naughty enough. And when the mother saw all that they had done she did not scold them as she had the day before or send them to bed, but she just broke down and cried, and then she looked at the children and said sadly—

"Unless you are good tomorrow, my poor Blue-Eyes and Turkey, I shall indeed have *to* go away and come back no more, and the new mother I told you of will come to you."

They did not believe her; yet their hearts ached when they saw how unhappy she looked, and they thought within themselves that when they once had seen the little man and woman dance, they would be good to the dear mother for ever afterwards; but they could not be good now till they had heard the sound of the peardrum, seen the little man and woman dance, and heard the secret told—then they would be satisfied.

The next morning, before the birds were stirring, before the sun had climbed high enough to look in at their bedroom window, or the flowers had wiped their eyes ready for the day, the children got up and crept out of the cottage and ran across the fields. They did not think the village girl would be up so very early, but their hearts had ached so much at the sight of the mother's sad face that they had not been able to sleep, and they longed to know if they had been naughty enough, and if they might just once hear the peardrum and see the little man and woman, and then go home and be good for ever.

To their surprise they found the village girl sitting by the heap of stones, just as if it were her natural home. They ran fast when they saw her, and they noticed that the box containing the little man and woman was open, but she closed it quickly when she saw them, and they heard the clicking of the spring that kept it fast.

"We have been very naughty," they cried. "We have done all the things you told us; now will you show us the little man and woman?" The girl looked at them curiously, then drew the yellow silk handkerchief she sometimes wore round her head out of her pocket, and began to smooth out the creases in it with her hands.

"You really seem quite excited," she said in her usual voice. "You should be calm; calmness gathers in and hides things like a big cloak, or like my shawl does here, for instance;" and she looked down at the ragged covering that hid the peardrum.

"We have done all the things you told us," the children cried again, "and we do so long to hear the secret;" but the girl only went on smoothing out her handkerchief.

"I am so very particular about my dress," she said. They could hardly listen to her in their excitement.

"But do tell if we may see the little man and woman," they entreated again. "We have been so very naughty, and mother says she will go away today and send home a new mother if we are not good."

"Indeed," said the girl, beginning to be interested and amused. "The things that people say are most singular and amusing. There is an endless variety in language." But the children did not understand, only entreated once more to see the little man, and woman.

"Well, let me see," the girl said at last, just as if she were relenting. "When did your mother say she would go?"

"But if she goes what shall we do?" they cried in despair. "We don't want her to go; we love her very much. Oh! what shall we do if she goes?"

"People go and people come; first they go and then they come. Perhaps she will go before she comes; she couldn't come before she goes. You had better go back and be good," the girl added suddenly; "you are really not clever enough to be anything else; and the little woman's secret is very important; she never tells it for make-believe naughtiness."

"But we did do all the things you told us," the children cried, despairingly.

"You didn't throw the looking-glass out of window, or stand the baby on its head."

"No, we didn't do that," the children gasped.

"I thought not," the girl said triumphantly. "Well, good-day. I shall not be here tomorrow. Good-day."

"Oh, but don't go away," they cried. "We are so unhappy; do let us see them just once."

"Well, I shall go past your cottage at eleven o'clock this morning," the girl said. "Perhaps I shall play the peardrum as I go by."

"And will you show us the man and woman?" they asked.

"Quite impossible, unless you have really deserved it; make-believe naughtiness is only spoilt goodness. Now if you break the looking-glass and do the things that are desired—"

"Oh, we will," they cried. "We will be very naughty till we hear you coming."

"It's waste of time, I fear," the girl said politely; "but of course I should not like to interfere with you. You see the little man and woman, being used to the best society, are very particular. Good-day," she said, just as she always said, and then quickly turned away, but she looked back and called out, "Eleven o'clock, I shall be quite punctual; I am very particular about my engagements."

Then again the children went home, and were naughty, oh, so very very naughty that the dear mother's heart ached, and her eyes filled with tears, and at last she went upstairs and slowly put on her best gown and her new sun-bonnet, and she dressed the baby all in its Sunday clothes, and then she came down and stood before Blue-Eyes and the Turkey, and just as she did so the Turkey threw the looking-glass out of window, and it fell with a loud crash upon the ground.

"Good-bye, my children," the mother said sadly, kissing them. "Good-bye, my Blue-Eyes; good-bye, my Turkey; the new mother will be home presently. Oh, my poor children!" and then weeping bitterly the mother took the baby in her arms and turned to leave the house.

"But, mother," the children cried, "we are—" and then suddenly the broken clock struck half-past ten, and they knew that in half an hour the village girl would come by playing on the peardrum. "But, mother, we will be good at half-past eleven, come back at half-past eleven," they cried, "and we'll both be good, we will indeed; we must be naughty till eleven o'clock." But the mother only picked up the little bundle in which she had tied up her cotton apron and a pair of old shoes, and went slowly out at the door. It seemed as if the children were spellbound, and they could not follow her. They opened the window wide, and called after her—

"Mother! mother! oh, dear mother, come back again! We will be good, we will be good now, we will be good for evermore if you will come back." But the mother only looked round and shook her head, and they could see the tears falling down her cheeks.

"Come back, dear mother!" cried Blue-Eyes; but still the mother went on across the fields.

"Come back, come back!" cried the Turkey; but still the mother went on. Just by the corner of the field she stopped and turned, and waved her handkerchief, all wet with tears, to the children at the window; she made the baby kiss its hand; and in a moment mother and baby had vanished from their sight.

Then the children felt their hearts ache with sorrow, and they cried bitterly just as the mother had done, and yet they could not believe that she had gone. Surely she would come back, they thought; she would not leave them altogether; but, oh, if she did—if she did—if she did. And then the broken clock struck eleven, and suddenly there was a sound—a quick, clanging, jangling sound, with a strange discordant one at intervals; and they looked at each other, while their hearts stood still, for they knew it was the peardrum. They rushed to the open window, and there they saw the village girl coming towards them from the fields, dancing along and playing as she did so. Behind her, walking slowly, and yet ever keeping the same distance from her, was the man with the dogs whom they had seen asleep by the Blue Lion, on the day they first saw the girl with the peardrum. He was playing on a flute that had a strange shrill sound; they could hear it plainly above the jangling of the peardrum. After the man followed the two dogs, slowly waltzing round and round on their hind legs.

"We have done all you told us," the children called, when they had recovered from their astonishment. "Come and see; and now show us the little man and woman."

The girl did not cease her playing or her dancing, but she called out in a voice that was half speaking half singing, and seemed to keep time to the strange music of the peardrum.

"You did it all badly. You threw the water on the wrong side of the fire, the tin things were not quite in the middle of the room, the clock was not broken enough, you did not stand the baby on its head."

Then the children, still standing spellbound by the window, cried out, entreating and wringing their hands, "Oh, but we have done everything you told us, and mother has gone away. Show us the little man and woman now, and let us hear the secret."

As they said this the girl was just in front of the cottage, but she did not stop playing. The sound of the strings seemed to go through their hearts. She did not stop dancing; she was already passing the cottage by. She did not stop singing, and all she said sounded like part of a terrible song. And still the man followed her, always at the same distance, playing shrilly on his flute; and still the two dogs waltzed round and round after him—their tails motionless, their legs straight, their collars clear and white and stiff. On they went, all of them together.

"Oh, stop!" the children cried, "and show us the little man and woman now."

But the girl sang out loud and clear, while the string that was out of tune twanged above her voice.

"The little man and woman are far away. See, their box is empty."

266

And then for the first time the children saw that the lid of the box was raised and hanging back, and that no little man and woman were in it.

"I am going to my own land," the girl sang, "to the land where I was born." And she went on towards the long straight road that led to the city many many miles away.

"But our mother is gone," the children cried; "our dear mother, will she ever come back?"

"*No*," sang the girl; "she'll never come back, she'll never come back. I saw her by the bridge: she took a boat upon the river; she is sailing to the sea; she will meet your father once again, and they will go sailing on, sailing on to the countries far away."

And when they heard this, the children cried out, but could say no more, for their hearts seemed to be breaking.

Then the girl, her voice getting fainter and fainter in the distance, called out once more to them. But for the dread that sharpened their ears they would hardly have heard her, so far was she away, and so discordant was the music.

"Your new mother is coming. She is already on her way; but she only walks slowly, for her tail is rather long, and her spectacles are left behind; but she is coming, she is coming—coming—coming."

The last word died away; it was the last one they ever heard the village girl utter. On she went, dancing on; and on followed the man, they could see that he was still playing, but they could no longer hear the sound of his flute; and on went the dogs round and round and round. On they all went, farther and farther away, till they were separate things no more, till they were just a confused mass of faded colour, till they were a dark misty object that nothing could define, till they had vanished altogether,—altogether and for ever.

Then the children turned, and looked at each other and at the little cottage home, that only a week before had been so bright and happy, so cosy and so spotless. The fire was out, and the water was still among the cinders; the baking-dish and cake-tin, the fish-slice and the saucepan lid, which the dear mother used to spend so much time in rubbing, were all pulled down from the nails on which they had hung so long, and were lying on the floor. And there was the clock all broken and spoilt, the little picture upon its face could be seen no more; and though it sometimes struck a stray hour, it was with the tone of a clock whose hours are numbered. And there was the baby's high chair, but no little baby to sit in it; there was the cupboard on the wall, and never a sweet loaf on its shelf; and there were the broken mugs, and the bits of bread tossed about, and the greasy boards which the mother had knelt down to scrub until they were white as snow. In the midst of all stood the children, looking at the wreck they had made, their hearts aching, their eyes blinded with tears, and their poor little hands clasped together in their misery.

"Oh, what shall we do?" cried Blue-Eyes. "I wish we had never seen the village girl and the nasty, nasty peardrum."

"Surely mother will come back," sobbed the Turkey. "I am sure we shall die if she doesn't come back."

"I don't know what we shall do if the new mother comes," cried Blue-Eyes. "I shall never, never like any other mother. I don't know what we shall do if that dreadful mother comes."

"We won't let her in," said the Turkey.

"But perhaps she'll walk in," sobbed Blue-Eyes.

Then Turkey stopped crying for a minute, to think what should be done.

"We will bolt the door," she said, "and shut the window; and we won't take any notice when she knocks."

So they bolted the door, and shut the window, and fastened it. And then, in spite of all they had said, they felt naughty again, and longed after the little man and woman they had never seen, far more than after the mother who had loved them all their lives. But then they did not really believe that their own mother would not come back, or that any new mother would take her place.

When it was dinner-time, they were very hungry, but they could only find some stale bread, and they had to be content with it.

"Oh, I wish we had heard the little woman's secret," cried the Turkey; "I wouldn't have cared then."

All through the afternoon they sat watching and listening for fear of the new mother; but they saw and heard nothing of her, and gradually they became less and less afraid lest she should come. Then they thought that perhaps when it was dark their own dear mother would come home; and perhaps if they asked her to forgive them she would. And then Blue-Eyes thought that if their mother did come she would be very cold, so they crept out at the back door and gathered in some wood, and at last, for the grate was wet, and it was a great deal of trouble to manage it, they made a fire. When they saw the bright fire burning, and the little flames leaping and playing among the wood and coal, they began to be happy again, and to feel certain that their own mother would return; and the sight of the pleasant fire reminded them of all the times she had waited for them to come from the post-office, and of how she had welcomed them, and comforted them, and given them nice warm tea and sweet bread, and talked to them. Oh, how sorry they were they had been naughty, and all for that nasty village girl! They did not care a bit about the little man and woman now, or want to hear the secret.

They fetched a pail of water and washed the floor; they found some rag, and rubbed the tins till they looked bright again, and, putting a footstool on a chair, they got up on it very carefully and hung up the things in their places; and then they picked up the broken mugs and made the room as neat as they could, till it looked more and more as if the dear mother's hands had been busy about it. They felt more and more certain she would return, she and the dear little baby together, and they thought they would set the tea-things for her, just as she had so often set them for her naughty children. They took down the tea-tray, and got out the cups, and put the kettle on the fire to boil, and made everything look as home-like as they could. There was no sweet loaf to put on the table, but perhaps the mother would bring something from the village, they thought. At last all was ready, and Blue-Eyes and the Turkey washed their faces and their hands, and then sat and waited, for of course they did not believe what the village girl had said about their mother sailing away.

Suddenly, while they were sitting by the fire, they heard a sound as of something heavy being dragged along the ground outside, and then there was a loud and terrible knocking at the door. The children felt their hearts stand still. They knew it could not be their own mother, for she would have turned the handle and tried to come in without any knocking at all.

"Oh, Turkey!" whispered Blue-Eyes, "if it should be the new mother, what shall we do?"

"We won't let her in," whispered the Turkey, for she was afraid to speak aloud, and again there came a long and loud and terrible knocking at the door.

"What shall we do? oh, what shall we do?" cried the children, in despair. "Oh, go away!" they called out. "Go away; we won't let you in; we will never be naughty any more; go away, go away!"

But again there came a loud and terrible knocking.

"She'll break the door if she knocks so hard," cried Blue-Eyes.

"Go and put your back to it," whispered the Turkey, "and I'll peep out of the window and try to see if it is really the new mother."

So in fear and trembling Blue-Eyes put her back against the door, and the Turkey went to the window, and, pressing her face against one side of the frame, peeped out. She could just see a black satin poke bonnet with a frill round the edge, and a long bony arm carrying a black leather bag. From beneath the bonnet there flashed a strange bright light, and Turkey's heart sank and her cheeks turned pale, for she knew it was the flashing of two glass eyes. She crept up to Blue-Eyes. "It is—it is—it is!" she whispered, her voice shaking with fear, "it is the new mother! She has come, and brought her luggage in a black leather bag that is hanging on her arm!"

"Oh, what shall we do?" wept Blue-Eyes; and again there was the terrible knocking.

"Come and put your back against the door too, Turkey," cried Blue-Eyes; "I am afraid it will break."

So together they stood with their two little backs against the door. There was a long pause. They thought perhaps the new mother had made up her mind that there was no one at home to let her in, and would go away, but presently the two children heard through the thin wooden door the new mother move a little, and then say to herself—"I must break open the door with my tail."

For one terrible moment all was still, but in it the children could almost hear her lift up her tail, and then, with a fearful blow, the little painted door was cracked and splintered.

With a shriek the children darted from the spot and fled through the cottage, and out at the back door into the forest beyond. All night long they stayed in the darkness and the cold, and all the next day and the next, and all through the cold, dreary days and the long dark nights that followed.

They are there still, my children. All through the long weeks and months have they been there, with only green rushes for their pillows and only the brown dead leaves to cover them, feeding on the wild strawberries in the summer, or on the nuts when they hang green; on the blackberries when they are no longer sour in the autumn, and in the winter on the little red berries that ripen in the snow. They wander about among the tall dark firs or beneath the great trees beyond. Sometimes they stay to rest beside the little pool near the copse where the ferns grow thickest, and they long and long, with a longing that is greater than words can say, to see their own dear mother again, just once again, to tell her that they'll be good for evermore—just once again.

And still the new mother stays in the little cottage, but the windows are closed and the doors are shut, and no one knows what the inside looks like. Now and then, when the darkness has fallen and the night is still, hand in hand Blue-Eyes and the Turkey creep up near to the home in which they once were so happy, and with beating hearts they watch and listen; sometimes a blinding flash comes through the window, and they know it is the light from the new mother's glass eyes, or they hear a strange muffled noise, and they know it is the sound of her wooden tail as she drags it along the floor.

THE HOARD OF THE GIBBELINS

Lord Dunsany (1878–1957)

In the history of modern fantasy, and in particular how adult fantasy emerged from the Victorian fairy tale, three writers stand out, George Macdonald, William Morris and Lord Dunsany. Of those Dunsany was not only the most prolific, but arguably the most influential. His works influenced the next generation or two of fantasists, notably H. P. Lovecraft, Clark Ashton Smith and Jack Vance, and because he lived for so long—he was still writing to within days of his death, after a career of close on sixty years—he continued to influence more recent writers. Long before Tolkien, Dunsany created his own fantasy world in *The Gods of Pegana* (1905) and several further collections such as *Time and the Gods* (1906) and *The Sword of Welleran* (1908). His stories are often short, sharp, sardonic and surreal, and they bring alive a world of mischief and chaos. His novels, especially *The Chronicles of Rodriquez* (1922), *The King of Elfland's Daughter* (1924) and *The Charwoman's Shadow* (1926) are deeper, more controlled, but no less wondrous. The story included here shows how Dunsany loved to play with convention and turn it inside out.

The Gibbelins eat, as is well known, nothing less good than man. Their evil tower is joined to Terra Cognita, to the lands we know, by a bridge. Their hoard is beyond reason; avarice has no use for it; they have a separate cellar for emeralds and a separate cellar for sapphires; they have filled a hole with gold and dig it up when they need it. And the only use that is known for their ridiculous wealth is to attract to their larder a continual supply of food. In times of famine they have even been known to scatter rubies abroad, a little trail of them to some city of Man, and sure enough their larders would soon be full again.

Their tower stands on the other side of that river known to Homer—*ho rhoos okeanoio*, as he called it—which surrounds the world. And where the river is narrow and fordable the tower was built by the Gibbelins' gluttonous sires, for they liked to see burglars rowing easily to their steps. Some nourishment that common soil has not the huge trees drained there with their colossal roots from both banks of the river.

There the Gibbelins lived and discreditably fed.

Alderic, Knight of the Order of the City and the Assault, hereditary Guardian of the King's Peace of Mind, a man not unremembered among makers of myth, pondered so long upon the Gibbelins' hoard that by now he deemed it his. Alas that I should say of so perilous a venture, undertaken at dead of night by a valourous man, that its motive was sheer avarice! Yet upon avarice only the Gibbelins relied to keep their larders full, and once in every hundred years sent spies into the cities of men to see how avarice did, and always the spies returned again to the tower saying that all was well.

It may be thought that, as the years went on and men came by fearful ends on that tower's wall, fewer and fewer would come to the Gibbelins' table: but the Gibbelins found otherwise.

Not in the folly and frivolity of his youth did Alderic come to the tower, but he studied carefully for several years the manner in which burglars met their doom when they went in search of the treasure that he considered his. *In every case they had entered by the door.*

He consulted those who gave advice on this quest; he noted every detail and cheerfully paid their fees, and determined to do nothing that they advised, for what were their clients now? No more than examples of the savoury art, and mere half-forgotten memories of a meal; and many, perhaps, no longer even that.

These were the requisites for the quest that these men used to advise: a horse, a boat, mail armour, and at least three men-at-arms. Some said, "Blow the horn at the tower door"; others said, "Do not touch it."

Alderic thus decided: he would take no horse down to the river's edge, he would not row along it in a boat, and he would go alone and by way of the Forest Unpassable.

How pass, you may say, the unpassable? This was his plan: there was a dragon he knew of who if peasants' prayers are heeded deserved to die, not alone because of the number of maidens he cruelly slew, but because he was bad for the crops; he ravaged the very land and was the bane of a dukedom.

Now Alderic determined to go up against him. So he took horse and spear and pricked till he met the dragon, and the dragon came out against him breathing bitter smoke. And to him Alderic shouted, "Hath foul dragon ever slain true knight?" And well the dragon knew that this had never been, and he hung his head and was silent, for he was glutted with blood. "Then," said the knight, "if thou would'st ever taste maiden's blood again thou shalt be my trusty steed, and if not, by this spear there shall befall thee all that the troubadours tell of the dooms of thy breed."

And the dragon did not open his ravening mouth, nor rush upon the knight, breathing out fire; for well he knew the fate of those that did these things, but he consented to the terms imposed, and swore to the knight to become his trusty steed.

It was on a saddle upon this dragon's back that Alderic afterwards sailed above the unpassable forest, even above the tops of those measureless trees, children of wonder. But first he pondered that subtle plan of his which was more profound than merely to avoid all that had been done before; and he commanded a blacksmith, and the blacksmith made him a pickaxe.

Now there was great rejoicing at the rumour of Alderic's quest, for all folk knew that he was a cautious man, and they deemed that he would succeed and enrich the world, and they rubbed their hands in the cities at the thought of largesse; and there was joy among all men in Alderic's country, except perchance among the lenders of money, who feared they would soon be paid. And there was rejoicing also because men hoped that when the Gibbelins were robbed of their hoard, they would shatter their high-built bridge and break the golden chains that bound them to the world, and drift back, they and their tower, to the moon, from which they had come and to which they rightly belonged. There was little love for the Gibbelins, though all men envied their hoard.

So they all cheered, that day when he mounted his dragon, as though he was already a conqueror, and what pleased them more than the good that they hoped he would do to the world was that he scattered gold as he rode away; for he would not need it, he said, if he found the Gibbelins' hoard, and he would not need it more if he smoked on the Gibbelins' table.

When they heard that he had rejected the advice of those that gave it, some said that the knight was mad, and others said he was greater than those what gave the advice, but none appreciated the worth of his plan.

He reasoned thus: for centuries men had been well advised and had gone by the cleverest way, while the Gibbelins came to expect them to come by boat and to look for them at the door whenever their larder was empty, even as a man looketh for a snipe in a marsh; but how, said Alderic, if a snipe should sit in the top of a tree, and would men find him there? Assuredly never! So Alderic decided to swim the river and not to go by the door, but to pick his way into the tower through the stone. Moreover, it was in his mind to work below the level of the ocean, the river (as Homer knew) that girdles the world, so that as soon as he made a hole in the wall the water should pour in, confounding the Gibbelins, and flooding the cellars, rumoured to be twenty feet in depth, and therein he would dive for emeralds as a diver dives for pearls.

And on the day that I tell of he galloped away from his home scattering largesse of gold, as I have said, and passed through many kingdoms, the dragon snapping at maidens as he went, but being unable to eat them because of the bit in his mouth, and earning no gentler reward than a spurthrust where he was softest. And so they came to the swart arboreal precipice of the unpassable forest. The dragon rose at it with a rattle of wings. Many a farmer near the edge of the worlds saw him up there where yet the twilight lingered, a faint, black, wavering line; and mistaking him for a row of geese going inland from the ocean, went into their houses cheerily rubbing their hands and saying that winter was coming, and that we should soon have snow. Soon even there the twilight faded away, and when they descended at the edge of the world it was night and the moon was shining. Ocean, the ancient river, narrow and shallow there, flowed by and made no murmur. Whether the Gibbelins banqueted or whether they watched by the door, they also made no murmur. And Alderic dismounted and took his armour off, and saying one prayer to his lady, swam with his pickaxe. He did not part from his sword, for fear that he met with a Gibbelin. Landed the other side, he began to work at once, and all went well with him. Nothing put out its head from any window, and all were lighted so that nothing within could see him in the dark. The blows of his pickaxe were dulled in the deep walls. All night he worked, no sound came to molest him, and at dawn the last rock swerved and tumbled inwards, and the river poured in after. Then Alderic took a stone, and went to the bottom step, and hurled the stone at the door; he heard the echoes roll into the tower, then he ran back and dived through the hole in the wall.

He was in the emerald-cellar. There was no light in the lofty vault above him, but, diving through twenty feet of water, he felt the floor all rough with emeralds, and open coffers full of them. By a faint ray of the moon he saw that the water was green with them, and easily filling a satchel, he rose again to the surface; and there were the Gibbelins waist-deep in the water, with torches in their hands! And, without saying a word, *or even smiling*, they neatly hanged him on the outer wall—and the tale is one of those that have not a happy ending.

THE THREE MARKED PENNIES

Mary E. Counselman (1911–1995)

Counselman was an American poet and short-story writer who became known as "The Queen of *Weird Tales*" because of the popularity of her thirty stories in that magazine. She contributed to many magazines, including *Collier's Weekly*, *Saturday Evening Post*, *Jungle Stories* and *Thrilling Mystery*, but it was her appearances in *Weird Tales* that made her work memorable. Her first story there was "The House of Shadows" (1933), and several stories, including "The Shot-Tower Ghost" (1949) and "The Green Window" (1949), were inspired by her own direct experiences. Her best-known story, "The Three Marked Pennies", which is reprinted here, was highlighted as one of the most popular ever published in *Weird Tales*. Several of her strange stories were collected in *Half in Shadow* (1964; reprinted with several different stories in 1978), whilst *African Yesterdays* (1975) brings together many of her stories based on native African folklore.

E veryone agreed, after it was over, that the whole thing was the conception of a twisted brain, a game of chess played by a madman—in which the pieces, instead of carved bits of ivory or ebony, were human beings.

It was odd that no one doubted the authenticity of the "contest." The public seems never for a moment to have considered it the prank of a practical joker, or even a publicity stunt. Jeff Haverty, editor of the *News*, advanced a theory that the affair was meant to be a clever, if rather elaborate, psychological experiment—which would end in the revealing of the originator's identity and a big laugh for everyone.

Perhaps it was the glamorous manner of announcement that gave the thing such widespread interest. Branton, the southern town of about thirty thousand people in which the affair occurred, awoke one April morning to find all its trees, telephone poles, house-sides, and storefronts plastered with a strange sign. There were scores of them, written on yellow copy-paper on an ordinary typewriter. The sign read:

> *"During this day of April 15, three pennies will find their way into the pockets of this city. On each penny there will be a well-defined mark. One is a square; one is a circle; and one is a cross. These three pennies will change hands often, as do all coins, and on the seventh day after this announcement (April 21) the possessor of each marked penny will receive a gift.*

"To the first: $100,000 in cash.

"To the second: A trip around the world.

"To the third: Death.

"The answer to this riddle lies in the marks on the three coins: circle, square, and cross. Which of these symbolizes wealth? Which, travel? Which, death? The answer is not an obvious one.

"To him who finds it and obtains the first penny, $100,000 will be sent without delay. To him who has the second penny, a first-class ticket for the earliest world-touring steamer to sail will be presented. But to the possessor of the third marked coin will be given—death. If you are afraid your penny is the third, give it away—but it may be the first or the second!

"Show your marked penny to the editor of the 'News' on April 21, giving your name and address. He will know nothing of this contest until he reads one of these signs. He is requested to publish the names of the three possessors of the coins April 21, with the mark on the penny each holds.

"It will do no good to mark a coin of your own, as the dates of the true coins will be sent to Editor Haverty."

By noon everyone had read the notice, and the city was buzzing with excitement. Clerks began to examine the contents of cash register drawers. Hands rummaged in pockets and purses. Stores and banks were flooded with customers wanting silver changed to coppers.

Jeff Haverty was the target for a barrage of queries, and his evening edition came with a lengthy editorial embodying all he knew about the mystery, which was exactly nothing. A note had come that morning with the rest of his mail—a note unsigned, and typewritten on the same yellow paper in a plain stamped envelope with the postmark of that city. It said merely: "*Circle—1920. Square—1909. Cross—1928. Please do not reveal these dates until after April 21.*"

Haverty complied with the request, and played up the story for all it was worth.

The first penny was found in the street by a small boy, who promptly took it to his father. His father, in turn, palmed it off hurriedly on his barber, who gave it in change to a patron before he noted the deep cross cut in the coin's surface.

The patron took it to his wife, who immediately paid it to the grocer. "It's too long a chance, honey!" she silenced her mate's protests. "I don't like the idea of that death-threat in the notice... and this certainly must be the third penny. What else could that little cross stand for? Crosses over graves—don't you see the significance?"

And when that explanation was wafted abroad, the cross-marked penny began to change hands with increasing rapidity.

The other two pennies bobbed up before dusk—one marked with a small perfect square, the other with a neat circle.

The square-marked penny was discovered in a slot-machine by the proprietor of the Busy Bee Café. There was no way it could have got there, he reported, mystified and a little frightened. Only four people, all of them old patrons, had been in the café that day. And not one of them had been near the slot-machine—located at the back of the place as it was, and filled with stale chewing-gum which, at a glance, was worth nobody's penny. Furthermore, the proprietor had examined the thing for a chance coin the night before and had left it empty when he locked up; yet there was the square-marked penny nestling alone in the slot-machine at closing time April fifteenth.

He had stared at the coin a long time before passing it in change to an elderly spinster.

"It ain't worth it," he muttered to himself. "I got a restaurant that's makin' me a thin livin', and I ain't in no hurry to get myself bumped off, on the long chance I might get that hundred thousand or that trip instead. No-sirree!"

The spinster took one look at the marked penny, gave a short mouselike squeak, and flung it into the gutter as though it were a tarantula.

"My land!" she quavered. "I don't want that thing in my pocket-book!"

But she dreamed that night of foreign ports, of dockhands jabbering in a brittle tongue, of barracuda fins cutting the surface of deep blue water, and the ruins of ancient cities.

A workman picked up the penny next morning and clung to it all day, dreaming of Harlem, before he succumbed at last to gnawing fear. And the square-marked penny changed hands once more.

The circle-marked penny was first noted in a stack of coins by a teller of the Farmer's Trust.

"We get marked coins every now and then," he said. "I didn't notice this one especially—it may have been here for days."

He pocketed it gleefully, but discovered with a twinge of dismay next morning that he had passed it out to someone without noticing it.

"I wanted to keep it!" he sighed. "For better or for worse!"

He glowered at the stacks of someone else's money before him, and wondered furtively how many tellers really escaped with stolen goods.

A fruit-seller had received the penny. He eyed it dubiously. "Mebbe you bring-a me those mon, heh?" He showed it to his fat, greasy wife, who made the sign of horns against the "evil eye."

"T'row away!" she commanded shrilly. "She iss bad lock!"

Her spouse shrugged and sailed the circle-marked coin across the street. A ragged child pounced on it and scuttered away to buy a twist of licorice. And the circle-marked penny changed hands once more—clutched at by avaricious fingers, stared at by eyes grown sick of familiar scenes, relinquished again by the power of fear.

Those who came into brief possession of the three coins were fretted by the drag and shove of conflicting advice.

"Keep it!" some urged. "Think! It may mean a trip around the world! Paris! China! London! Oh, why couldn't I have got the thing?"

"Give it away!" others admonished. "Maybe it's the third penny—you can't tell. Maybe the symbols don't mean what they seem to, and the square one is the death-penny! I'd throw it away, if I were you."

"No! No!" still others cried. "Hang on to it! It may bring you $100,000. *A hundred thousand dollars!* In these times! Why, fellow, you'd be the same as a millionaire!"

The meaning of the three symbols was on everyone's tongue, and no one agreed with his neighbour's solution to the riddle.

"It's as plain as the nose on my face," one man would declare. "The circle represents the globe—the travel-penny, see?"

"No, no. The cross means that. 'Cross' the seas, don't you get it? Sort of a pun effect. The circle means money—shape of a coin, understand?"

"And the square one—?"

"A grave. A square hole for a coffin, see? Death. It's quite simple. I wish I could get hold of that circle one!"

"You're crazy! The cross one is for death—everybody says so. And believe me, everybody's getting rid of it as soon as they get it! It may be a joke of some kind... no danger at all... but I wouldn't like to be the holder of that cross-marked penny when April twenty-first rolls around!"

"I'd keep it and wait till the other two had got what was due them. Then, if mine turned out to be the wrong one, I'd throw it away!" one man said importantly.

"But he won't pay up till all three pennies are accounted for, I shouldn't think," another answered him. "And maybe the offer doesn't hold good after April twenty-first—and you'd be losing the hundred thousand dollars or a world tour just because you're scared to find out!"

"That's a big stake, man," another murmured. "But frankly, I wouldn't like to take the chance. He might give me his third gift!"

"He" was how everyone designated the unknown originator of the contest; though, of course, there was no more clue to his sex than to his identity.

"He must be rich," some said, "to offer such expensive prizes."

"And crazy!" others exploded, "threatening to kill the third one. He'll never get away with it!"

"But clever," still others admitted, "to think up the whole business. He knows human nature, whoever he is. I'm inclined to agree with Haverty—it's all a sort of psychological experiment. He's trying to see whether desire for travel or greed for money is stronger than fear of death."

"Does he mean to pay up, do you think?"

"That remains to be seen!"

On the sixth day, Branton had reached a pitch of excitement amounting almost to hysteria. No one could work for wondering about the outcome of the bizarre test on the morrow.

It was known that a grocer's delivery boy held the square-marked coin, for he had been boasting of his indifference as to whether or not the square did represent a yawning grave. He exhibited the penny freely, making jokes about what he intended to do with his hundred thousand dollars—but on the morning of the last day he lost his nerve. Seeing a blind beggar woman huddled in her favourite corner between two shops, he passed close to her and surreptitiously dropped the cent piece into her box of pencils.

"I had it!" he wailed to a friend after he had reached his grocery. "I had it right here in my pocket last night, and now it's gone! See, I've got a hole in the dam' thing—the penny must have dropped out!"

It was also known who held the circle-marked penny. A young soda-clerk, with the sort of ready smile that customers like to see across a marble counter, had discovered the coin and fished it from the cash drawer, exulting over his good fortune.

"Bud Skinner's got the circle penny," people told one another, wavering between anxiety and gladness. "I hope the kid *does* get that world tour—it'd tickle him so! He seems to get such a kick out of life; it's a sin he has to be stuck in this slow burg!"

Finally it was found who held the cross-marked cent piece. "Carlton... poor devil!" people murmured in subdued tones. "Death would be a godsend to him. Wonder he hasn't shot himself before this. Guess he just hasn't the nerve."

The man with the cross-marked penny smiled bitterly. "I hope this blasted little symbol means what they all think it means!" he confided to a friend.

At last the eagerly awaited day came. A crowd formed in the street outside the newspaper office to see the three possessors of the three marked coins show Haverty their pennies and give him their names to publish. For their benefit the editor met the trio on the sidewalk outside the building, so that all might see them.

The evening edition ran the three people's photographs, with the name, address, and the mark on each one's penny under each picture. Branton read... and held its breath.

*

On the morning of April twenty-second, the old blind beggar woman sat in her accustomed place, musing on the excitement of the previous day, when several people had led her—she knew by the odour of fish from the market across the street—to the newspaper office. There someone had asked her name and many other puzzling things which had bewildered her until she had almost burst into tears.

"Let me alone!" she had whimpered. "I ask only enough food to keep from starving, and a place to sleep. Why are you pushing me around like this and yelling at me? Let me go back to my corner! I don't like all this confusion and strangeness that I can't see—it frightens me!"

Then they had told her something about a marked penny they had found in her alms-box, and other things about a large sum of money and some impending danger that threatened her. She was glad when they led her back to her cranny between the shops.

Now as she sat in her accustomed spot, nodding comfortably and humming a little under her breath, a paper fluttered down into her lap. She felt the stiff oblong, knew it was an envelope, and called a bystander to her side.

"Open this for me, will you?" she requested. "Is it a letter? Read it to me."

The bystander tore open the envelope and frowned. "It's a note," he told her. "Typewritten, and it's not signed. It just says—what the devil?—just says: '*The four corners of the earth are exactly the same.*' And... hey! look at this!... oh, I'm sorry; I forgot you're... it's a steamship ticket for a world tour! Look, didn't you have one of the marked pennies?"

The blind woman nodded drowsily. "Yes, the one with the square, they said." She sighed faintly. "I had hoped I would get the money, or... the other, so I would never have to beg again."

"Well, here's your ticket." The bystander held it out to her uncertainly. "Don't you want it?" as the beggar made no move to take it.

"No," snapped the blind woman. "What good would it be to me?" She seized the ticket in sudden rage, and tore it into bits.

At nearly the same hour, Kenneth Carlton was receiving a fat manila envelope from the postman. He frowned as he squinted at the local postmark over the stamp. His friend Evans stood beside him, paler than Carlton.

"Open it, open it!" he urged. "Read it—no, don't open it, Ken. I'm scared! After all... it's a terrible way to go. Not knowing where the blow's coming from, and—"

Carlton emitted a macabre chuckle, ripping open the heavy envelope. "It's the best break I've had in years, Jim. I'm glad! Glad, Jim, do you hear? It will be quick, I hope... and painless. What's this, I wonder. A treatise on how to blow off the top of your head?" He shook the contents of the letter onto a table, and then, after a moment, he began to laugh... mirthlessly... hideously.

His friend stared at the little heap of crisp bills, all of a larger denomination than he had ever seen before. "The money! You get the hundred thousand, Ken! I can't believe..." He broke off to snatch up a slip of yellow paper among the bills. "*Wealth is the greatest cross a man can bear,*" he read aloud the typewritten words. "It doesn't make sense... wealth? Then... the cross-mark stood for wealth? I don't understand."

Carlton's laughter cracked. "He has depth, that bird—whoever he is! Nice irony there, Jim—wealth being a burden instead of the blessing most people consider it. I suppose he's right, at that. But I wonder if he knows the really ironic part of this act of his little play? A hundred thousand dollars to a man with—cancer. Well, Jim, I have a month or less to spend it in... one more damnable month to suffer through before it's all over!"

His terrible laughter rose again, until his friend had to clap hands to ears, shutting out the sound.

But the strangest part of the whole affair was Bud Skinner's death. Just after the rush hour at noon, he had found a small package, addressed to him, on a back counter in the drug store. Eagerly he tore off the brown paper wrappings, a dozen or so friends crowding around him.

A curiously wrought silver box was what he found. He pressed the catch with trembling fingers and snapped back the lid. An instant later his face took on a queer expression—and he slid noiselessly to the tile floor of the drug store.

The ensuing police investigation unearthed nothing at all, except that young Skinner had been poisoned with *crotalin*—snake venom—administered through a pin-prick on his thumb when he pressed the trick catch on the little silver box. This, and the typewritten note in the otherwise empty box: "*Life ends where it began—nowhere,*" were all they found as an explanation of the clerk's death. Nor was anything else ever brought to light about the mysterious contest of the three marked pennies—which are probably still in circulation somewhere in the United States.

Copyright Acknowledgements and Story Sources

All the stories in this anthology are in the public domain unless otherwise noted. Every effort has been made to trace copyright holders and the publisher apologizes for any errors or omissions and would be pleased to be notified of any corrections to be incorporated in reprints or future editions. The following gives the first publication details for each story. They are listed in alphabetical order of author.

"Johnson Looked Back" by Thomas Burke, first published in *Collier's Weekly*, 14 October 1933.

"The New Mother" by Lucy Clifford, first published in *Anyhow Stories: Moral and Otherwise*, London: Macmillan, 1882.

"The Three Marked Pennies" by Mary E. Counselman, first published in *Weird Tales*, August 1934. Unable to trace author's estate.

"The Hoard of the Gibbelins" by Lord Dunsany, first published in *The Sketch*, 25 January 1911, reprinted by permission of Curtis Brown, Ltd., on behalf of the author's estate.

"The Woman in Red" and "Unmasked" by Muriel Campbell Dyar, first published in *The Black Cat*, November 1899 and March 1900 respectively.

"The Thing in the Cellar" by David H. Keller, first published in *Weird Tales*, March 1932. Unable to trace author's estate.

"The White People" by Arthur Machen, first published in *The Horlick's Magazine*, January 1904.

BRITISH LIBRARY TALES OF THE WEIRD

*The Face in the Glass: The Gothic
Tales of Mary Elizabeth Braddon*
Edited by Greg Buzwell

*The Platform Edge:
Uncanny Tales of the Railways*
Edited by Mike Ashley

*The Weird Tales of
William Hope Hodgson*
Edited by Xavier Aldana Reyes

*Glimpses of the Unknown:
Lost Ghost Stories*
Edited by Mike Ashley

British Library Tales of the Weird collects a thrilling array of uncanny story-telling, from the realms of gothic, supernatural and horror fiction. With stories ranging from the 19th century to the present day, this series revives long-lost material from the Library's vaults to thrill again alongside beloved classics of the weird fiction genre.